HERE AGAIN! THE IRREPRESSIBLE
ARCHIE AND THE INCOMPARABLE
NERO WOLFE IN THREE OF THEIR
UNIQUE EXERCISES IN MURDER!

1. A DOSE OF POISON—There were twelve
suspects—and they just happened to be the
twelve most beautiful models in New York!

2. A DEADLY LASSO—The most famous
cowboy of them all . . . but the rope was
around his own neck!

3. A BUTCHER KNIFE—Archie saw it—still
stuck in the dame's ribs—and the
corpse was at Nero's door!

"All three are ingenious and colorful, with as
much plot-interest as a full-length mystery."
—The New York Times

Published by Bantam Books, Inc.

A NERO WOLFE THREESOME

THREE AT WOLFE'S DOOR

BY REX STOUT

BANTAM BOOKS · LONDON
TORONTO
NEW YORK

THREE AT WOLFE'S DOOR

*A Bantam Book / published by arrangement with
The Viking Press, Inc.*

PRINTING HISTORY

*Viking edition published April 1960
Mystery Guild edition published July 1960*
"Method Three for Murder" *appeared serially in* THE SATURDAY
EVENING POST. © *1960 by The Curtis Publishing Company.*
Bantam edition published August 1961
2nd printing .... January 1968

*Bantam Books are published by Bantam Books, Inc., a subsidiary
of Grosset & Dunlap, Inc. Its trade-mark, consisting of the words
"Bantam Books" and the portrayal of a bantam, is registered in the
United States Patent Office and in other countries. Marca Registrada.
Bantam Books, Inc., 271 Madison Avenue, New York, N.Y. 10016.*

PRINTED IN THE UNITED STATES OF AMERICA

CONTENTS

POISON À LA CARTE

I slanted my eyes down to meet her big brown ones, which were slanted up. "No," I said, "I'm neither a producer nor an agent. My name's Archie Goodwin, and I'm here because I'm a friend of the cook. My reason for wanting it is purely personal."

"I know," she said, "it's my dimples. Men often swoon."

I shook my head. "It's your earrings. They remind me of a girl I once loved in vain. Perhaps if I get to know you well enough—who can tell?"

"Not me," she declared. "Let me alone. I'm nervous, and I don't want to spill the soup. The name is Nora Jaret, without an H, and the number is Stanhope five, six-six-two-one. The earrings were a present from Sir Laurence Olivier. I was sitting on his knee."

I wrote the number down in my notebook, thanked her, and looked around. Most of the collection of attractive young females were gathered in an alcove between two cupboards, but one was over by a table watching Felix stir something in a bowl. Her profile was fine and her hair was the color of corn silk just before it starts to turn. I crossed to her, and when she turned her head I spoke. "Good evening, Miss—Miss?"

"Annis," she said. "Carol Annis."

I wrote it down, and told her my name. "I am not blunt by nature," I said, "but you're busy, or soon will be, and there isn't time to talk up to it. I was standing watching you, and all of a sudden I had an impulse to ask you for your phone number, and I'm no good at fighting impulses. Now that you're close up it's even stronger, and I guess we'll have to humor it."

But I may be giving a wrong impression. Actually I had no special hankering that Tuesday evening for new telephone numbers; I was doing it for Fritz. But that could give a wrong impression too, so I'll have to explain.

One day in February, Lewis Hewitt, the millionaire and orchid fancier for whom Nero Wolfe had once handled a tough problem, had told Wolfe that the Ten for Aristology wanted Fritz Brenner to cook their annual dinner, to be given as usual on April first, Brillat-Savarin's birthday. When Wolfe said he had never heard of the Ten for Aristology, and Hewitt explained that it was a group of ten men pursuing the ideal of perfection in food and drink, and he was one of them. Wolfe had swiveled to the dictionary on its stand at a corner of his desk, and after consulting it had declared that "aristology" meant the science of dining, and therefore the Ten were witlings, since dining was not a science but an art. After a long argument Hewitt had admitted he was licked and had agreed that the name should be changed, and Wolfe had given him permission to ask Fritz to cook the dinner.

In fact Wolfe was pleased, though of course he wouldn't say so. It took a big slice of his income as a private detective to pay Fritz Brenner, chef and housekeeper in the old brownstone on West 35th Street—about the same as the slice that came to me as his assistant detective and man Friday, Saturday, Sunday, Monday, Tuesday, Wednesday, and Thursday—not to mention what it took to supply the kitchen with the raw materials of Fritz's productions. Since I am also the bookkeeper, I can certify that for the year 1957 the kitchen and Fritz cost only slightly less than the plant rooms on the roof bulging with orchids. So when Hewitt made it clear that the Ten, though they might be dubs at picking names, were true and trustworthy gourmets, that the dinner would be at the home of Benjamin Schriver, the shipping magnate, who wrote a letter to the *Times* every year on September first denouncing the use of horseradish on oysters, and that the cook would have a free hand on the menu and the Ten would furnish whatever he desired, Wolfe pushed a button to summon Fritz. There was a little hitch when Fritz refused to commit himself until he had seen the Schriver kitchen, but Hewitt settled that by escorting him out front to his Heron town car and driving him down to Eleventh Street to inspect the kitchen.

That's where I was that Tuesday evening, April first, collecting phone numbers: in the kitchen of the four-story Schriver house on Eleventh Street west of Fifth Avenue. Wolfe and I had been invited by Schriver, and though Wolfe dislikes eating with strangers and thinks that more than six at table spoils a meal, he knew Fritz's feelings would be hurt if he didn't go; and besides, if he stayed home who would cook his dinner? Even so, he would probably have balked if he had learned of one detail which Fritz and I knew about but had carefully kept from him: that the table was to be served by twelve young women, one for each guest.

When Hewitt had told me that, I had protested that I wouldn't be responsible for Wolfe's conduct when the orgy got under way, that he would certainly stamp out of the house when the girls started to squeal. Good lord, Hewitt said, nothing like that; that wasn't the idea at all. It was merely that the Ten had gone to ancient Greece not only for their name but also for other precedents. Hebe, the goddess of youth, had been cupbearer to the gods, so it was the custom of the Ten for Aristology to be waited on by maidens in appropriate dress. When I asked where they got the maidens he said through a theatrical agency, and added that at that time of year there were always hundreds of young actresses out of a job glad to grab at a chance to make fifty bucks, with a good meal thrown in, by spending an evening carrying food, one plate at a time. Originally they had hired experienced waitresses from an agency, but they had tripped on their *stolas*.

Wolfe and I had arrived at seven on the dot, and after we had met our host and the rest of the Ten, and had sampled oysters and our choice of five white wines, I had made my way to the kitchen to see how Fritz was making out. He was tasting from a pot on the range, with no more sign of fluster than if he had been at home getting dinner for Wolfe and me. Felix and Zoltan, from Rusterman's, were there to help, so I didn't ask if I was needed.

And there were the Hebes, cupbearers to the gods, twelve of them, in their stolas, deep rich purple, flowing garments to their ankles. Very nice. It gave me an idea. Fritz likes to pretend that he has reason to believe that no damsel is safe within a mile of me, which doesn't make sense since you can't tell much about them a mile off, and I thought it would do him good to see me operate at close quarters. Also it was a challenge and an interesting sociological experiment. The first two had been a cinch: one named Fern Faber, so she said, a tall self-made blonde with a wide lazy mouth, and Nora Jaret with the big brown eyes and dimples. Now I was after this Carol Annis with hair like corn silk.

"I have no sense of humor," she said, and turned back to watch Felix stir.

I stuck. "That's a different kind of humor and an impulse like mine isn't funny. It hurts. Maybe I can guess it. Is it Hebe one, oh-oh-oh-oh?"

No reply.

"Apparently not. Plato two, three-four-five-six?"

She said, without turning her head, "It's listed. Gorham eight, three-two-one-seven." Her head jerked to me. "Please?" It jerked back again.

It rather sounded as if she meant please go away, not please ring her as soon as possible, but I wrote it down anyway, for the record, and moved off. The rest of them were still grouped in the alcove, and I crossed over. The deep purple of the stolas was a good contrast for their pretty young faces topped by nine different colors and styles of hairdos. As I came up the chatter stopped and the faces turned to me.

"At ease," I told them. "I have no official standing. I am merely one of the guests, invited because I'm a friend of the cook, and I have a personal problem. I would prefer to discuss it with each of you separately and privately, but since there isn't time for that I am—"

"I know who you are," one declared. "You're a detective and you work for Nero Wolfe. You're Archie Goodwin."

She was a redhead with milky skin. "I don't deny it," I told her, "but I'm not here professionally. I don't ask if I've met you because if I had I wouldn't have forgot—"

"You haven't met me. I've seen you and I've seen your picture. You like yourself. Don't you?"

"Certainly. I string along with the majority. We'll take a vote. How many of you like yourselves? Raise your hands."

A hand went up with a bare arm shooting out of the purple folds, then two more, then the rest of them, including the redhead.

"Okay," I said, "that's settled. Unanimous. My problem is that I decided to look you over and ask the most absolutely irresistibly beautiful and fascinating one of the bunch for her phone number, and I'm stalled. You are all it. In beauty and fascination you are all far beyond the wildest dreams of any poet, and I'm not a poet. So obviously I'm in a fix. How can I possibly pick on one of you, any one, when—"

"Nuts." It was the redhead. "Me, of course. Peggy Choate. Argyle two, three-three-four-eight. Don't call before noon."

"That's not fair," a throaty voice objected. It came from one who looked a little too old for Hebe, and just a shade too plump. It went on, "Do I call you Archie?"

"Sure, that's my name."

"All right, Archie, have your eyes examined." She lifted an arm, baring it, to touch the shoulder of one beside her. "We admit we're all beautiful, but we're not in the same class as Helen Iacono. Look at her!"

I was doing so, and I must say that the throaty voice had a point. Helen Iacono, with deep dark eyes, dark velvet skin, and wavy silky hair darker than either skin or eyes, was unquestionably rare and special. Her lips were parted enough to show the gleam of white teeth, but she wasn't laughing. She wasn't reacting at all, which was remarkable for an actress.

"It may be," I conceded, "that I am so dazzled by the collective radiance that I am blind to the glory of any single star. Perhaps I'm a poet after all, I sound like one. My feeling that I must have the phone numbers of *all* of you is certainly no reflection on Helen Iacono. I admit that that will not completely solve the problem, for tomorrow I must face the question which one to call first. If I feel as I do right now I would have to dial all the numbers simultaneously, and that's impossible. I hope to heaven it doesn't end in a stalemate. What if I can never decide which one to call first? What if it drives me mad? Or what if I gradually sink—"

I turned to see who was tugging at my sleeve. It was Benjamin Schriver, the host, with a grin on his ruddy round face. He said, "I hate to interrupt your speech, but perhaps you can finish it later. We're ready to sit. Will you join us?"

II

The dining room, on the same floor as the kitchen, three feet or so below street level, would have been too gloomy for my taste if most of the dark wood paneling hadn't been covered with pictures of geese, pheasants, fish, fruit, vegetables, and other assorted edible objects; and also it helped that the tablecloth was white as snow, the wineglasses, seven of them at each place, glistened in the soft light from above, and the polished silver shone. In the center was a low gilt bowl, or maybe gold, two feet long, filled with clusters of Phalaenopsis Aphrodite, donated by Wolfe, cut by him that afternoon from some of his most treasured plants.

As he sat he was scowling at them, but the scowl was not for the orchids; it was for the chair, which, though a little fancy, was perfectly okay for you or me but not for his seventh of a ton. His fundament lapped over at both sides. He erased the scowl when Schriver, at the end of the table, complimented him on the flowers, and Hewitt, across from him, said he had never seen Phalaenopsis better grown, and the others joined in the chorus, all but the aristologist who sat between Wolfe and me. He was a Wall Street character and a well-known theatrical angel named Vincent Pyle, and was living up to his reputation as an original by wearing a dinner jacket, with tie to match, which looked black until you had the light at a certain slant and then you saw that it was green. He eyed the orchids with his head cocked and his mouth puckered, and said, "I don't care for flowers with spots and streaks. They're messy."

I thought, but didn't say, Okay, drop dead. If I had known that that was what he was going to do in about three hours I might not even have thought it. He got a rise, not from Wolfe or me, or Schriver or Hewitt, but from three others who thought flowers with spots and streaks were wonderful: Adrian Dart, the actor who had turned down an offer of a million a week, more or less, from Hollywood; Emil Kreis, Chairman of the Board of Codex Press, book publishers; and Harvey M. Leacraft, corporation lawyer.

Actually, cupbearers was what the Hebes were not. The wines, beginning with the Montrachet with the first course, were poured by Felix; but the girls delivered the food, with different routines for different items. The first course, put on individual plates in the kitchen, with each girl bringing in a plate for her aristologist, was small *blinis* sprinkled with chopped chives, piled with caviar, and topped with sour cream—the point, as far as Fritz was concerned, being that he had made the blinis, starting on them at eleven that morning, and also the sour cream, starting on that Sunday evening. Fritz's sour cream is very special, but Vincent Pyle had to get in a crack. After he had downed all of his blinis he remarked, loud enough to carry around the table, "A new idea, putting sand in. Clever. Good for chickens, since they need grit."

The man on my left, Emil Kreis, the publisher, muttered at my ear, "Ignore him. He backed three flops this season."

The girls, who had been coached by Fritz and Felix that afternoon, handled the green turtle soup without a splash. When they had brought in the soup plates Felix brought the bowl, and each girl ladled from it as Felix held it by the plate. I asked Pyle cordially, "Any sand?" but he said no, it was delicious, and cleaned it up.

I was relieved when I saw that the girls wouldn't dish the fish—flounders poached in dry white wine, with a mussel-and-mushroom sauce that was one of Fritz's specialties. Felix did the dishing at a side table, and the girls merely carried. With the first taste of the sauce there were murmurs of appreciation, and Adrian Dart, the actor, across from Wolfe, sang out, "Superb!" They were making various noises of satisfaction, and Leacraft, the lawyer, was asking Wolfe if Fritz would be willing to give him the recipe, when Pyle, on my right, made a face and dropped his fork on his plate with a clatter. I thought he was putting on an act, and still thought so when his head drooped and I heard him gnash his teeth, but then his shoulders sagged and he clapped a hand to his mouth, and that seemed to be overdoing it. Two or three of them said something, and he pushed his chair back, got to his feet, said, "You must excuse me, I'm sorry," and headed for the door to the hall. Schriver arose and followed him out. The others exchanged words and glances.

Hewitt said, "A damn shame, but I'm going to finish this,"

and used his fork. Someone asked if Pyle had a bad heart, and someone else said no. They all resumed with the flounder, and the conversation, but the spirit wasn't the same.

When, at a signal from Felix, the maidens started removing the plates, Lewis Hewitt got up and left the room, came back in a couple of minutes, sat, and raised his voice. "Vincent is in considerable pain, and a doctor has come. There is nothing we can do, and Ben wishes us to proceed. He will rejoin us when—when he can."

"What is it?" someone asked.

Hewitt said the doctor didn't know. Zoltan entered bearing an enormous covered platter, and the Hebes gathered at the side table, and Felix lifted the cover and began serving the roast pheasant, which had been larded with strips of pork soaked for twenty hours in Tokay, and then—but no. What's the use? The annual dinner of the Ten for Aristology was a flop. Since for years I have been eating three meals a day cooked by Fritz Brenner I would like to show my appreciation by getting in print some idea of what he can do in the way of victuals, but it won't do here. Sure, the pheasant was good enough for gods if there had been any around, and so was the suckling pig, and the salad, with a dressing which Fritz calls Devil's Rain, and the chestnut croquettes, and the cheese —only the one kind, made in New Jersey by a man named Bill Thompson under Fritz's supervision; and they were all eaten, more or less. But Hewitt left the room three more times and the last time was gone a good ten minutes, and Schriver didn't rejoin the party at all, and while the salad was being served Emil Kreis went out and didn't come back.

When, as coffee and brandy were being poured and cigars and cigarettes passed, Hewitt left his chair for the fifth time, Nero Wolfe got up and followed him out. I lit a cigar just to be doing something, and tried to be sociable by giving an ear to a story Adrian Dart was telling, but by the time I finished my coffee I was getting fidgety. By the glower that had been deepening on Wolfe's face for the past hour I knew he was boiling, and when he's like that, especially away from home, there's no telling about him. He might even have had the idea of aiming the glower at Vincent Pyle for ruining Fritz's meal. So I put what was left of the cigar in a tray, arose, and headed for the door, and was halfway to it when here he came, still glowering.

"Come with me," he snapped, and kept going.

The way to the kitchen from the dining room was through a pantry, twenty feet long, with counters and shelves and cupboards on both sides. Wolfe marched through with me behind. In the kitchen the twelve maidens were scattered around on chairs and stools at tables and counters, eating. A woman was busy at a sink. Zoltan was busy at a refrigerator. Fritz, who was pouring a glass of wine, presumably for himself, turned as Wolfe entered and put the bottle down.

Wolfe went to him, stood, and spoke. "Fritz. I offer my apologies. I permitted Mr. Hewitt to cajole you. I should have known better. I beg your pardon."

Fritz gestured with his free hand, the wineglass steady in the other. "But it is not to pardon, only to regret. The man got sick, that's a pity, only not from my cooking. I assure you."

"You don't need to. Not from your cooking as it left you, but as it reached him. I repeat that I am culpable, but I won't dwell on that now; it can wait. There is an aspect that is exigent." Wolfe turned. "Archie. Are those women all here?"

I had to cover more than half a circle to count them, scattered as they were. "Yes, sir, all present. Twelve."

"Collect them. They can stand"—he pointed to the alcove—"over there. And bring Felix."

It was hard to believe. They were eating; and for him to interrupt a man, or even a woman, at a meal, was unheard of. Not even me. Only in an extreme emergency had he ever asked me to quit food before I was through. Boiling was no name for it. Without even bothering to raise a brow, I turned and called out, "I'm sorry, ladies, but if Mr. Wolfe says it's urgent that settles it. Over there, please? All of you." Then I went through the pantry corridor, pushed the two-way door, caught Felix's eye, and wiggled a beckoning finger at him, and he came. By the time we got to the kitchen the girls had left the chairs and stools and were gathering at the alcove, but not with enthusiasm. There were mutterings, and some dirty looks for me as I approached with Felix. Wolfe came, with Zoltan, and stood, tight-lipped, surveying them.

"I remind you," he said, "that the first course you brought to the table was caviar on blinis topped with sour cream. The portion served to Mr. Vincent Pyle, and eaten by him, contained arsenic. Mr. Pyle is in bed upstairs, attended by three doctors, and will probably die within an hour. I am speaking—"

He stopped to glare at them. They were reacting, or acting, no matter which. There were gasps and exclamations, and one of them clutched her throat, and another, baring her arms, clapped her palms to her ears. When the glare had restored order Wolfe went on, "You will please keep quiet and listen. I am speaking of conclusions formed by me. My conclusion that Mr. Pyle ate arsenic is based on the symptoms: burning throat, faintness, intense burning pain in the stomach, dry mouth, cool skin, vomiting. My conclusion that the arsenic was in the first course is based, first, on the amount of time it takes arsenic to act; second, on the fact that it is highly unlikely it could have been put in the soup or the fish; and third, that Mr. Pyle complained of sand in the cream or caviar. I admit the possibility that one or both of my conclusions will be proven wrong, but I regard it as remote and I am acting on them." His head turned. "Fritz. Tell me about the caviar from the moment it was put on the individual plates. Who did that?"

I had once told Fritz that I could imagine no circumstances in which he would look really unhappy, but now I wouldn't have to try. He was biting his lips, first the lower and then the upper. He began, "I must assure you—"

"I need no assurance from you, Fritz. Who put it on the plates?"

"Zoltan and I did." He pointed. "At that table."

"And left them there? They were taken from that table by the women?"

"Yes, sir."

"Each woman took one plate?"

"Yes, sir. I mean, they were told to. I was at the range."

Zoltan spoke up. "I watched them, Mr. Wolfe. They each took one plate. And believe me, nobody put any arsenic—"

"Please, Zoltan. I add another conclusion: that no one put arsenic in one of the portions and then left to chance which one of the guests would get it. Surely the poisoner intended it to reach a certain one—either Mr. Pyle, or, as an alternative, some other one and it went to Mr. Pyle by mishap. In any case, it was the portion Pyle ate that was poisoned, and whether he got it by design or by mischance is for the moment irrelevant." His eyes were at the girls. "Which one of you took that plate to Mr. Pyle?"

No reply. No sound, no movement.

Wolfe grunted. "Pfui. If you didn't know his name, you do now. The man who left during the fish course and who is now dying. Who served him?"

No reply; and I had to hand it to them that no pair of eyes left Wolfe to fasten on Peggy Choate, the redhead. Mine did. "What the heck," I said. "Speak up, Miss Choate."

"I didn't!" she cried.

"That's silly. Of course you did. Twenty people can swear to it. I looked right at you while you were dishing his soup. And when you brought the fish—"

"But I didn't take him that first thing! He already had some! I didn't!"

Wolfe took over. "Your name is Choate?"

"Yes." Her chin was up. "Peggy Choate."

"You deny that you served the plate of caviar, the first course, to Mr. Pyle?"

"I certainly do."

"But you were supposed to? You were assigned to him?"

"Yes. I took the plate from the table there and went in with it, and started to him, and then I saw that he had some, and I thought I had made a mistake. We hadn't seen the guests. That man"—she pointed to Felix—"had shown us which chair our guest would sit in, and mine was the second from the right on this side as I went in, but that one had already been served, and I thought someone else had made a mistake or I was mixed up. Anyway, I saw that the man next to him, on his right, hadn't been served, and I gave it to him. That was you. I gave it to you."

"Indeed." Wolfe was frowning at her. "Who was assigned to me?"

That wasn't put on. He actually didn't know. He had never looked at her. He had been irritated that females were serving, and besides, he hates to twist his neck. Of course I could have told him, but Helen Iacono said, "I was."

"Your name, please?"

"Helen Iacono." She had a rich contralto that went fine with the deep dark eyes and dark velvet skin and wavy silky hair.

"Did you bring me the first course?"

"No. When I went in I saw Peggy serving you, and a man on the left next to the end didn't have any, so I gave it to him."

"Do you know his name?"

"I do," Nora Jaret said. "From the card. He was mine." Her big brown eyes were straight at Wolfe. "His name is Kreis. He had his when I got there. I was going to take it back to the kitchen, but then I thought, someone had stage fright but I haven't, and I gave it to the man at the end."

"Which end?"

"The left end. Mr. Schriver. He came and spoke to us this afternoon."

She was corroborated by Carol Annis, the one with hair like corn silk who had no sense of humor. "That's right," she said. "I saw her. I was going to stop her, but she had already put the plate down, so I went around to the other side of the table with it when I saw that Adrian Dart didn't have any. I didn't mind because it was him."

"You were assigned to Mr. Schriver?"

"Yes. I served him the other courses, until he left."

It was turning into a ring-around-a-rosy, but the squat was bound to come. All Wolfe had to do was get to one who couldn't claim a delivery, and that would tag her. I was rather hoping it wouldn't be the next one, for the girl with the throaty voice had been Adrian Dart's, and she had called me Archie and had given Helen Iacono a nice tribute. Would she claim she had served Dart herself?

No. She answered without being asked. "My name is Lucy Morgan," she said, "and I had Adrian Dart, and Carol got to him before I did. There was only one place that didn't have one, on Dart's left, the next but one, and I took it there. I don't know his name."

I supplied it. "Hewitt. Mr. Lewis Hewitt." A better name for it than ring-around-a-rosy would have been passing-the-buck. I looked at Fern Faber, the tall self-made blonde with a wide lazy mouth who had been my first stop on my phone-number tour. "It's your turn, Miss Faber," I told her. "You had Mr. Hewitt. Yes?"

"I sure did." Her voice was pitched so high it threatened to squeak.

"But you didn't take him his caviar?"

"I sure didn't."

"Then who did you take it to?"

"Nobody."

I looked at Wolfe. His eyes were narrowed at her. "What did you do with it, Miss Faber?"

"I didn't do anything with it. There wasn't any."

"Nonsense. There are twelve of you, and there were twelve at the table, and each got a portion. How can you say there wasn't any?"

"Because there wasn't. I was in the john fixing my hair, and when I came back in she was taking the last one from the table, and when I asked where mine was he said he didn't know, and I went to the dining room and they all had some."

"Who was taking the last one from the table?"

She pointed to Lucy Morgan. "Her."

"Whom did you ask where yours was?"

She pointed to Zoltan. "Him."

Wolfe turned. "Zoltan?"

"Yes, sir. I mean, yes, sir, she asked where hers was. I had turned away when the last one was taken. I don't mean I know where she had been, just that she asked me that.

I asked Fritz if I should go in and see if they were one short
and he said no, Felix was there and would see to it."

Wolfe went back to Fern Faber. "Where is that room where
you were fixing your hair?"

She pointed toward the pantry. "In there."

"The door's around the corner," Felix said.

"How long were you in there?"

"My God, I don't know, do you think I timed it? When
Archie Goodwin was talking to us, and Mr. Schriver came
and said they were going to start, I went pretty soon after
that."

Wolfe's head jerked to me. "So that's where you were. I
might have known there were young women around. Sup-
posing that Miss Faber went to fix her hair shortly after you
left—say three minutes—how long was she at it, if the last
plate had been taken from the table when she returned to the
kitchen?"

I gave it a thought. "Fifteen to twenty minutes."

He growled at her, "What was wrong with your hair?"

"I didn't say anything was wrong with it." She was getting
riled. "Look, Mister, do you want all the details?"

"No." Wolfe surveyed them for a moment, not amiably,
took in enough air to fill all his middle—say two bushels—
let it out again, turned his back on them, saw the glass of
wine Fritz had left on a table, went and picked it up, smelled
it, and stood gazing at it. The girls started to make noises,
and, hearing them, he put the glass down and came back.

"You're in a pickle," he said. "So am I. You heard me
apologize to Mr. Brenner and avow my responsibility for his
undertaking to cook that meal. When, upstairs, I saw that
Mr. Pyle would die, and reached the conclusions I told you
of, I felt myself under compulsion to expose the culprit. I
am committed. When I came down here I thought it would
be a simple matter to learn who had served poisoned food to
Mr. Pyle, but I was wrong. It's obvious now that I have to
deal with one who is not only resourceful and ingenious, but
also quick-witted and audacious. While I was closing in on
her just now, as I thought, inexorably approaching the point
where she would either have to contradict one of you or deny
that she had served the first course to anyone, she was fleer-
ing at me inwardly, and with reason, for her coup had worked.
She had slipped through my fingers, and—"

"But she didn't!" It came from one of them whose name I
didn't have. "She said she didn't serve anybody!"

Wolfe shook his head. "No. Not Miss Faber. She is the
only one who is eliminated. She says she was absent from this
room during the entire period when the plates were being

taken from the table, and she wouldn't dare to say that if she had in fact been here and taken a plate and carried it in to Mr. Pyle. She would certainly have been seen by some of you."

He shook his head again. "Not her. But it could have been any other one of you. You—I speak now to that one, still to be identified—you must have extraordinary faith in your attendant godling, even allowing for your craft. For you took great risks. You took a plate from the table—not the first probably, but one of the first—and on your way to the dining room you put arsenic in the cream. That wasn't difficult; you might even have done it without stopping if you had the arsenic in a paper spill. You could get rid of the spill later, perhaps in the room which Miss Faber calls a john. You took the plate to Mr. Pyle, came back here immediately, got another plate, took it to the dining room, and gave it to one who had not been served. I am not guessing; it had to be like that. It was a remarkably adroit stratagem, but you can't possibly be impregnable."

He turned to Zoltan. "You say you watched as the plates were taken, and each of them took only one. Did one of them come back and take another?"

Zoltan looked fully as unhappy as Fritz. "I'm thinking, Mr. Wolfe. I can try to think, but I'm afraid it won't help. I didn't look at their faces, and they're all dressed alike. I guess I didn't watch very close."

"Fritz?"

"No, sir. I was at the range."

"Then try this, Zoltan. Who were the first ones to take plates—the first three or four?"

Zoltan slowly shook his head. "I'm afraid it's no good, Mr. Wolfe. I could try to think, but I couldn't be sure." He moved his eyes right to left and back again, at the girls. "I tell you, I wasn't looking at their faces." He extended his hands, palms up. "You will consider, Mr. Wolfe, I was not thinking of poison. I was only seeing that the plates were carried properly. Was I thinking which one has got arsenic? No."

"I took the first plate," a girl blurted—another whose name I didn't know. "I took it in and gave it to the man in my chair, the one at the left corner at the other side of the table, and I stayed there. I never left the dining room."

"Your name, please?"

"Marjorie Quinn."

"Thank you. Now the second plate. Who took it?"

Apparently nobody. Wolfe gave them ten seconds, his eyes moving to take them all in, his lips tight. "I advise you," he said, "to jog your memories, in case it becomes necessary to establish the order in which you took the plates by dragging it out of you. I hope it won't come to that." His head turned. "Felix, I have neglected you purposely, to give you time to reflect. You were in the dining room. My expectation was that after I had learned who had served the first course to Mr. Pyle you would corroborate it, but now that there is nothing for you to corroborate I must look to you for the fact itself. I must ask you to point her out."

In a way Wolfe was Felix's boss. When Wolfe's oldest and dearest friend, Marko Vukcic, who had owned Rusterman's restaurant, had died, his will had left the restaurant to members of the staff in trust, with Wolfe as the trustee, and Felix was the maître d'hôtel. With that job at the best restaurant in New York, naturally Felix was both bland and commanding, but now he was neither. If he felt the way he looked, he was miserable.

"I can't," he said.

"Pfui! You, trained as you are to see everything?"

"That is true, Mr. Wolfe. I knew you would ask me this, but I can't. I can only explain. The young woman who just spoke, Marjorie Quinn, was the first one in with a plate, as she said. She did not say that as she served it one of the blinis slid off onto the table, but it did. As I sprang toward her she was actually about to pick it up with her fingers, and I jerked her away and put it back on the plate with a fork, and I gave her a look. Anyway, I was not myself. Having women as waiters was bad enough, and not only that, they were without experience. When I recovered command of myself I saw the red-headed one, Choate, standing back of Mr. Pyle, to whom she had been assigned, with a plate in her hand, and I saw that he had already been served. As I moved forward she stepped to the right and served the plate to you. The operation was completely upset, and I was helpless. The dark-skinned one, Iacono, who was assigned to you, served Mr. Kreis, and the—"

"If you please." Wolfe was curt. "I have heard them, and so have you. I have always found you worthy of trust, but it's possible that in your exalted position, maître d'hôtel at Rusterman's, you would rather dodge than get involved in a poisoning. Are you dodging, Felix?"

"Good God, Mr. Wolfe, I *am* involved!"

"Very well. I saw that woman spill the blini and start her fingers for it, and I saw you retrieve it. Yes, you're involved, but not as I am." He turned to me. "Archie. You are commonly my first resort, but now you are my last. You sat next to Mr. Pyle. Who put that plate before him?"

Of course I knew that was coming, but I hadn't been beating my brain because there was no use. I said merely but positively, "No." He glared at me and I added, "That's all, just no, but like Felix I can explain. First, I would have had to turn around to see her face, and that's bad table manners. Second, I was watching Felix rescue the blini. Third, there was an argument going on about flowers with spots and streaks, and I was listening to it and so were you. I didn't even see her arm."

Wolfe stood and breathed. He shut his eyes and opened them again, and breathed some more. "Incredible," he muttered. "The wretch had incredible luck."

"I'm going home," Fern Faber said. "I'm tired."

"So am I," another one said, and was moving, but Wolfe's eyes pinned her. "I advise you not to," he said. "It is true that Miss Faber is eliminated as the culprit, and also Miss Quinn, since she was under surveillance by Felix while Mr. Pyle was being served, but I advise even them to stay. When Mr. Pyle dies the doctors will certainly summon the police, and it would be well for all of you to be here when they arrive. I had hoped to be able to present them with an exposed murderer. Confound it! There is still a chance. Archie, come with me. Fritz, Felix, Zoltan, remain with these women. If one or more of them insist on leaving do not detain them by force, but have the names and the times of departure. If they want to eat feed them. I'll be—"

"I'm going home," Fern Faber said stubbornly.

"Very well, go. You'll be got out of bed by a policeman before the night's out. I'll be in the dining room, Fritz. Come, Archie."

He went and I followed, along the pantry corridor and through the two-way door. On the way I glanced at my wrist watch: ten past eleven. I rather expected to find the dining room empty, but it wasn't. Eight of them were still there, the only ones missing being Schriver and Hewitt, who were probably upstairs. The air was heavy with cigar smoke. All of them but Adrian Dart were at the table with their chairs pushed back at various angles, with brandy glasses and cigars. Dart was standing with his back to a picture of honkers on the wing, holding forth. As we entered he stopped and heads turned.

Emil Kreis spoke. "Oh, there you are. I was coming to the kitchen but didn't want to butt in. Schriver asked me to apologize to Fritz Brenner. Our custom is to ask the chef to join us with champagne, which is barbarous but gay, but of course in the circumstances . . ." He let it hang, and added, "Shall I explain to him? Or will you?"

"I will." Wolfe went to the end of the table and sat. He had been on his feet for nearly two hours—all very well for his twice-a-day sessions in the plant rooms, but not elsewhere. He looked around. "Mr. Pyle is still alive?"

"We hope so," one said. "We sincerely hope so."

"I ought to be home in bed," another one said. "I have a hard day tomorrow. But it doesn't seem . . ." He took a puff on his cigar.

Emil Kreis reached for the brandy bottle. "There's been no word since I came down." He looked at his wrist. "Nearly an hour ago. I suppose I should go up. It's so damned unpleasant." He poured brandy.

"Terrible," one said. "Absolutely terrible. I understand you were asking which one of the girls brought him the caviar. Kreis says you asked him."

Wolfe nodded. "I also asked Mr. Schriver and Mr. Hewitt. And Mr. Goodwin and Mr. Brenner, and the two men who came to help at my request. And the women themselves. After more than an hour with them I am still at fault. I have discovered the artifice the culprit used, but not her identity."

"Aren't you a bit premature?" Leacraft, the lawyer, asked. "There may be no culprit. An acute and severe gastric disturbance may be caused—"

"Nonsense. I am too provoked for civility, Mr. Leacraft. The symptoms are typical of arsenic, and you heard Mr. Pyle complain of sand, but that's not all. I said I have discovered the artifice. None of them will admit serving him the first course. The one assigned to him found he had already been served and served me instead. There is indeed a culprit. She put arsenic in the cream *en passant*, served it to Mr. Pyle, returned to the kitchen for another portion, and came and served it to someone else. That is established."

"But then," the lawyer objected, "one of them served no one. How could that be?"

"I am not a tyro at inquiry, Mr. Leacraft. I'll ravel it for you later if you want, but now I want to get on. It is no conjecture that poison was given to Mr. Pyle by the woman who brought him the caviar; it is a fact. By a remarkable combination of cunning and luck she has so far eluded identification, and I am appealing to you. All of you. I ask you to close your eyes and recall the scene. We are here at table, discussing the orchids—the spots and streaks. The woman serving that place"—he pointed—"lets a blini slip from the plate and Felix retrieves it. It helps to close your eyes. Just about then a woman enters with a plate, goes to Mr. Pyle, and puts it before him. I appeal to you: which one?"

Emil Kreis shook his head. "I told you upstairs, I don't know. I didn't see her. Or if I did, it didn't register."

Adrian Dart, the actor, stood with his eyes closed, his chin up, and his arms folded, a fine pose for concentration. The others, even Leacraft, had their eyes closed too, but of course they couldn't hold a candle to Dart. After a long moment the eyes began to open and heads to shake.

"It's gone," Dart said in his rich musical baritone. "I must have seen it, since I sat across from him, but it's gone. Utterly."

"I didn't see it," another said. "I simply didn't see it."

"I have a vague feeling," another said, "but it's too damn vague. No."

They made it unanimous. No dice.

Wolfe put his palms on the table. "Then I'm in for it," he said grimly. "I am your guest, gentlemen, and would not be offensive, but I am to blame that Fritz Brenner was enticed to this deplorable fiasco. If Mr. Pyle dies, as he surely will—"

The door opened and Benjamin Schriver entered. Then Lewis Hewitt, and then the familiar burly frame of Sergeant Purley Stebbins of Manhattan Homicide West.

Schriver crossed to the table and spoke. "Vincent is dead. Half an hour ago. Doctor Jameson called the police. He thinks that it is practically certain—"

"Hold it," Purley growled at his elbow. "I'll handle it if you don't mind."

"My God," Adrian Dart groaned, and shuddered magnificently.

That was the last I heard of the affair from an aristologist.

III

"I did not!" Inspector Cramer roared. "Quit twisting my words around! I didn't charge you with complicity! I merely said you're concealing something, and what the hell is that to scrape your neck? You always do!"

It was a quarter to two Wednesday afternoon. We were in the office on the first floor of the old brownstone on West 35th Street—Wolfe in his oversized chair. The daily schedule was messed beyond repair. When we had finally got home, at five o'clock in the morning, Wolfe had told Fritz to forget about breakfast until further notice, and had sent me up to the plant rooms to leave a note for Theodore saying that he would not appear at nine in the morning and perhaps not at all. It had been not at all. At half past eleven he had buzzed on the house phone to tell Fritz to bring up the breakfast tray with four eggs and ten slices of bacon instead of two and five, and it was past one o'clock when the sounds came of his elevator and then his footsteps in the hall, heading for the office.

If you think a problem child is tough, try handling a problem elephant. He is plenty knotty even when he is himself, and that day he was really special. After looking through the mail, glancing at his desk calendar, and signing three checks I had put on his desk, he had snapped at me, "A fine prospect. Dealing with them singly would be interminable. Will you have them all here at six o'clock?"

I kept calm. I merely asked, "All of whom?"

"You know quite well. Those women."

I still kept calm. "I should think ten of them would be enough. You said yourself that two of them can be crossed off."

"I need them all. Those two can help establish the order in which the plates were taken."

I held on. I too was short on sleep, shorter even than he, and I didn't feel up to a fracas. "I have a suggestion," I said. "I suggest that you postpone operations until your wires are connected again. Counting up to five hundred might help. You know damn well that all twelve of them will spend the afternoon either at the District Attorney's office or receiving official callers at their homes—probably most of them at the DA's office. And probably they'll spend the evening there too. Do you want some aspirin?"

"I want *them*," he growled.

I could have left him to grope back to normal on his own and gone up to my room for a nap, but after all he pays my salary. So I picked up a sheet of paper I had typed and got up and handed it to him. It read:

	Assigned to	*Served*
Peggy Choate	Pyle	Wolfe
Helen Iacono	Wolfe	Kreis
Nora Jaret	Kreis	Schriver
Carol Annis	Schriver	Dart
Lucy Morgan	Dart	Hewitt
Fern Faber	Hewitt	No one

"Fern Faber's out," I said, "and I realize it doesn't have to be one of those five, even though Lucy Morgan took the last plate. Possibly one or two others took plates after Peggy Choate did, and served the men they were assigned to. But it seems—"

I stopped because he had crumpled it and dropped it in the wastebasket. "I heard them," he growled. "My faculties, including my memory, are not impaired. I am merely ruffled beyond the bounds of tolerance."

For him that was an abject apology, and a sign that he

was beginning to regain control. But a few minutes later, when the bell rang, and after a look through the one-way glass panel of the front door I told him it was Cramer, and he said to admit him, and Cramer marched in and planted his fanny on the red leather chair and opened up with an impolite remark about concealing facts connected with a murder, Wolfe had cut loose; and Cramer asked him what the hell was that to scrape his neck, which was a new one to me but sounded somewhat vulgar for an inspector. He had probably picked it up from some hoodlum.

Ruffling Cramer beyond the bounds of tolerance did Wolfe good. He leaned back in his chair. "Everyone conceals something," he said placidly. "Or at least omits something, if only because to include everything is impossible. During those wearisome hours, nearly six of them, I answered all questions, and so did Mr. Goodwin. Indeed, I thought we were helpful. I thought we had cleared away some rubble."

"Yeah." Cramer wasn't grateful. His big pink face was always a little pinker than normal, not with pleasure, when he was tackling Wolfe. "You had witnessed the commission of a murder, and you didn't notify—"

"It wasn't a murder until he died."

"All right, a felony. You not only failed to report it, you—"

"That a felony had been committed was my conclusion. Others present disagreed with me. Only a few minutes before Mr. Stebbins entered the room Mr. Leacraft, a member of the bar and therefore himself an officer of the law, challenged my conclusion."

"You should have reported it. You're a licensed detective. Also you started an investigation, questioning the suspects—"

"Only to test my conclusion. I would have been a ninny to report it before learning—"

"Damn it," Cramer barked, "will you let me finish a sentence? Just one?"

Wolfe's shoulders went up an eighth of an inch and down again. "Certainly, if it has import. I am not baiting you, Mr. Cramer. But I have already replied to these imputations, to you and Mr. Stebbins and an assistant district attorney. I did not wrongly delay reporting a crime, and I did not usurp the function of the police. Very well, finish a sentence."

"You knew Pyle was dying. You said so."

"Also my own conclusion. The doctors were still trying to save him."

Cramer took a breath. He looked at me, saw nothing inspiring, and returned to Wolfe. "I'll tell you why I'm here. Those three men—the cook, the man that helped him, and the man in the dining room—Fritz Brenner, Felix Courbet, and Zoltan Mahany—were all supplied by you. All close to you. I want to know about them, or at least two of them. I might as well leave Fritz out of it. In the first place, it's hard to believe that Zoltan doesn't know who took the first two or three plates or whether one of them came back for a second one, and it's also hard to believe that Felix doesn't know who served Pyle."

"It is indeed," Wolfe agreed. "They are highly trained men. But they have been questioned."

"They sure have. It's also hard to believe that Goodwin didn't see who served Pyle. He sees everything."

"Mr. Goodwin is present. Discuss it with him."

"I have. Now I want to ask your opinion of a theory. I know yours, and I don't reject it, but there are alternatives. First a fact. In a metal trash container in the kitchen—not a garbage pail—we found a roll of paper, ordinary white paper that had been rolled into a tube, held with tape, smaller at one end. The laboratory has found particles of arsenic inside. The only two fingerprints on it that are any good are Zoltan's. He says he saw it on the kitchen floor under a table some time after the meal had started, he can't say exactly when, and he picked it up and dropped it in the container, and his prints are on it because he pinched it to see if there was anything in it."

Wolfe nodded. "As I surmised. A paper spill."

"Yeah. I don't say it kills your theory. She could have shaken it into the cream without leaving prints, and she certainly wouldn't have dropped it on the floor if there was any chance it had her prints. But it *has* got Zoltan's. What's wrong with the theory that Zoltan poisoned one of the portions and saw that it was taken by a certain one? I'll answer that myself. There are two things wrong with it. First, Zoltan claims he didn't know which guest any of the girls were assigned to. But Felix knew, and they could have been in collusion. Second, the girls all deny that Zoltan indicated which plate they were to take, but you know how that is. He could have done it without her knowing it. What else is wrong with it?"

"It's not only untenable, it's egregious," Wolfe declared. "Why, in that case, did one of them come back for another plate?"

"She was confused. Nervous. Dumb."

"Bosh. Why doesn't she admit it?"

"Scared."

"I don't believe it. I questioned them before you did." Wolfe waved it away. "Tommyrot, and you know it. My theory is not a theory; it is a reasoned conviction. I hope it is being acted on. I suggested to Mr. Stebbins that he examine their garments to see if some kind of pocket had been made in one of them. She had to have it readily available."

"He did. They all had pockets. The laboratory has found no trace of arsenic." Cramer uncrossed his legs. "We're following up your theory all right; we might even have hit on it ourselves in a week or two. But I wanted to ask you about those men. You know them."

"I do, yes. But I do not answer for them. They may have a dozen murders on their souls, but they had nothing to do with the death of Mr. Pyle. If you are following up my theory—my conviction, rather—I suppose you have learned the order in which the women took the plates."

Cramer shook his head. "We have not, and I doubt if we will. All we have is a bunch of contradictions. You had them good and scared before we got to them. We do have the last five, starting with Peggy Choate, who found that Pyle had been served and gave it to you, and then—but you know them. You got that yourself."

"No. I got those five, but not that they were the last. There might have been others in between."

"There weren't. It's pretty well settled that those five were the last. After Peggy Choate the last four plates were taken by Helen Iacono, Nora Jaret, Carol Annis, and Lucy Morgan. Then that Fern Faber, who had been in the can, but there was no plate for her. It's the order in which they took them before that, the first seven, that we can't pry out of them—except the first one, that Marjorie Quinn. You couldn't either."

Wolfe turned a palm up. "I was interrupted."

"You were not. You left them there in a huddle, scared stiff, and went to the dining room to start in on the men. Your own private murder investigation, and to hell with the law. I was surprised to see Goodwin here when I rang the bell just now. I supposed you'd have him out running errands like calling at the agency they got the girls from. Or getting a line on Pyle to find a connection between him and one of them. Unless you're no longer interested?"

"I'm interested willy-nilly," Wolfe declared. "As I told the assistant district attorney, it is on my score that a man was poisoned in food prepared by Fritz Brenner. But I do not send Mr. Goodwin on fruitless errands. He is one and you have dozens, and if anything is to be learned at the agency or by inquiry into Mr. Pyle's associations your army will dig it up. They're already at it, of course, but if they had started a trail you wouldn't be here. If I send Mr. Goodwin—"

The doorbell rang and I got up and went to the hall. At the rear the door to the kitchen swung open part way and Fritz poked his head through, saw me, and withdrew. Turning to the front for a look through the panel, I saw that I had exaggerated when I told Wolfe that all twelve of them would be otherwise engaged. At least one wasn't. There on the stoop was Helen Iacono.

IV

It had sounded to me as if Cramer had about said his say and would soon be moving along, and if he bumped into Helen Iacono in the hall she might be too embarrassed to give me her phone number, if that was what she had come for, so as I opened the door I pressed a finger to my lips and *sshh*ed at her, and then crooked the finger to motion her in. Her deep dark eyes looked a little startled, but she stepped across the sill, and I shut the door, turned, opened the first door on the left, to the front room, motioned to her to enter, followed, and closed the door.

"What's the matter?" she whispered.

"Nothing now," I told her. "This is soundproofed. There's a police inspector in the office with Mr. Wolfe and I thought you might have had enough of cops for a while. Of course if you want to meet him—"

"I don't. I want to see Nero Wolfe."

"Okay, I'll tell him as soon as the cop goes. Have a seat. It shouldn't be long."

There is a connecting door between the front room and the office, but I went around through the hall, and here came Cramer. He was marching by without even the courtesy of a grunt, but I stepped to the front to let him out, and then went to the office and told Wolfe, "I've got one of them in the front room. Helen Iacono, the tawny-skinned Hebe who had you but gave her caviar to Kreis. Shall I keep her while I get the rest of them?"

He made a face. "What does she want?"

"To see you."

He took a breath. "Confound it. Bring her in."

I went and opened the connecting door, told her to come, and escorted her across to the red leather chair. She was more ornamental in it than Cramer, but not nearly as impressive as she had been at first sight. She was puffy around the eyes and her skin had lost some glow. She told Wolfe she hadn't had any sleep. She said she had just left the District Attorney's office, and if she went home her mother would be at her again, and her brothers and sisters would come home from school and make noise, and anyway she had decided she had to see Wolfe. Her mother was old-fashioned and didn't want her to be an actress. It was beginning to sound as if what she was after was a place to take a nap, but then Wolfe got a word in.

He said drily, "I don't suppose, Miss Iacono, you came to consult me about your career."

"Oh, no. I came because you're a detective and you're very clever and I'm afraid. I'm afraid they'll find out something I did, and if they do I won't have any career. My parents won't let me even if I'm still alive. I nearly gave it away already when they were asking me questions. So I decided to tell you about it and then if you'll help me I'll help you. If you promise to keep my secret."

"I can't promise to keep a secret if it is a guilty one—if it is a confession of a crime or knowledge of one."

"It isn't."

"Then you have my promise, and Mr. Goodwin's. We have kept many secrets."

"All right. I stabbed Vincent Pyle with a knife and got blood on me."

I stared. For half a second I thought she meant that he hadn't died of poison at all, that she had sneaked upstairs and stuck a knife in him, which seemed unlikely since the doctors would probably have found the hole.

Apparently she wasn't going on, and Wolfe spoke. "Ordinarily, Miss Iacono, stabbing a man is considered a crime. When and where did this happen?"

"It wasn't a crime because it was in self-defense." Her rich contralto was as composed as if she had been telling us the multiplication table. Evidently she saved the inflections for her career. She was continuing. "It happened in January, about three months ago. Of course I knew about him, everybody in show business does. I don't know if it's true that he backs shows just so he can get girls, but it might as well be. There's a lot of talk about the girls he gets, but nobody really knows because he was always very careful about it. Some of the girls have talked but he never did. I don't mean just taking them out, I mean the last ditch. We say that on Broadway. You know what I mean?"

"I can surmise."

"Sometimes we say the last stitch, but it means the same thing. Early last winter he began on me. Of course I knew about his reputation, but he was backing *Jack in the Pulpit* and they were about to start casting, and I didn't know it was going to be a flop, and if a girl expects to have a career she has to be sociable. I went out with him a few times, dinner and dancing and so forth, and then he asked me to his apartment, and I went. He cooked the dinner himself—I said he was very careful. Didn't I?"

"Yes."

"Well, he was. It's a penthouse on Madison Avenue, but no one else was there. I let him kiss me. I figure it like this, an actress gets kissed all the time on the stage and the screen and TV, and what's the difference? I went to his apartment three times and there was no real trouble, but the fourth time, that was in January, he turned into a beast right before my eyes, and I had to do something, and I grabbed a knife from the table and stabbed him with it. I got blood on my dress, and when I got home I tried to get it out but it left a stain. It cost forty-six dollars."

"But Mr. Pyle recovered."

"Oh, yes. I saw him a few times after that, I mean just by accident, but he barely spoke and so did I. I don't think he ever told anyone about it, but what if he did? What if the police find out about it?"

Wolfe grunted. "That would be regrettable, certainly. You would be pestered even more than you are now. But if you have been candid with me you are not in mortal jeopardy. The police are not simpletons. You wouldn't be arrested for murdering Mr. Pyle last night, let alone convicted, merely because you stabbed him in self-defense last January."

"Of course I wouldn't," she agreed. "That's not it. It's my mother and father. They'd find out about it because they would ask them questions, and if I'm going to have a career I would have to leave home and my family, and I don't want to. Don't you see?" She came forward in the chair. "But if they find out right away who did it, who poisoned him, that would end it and I'd be all right. Only I'm afraid they won't find out right away, but I think you could if I help you, and you said last night that you're committed. I can't offer to help the police because they'd wonder why."

"I see." Wolfe's eyes were narrowed at her. "How do you propose to help me?"

"Well, I figure it like this." She was on the edge of the chair. "The way you explained it last night, one of the girls poisoned him. She was one of the first ones to take a plate in, and then she came back and got another one. I don't quite understand why she did that, but you do, so all right. But if she came back for another plate that took a little time, and she must have been one of the last ones, and the police have got it worked out who were the last five. I know that because of the questions they asked this last time. So it was Peggy Choate or Nora Jaret or Carol Annis or Lucy Morgan."

"Or you."

"No, it wasn't me." Just matter-of-fact. "So it was one of them. And she didn't poison him just for nothing, did she? You'd have to have a very good reason to poison a man, I know I would. So all we have to do is find out which one had a good reason, and that's where I can help. I don't know Lucy Morgan, but I know Carol a little, and I know Nora and Peggy even better. And now we're in this together, and I can pretend I want to talk about it. I can talk about him because I had to tell the police I went out with him a few times, because I was seen with him and they'd find out, so I thought I'd better tell them. Dozens of girls went out with him, but he was so careful that nobody knows which ones went to the last ditch except the ones that talked. And I can find out which one of those four girls had a reason, and tell you, and that will end it."

I was congratulating myself that I hadn't got her phone number; and if I had got it, I would have crossed it off without a pang. I don't say that a girl must have true nobility of character before I'll buy her a lunch, but you have to draw the line somewhere. Thinking that Wolfe might be disgusted enough to put into words the way I felt, I horned in. "I have a suggestion, Miss Iacono. You could bring them here, all four of them, and let Mr. Wolfe talk it over with them. As you say, he's very clever."

She looked doubtful. "I don't believe that's a good idea. I think they'd be more apt to say things to me, just one at a time. Don't you think so, Mr. Wolfe?"

"You know them better than I do," he muttered. He was controlling himself.

"And then," she said, "when we find out which one had a reason, and we tell the police, I can say that I saw her going back to the kitchen for another plate. Of course just where I saw her, where she was and where I was, that will depend on who she is. I saw you, Mr. Wolfe, when I said you could if I helped you, I saw the look on your face. You didn't think a twenty-year-old girl could help, did you?"

He had my sympathy. Of course what he would have liked to say was that it might well be that a twenty-year-old hellcat could help, but that wouldn't have been tactful.

"I may have been a little skeptical," he conceded. "And it's possible that you're over-simplifying the problem. We have to consider all the factors. Take one: her plan must

have been not only premeditated but also thoroughly rigged,
since she had the poison ready. So she must have known
that Mr. Pyle would be one of the guests. Did she?"

"Oh, yes. We all did. Mr. Buchman at the agency showed
us a list of them and told us who they were, only of course
he didn't have to tell us who Vincent Pyle was. That was
about a month ago, so she had plenty of time to get the
poison. Is that arsenic very hard to get?"

"Not at all. It is in common use for many purposes. That
is of course one of the police lines of inquiry, but she knew
it would be and she is no bungler. Another point: when Mr.
Pyle saw her there, serving food, wouldn't he have been on
his guard?"

"But he didn't see her. They didn't see any of us before.
She came up behind him and gave him that plate. Of course
he saw her afterwards, but he had already eaten it."

Wolf persisted. "But then? He was in agony, but he was
conscious and could speak. Why didn't he denounce her?"

She gestured impatiently. "I guess you're not as clever as
you're supposed to be. He didn't know she had done it.
When he saw her she was serving another man, and—"

"What other man?"

"I don't know. How do I know? Only it wasn't you, because I served you. And anyway, maybe he didn't know she
wanted to kill him. Of course she had a good reason, I know
that, but maybe he didn't know she felt like that. A man
doesn't know how a girl feels—anyhow, some girls. Look at
me. He didn't know I would never dream of going to the last
ditch. He thought I would give up my honor and my virtue
just to get a part in that play he was backing, and anyhow
it was a flop." She gestured again. "I thought you wanted to
get her. All you do is make objections."

Wolfe rubbed the side of his nose. "I do want to get her,
Miss Iacono. I intend to. But like Mr. Pyle, though from a
different motive, I am very careful. I can't afford to botch it.
I fully appreciate your offer to help. You didn't like Mr.
Goodwin's suggestion that you get them here in a body for
discussion with me, and you may be right. But I don't like
your plan, for you to approach them singly and try to pump
them. Our quarry is a malign and crafty harpy, and I will not
be a party to your peril. I propose an alternative. Arrange
for Mr. Goodwin to see them, together with you. Being a
trained investigator, he knows how to beguile, and the peril,
if any, will be his. If they are not available at the moment,
arrange it for this evening—but not here. Perhaps one of
them has a suitable apartment, or if not, a private room at

some restaurant would do. At my expense, of course. Will you?"

It was her turn to make objections, and she had several. But when Wolfe met them, and made it plain that he would accept her as a colleague only if she accepted his alternative, she finally gave in. She would phone to let me know how she was making out with the arrangements. From her manner, when she got up to go, you might have thought she had been shopping for some little item, say a handbag, and had graciously deferred to the opinion of the clerk. After I graciously escorted her out and saw her descend the seven steps from the stoop to the sidewalk, I returned to the office and found Wolfe sitting with his eyes closed and his fists planted on the chair arms.

"Even money," I said.

"On what?" he growled.

"On her against the field. She knows damn well who had a good reason and exactly what it was. It was getting too hot for comfort and she decided that the best way to duck was to wish it on some dear friend."

His eyes opened. "She would, certainly. A woman whose conscience has no sting will stop at nothing. But why come to me? Why didn't she cook her own stew and serve it to the police?"

"I don't know, but for a guess she was afraid the cops would get too curious and find out how she had saved her honor and her virtue and tell her mother and father, and father would spank her. Shall I also guess why you proposed your alternative instead of having her bring them here for you?"

"She wouldn't. She said so."

"Of course she would, if you had insisted. That's your guess. Mine is that you're not desperate enough yet to take on five females in a bunch. When you told me to bring the whole dozen you knew darned well it couldn't be done, not even by me. Okay, I want instructions."

"Later," he muttered, and closed his eyes.

V

It was on the fourth floor of an old walk-up in the West Nineties near Amsterdam Avenue. I don't know what it had in the way of a kitchen or bedroom—or bedrooms—because the only room I saw was the one we were sitting in. It was medium-sized, and the couch and chairs and rugs had a homey look, the kind of homeyness that furniture gets by being used by a lot of different people for fifty or sixty years.

The chair I was on had a wobbly leg, but that's no problem if you keep it in mind and make no sudden shifts. I was more concerned about the spidery little stand at my elbow on which my glass of milk was perched. I can always drink milk and had preferred it to Bubble-Pagne, registered trademark, a dime a bottle, which they were having. It was ten o'clock Wednesday evening.

The hostesses were the redhead with milky skin, Peggy Choate, and the one with big brown eyes and dimples, Nora Jaret, who shared the apartment. Carol Annis, with the fine profile and the corn-silk hair, had been there when Helen Iacono and I arrived, bringing Lucy Morgan and her throaty voice after detouring our taxi to pick her up at a street corner. They were a very attractive collection, though of course not as decorative as they had been in their ankle-length purple stolas. Girls always look better in uniforms or costumes. Take nurses or elevator girls or Miss Honeydew at a melon festival.

I was now calling her Helen, not that I felt like it, but in the detective business you have to be sociable, of course preserving your honor and virtue. In the taxi, before picking up Lucy Morgan, she told me she had been thinking it over and she doubted if it would be possible to find out which one of them had a good reason to kill Pyle, or thought she had, because Pyle had been so very careful when he had a girl come to his penthouse. The only way would be to get one of them to open up, and Helen doubted if she could get her to, since she would be practically confessing murder, and she was sure I couldn't. So the best way would be for Helen and me, after spending an evening with them, to talk it over and decide which one was the most likely, and then she would tell Wolfe she had seen her going back to the kitchen and bringing another plate, and Wolfe would tell the police, and that would do it.

No, I didn't feel like calling her Helen. I would just as soon have been too far away from her to call her at all.

Helen's declared object in arranging the party—declared to them—was to find out from me what Nero Wolfe and the cops had done and were doing, so they would know where they stood. Helen was sure I would loosen up, she had told them, because she had been to see me and found me very nice and sympathetic. So the hostesses were making it sort of festive and intimate by serving Bubble-Pagne, though I preferred milk. I had a suspicion that at least one of them, Lucy Morgan, would have preferred whisky or gin or rum or vodka, and maybe they all would, but that might have made me suspect that they were not just a bunch of wholesome, hard-working artists.

They didn't look festive. I wouldn't say they were haggard, but much of the bloom was off. And they hadn't bought Helen's plug for me that I was nice and sympathetic. They were absolutely skeptical, sizing me up with sidewise looks, especially Carol Annis, who sat cross-legged on the couch with her head cocked. It was she who asked me, after a few remarks had been made about how awful it had been and still was, how well I knew the chef and the other man in the kitchen. I told her she could forget Fritz. He was completely above suspicion, and anyway he had been at the range while the plates were taken. As for Zoltan, I said that though I had known him a long while we were not intimate, but that was irrelevant because, granting that he had known which guest each girl would serve, if he poisoned one of the portions and saw that a certain girl got it, why did she or some other girl come back for another plate?

"There's no proof that she did," Carol declared. "Nobody saw her."

"Nobody *noticed* her." I wasn't aggressive; I was supposed to be nice and sympathetic. "She wouldn't have been noticed leaving the dining room because the attention of the girls who were in there was on Felix and Marjorie Quinn, who had spilled a blini, and the men wouldn't notice her. The only place she would have been noticed was in the corridor through the pantry, and if she met another girl there she could have stopped and been patting her hair or something. Anyhow, one of you must have gone back for a second plate, because when Fern Faber went for hers there wasn't any."

"Why do you say one of us?" Nora demanded. "If you mean one of us here. There were twelve."

"I do mean one of you here, but I'm not saying it, I'm just quoting the police. They think it was one of you here because you were the last five."

"How do you know what they think?"

"I'm not at liberty to say. But I do."

"I know what I think," Carol asserted. She had uncrossed her legs and slid forward on the couch to get her toes on the floor. "I think it was Zoltan. I read in the *Gazette* that he's a chef at Rusterman's, and Nero Wolfe is the trustee and so he's the boss there, and I think Zoltan hated him for some reason and tried to poison him, but he gave the poisoned plate to the wrong girl. Nero Wolfe sat right next to Pyle."

There was no point in telling her that she was simply ignoring the fact that one of them had gone back for a second helping, so I just said, "Nobody can stop you thinking. But I doubt very much if the police would buy that."

"What would they buy?" Peggy asked.

My personal feelings about Peggy were mixed. For, she had recognized me and named me. Against, she had accused me of liking myself. "Anything that would fit," I told her. "As I said, they think it was one of you five that went back for more, and therefore they have to think that one of you gave the poison to Pyle, because what other possible reason could you have had for serving another portion? They wouldn't buy anything that didn't fit into that. That's what rules out everybody else, including Zoltan." I looked at Carol. "I'm sorry, Miss Annis, but that's how it is."

"They're a bunch of dopes," Lucy Morgan stated. "They get an idea and then they haven't got room for another one." She was on the floor with her legs stretched out, her back against the couch. "I agree with Carol, there's no proof that any of us went back for another plate. That Zoltan said he didn't see anyone come back. Didn't he?"

"He did. He still does."

"Then he's a dope too. And he said no one took two plates. Didn't he?"

"Right. He still does."

"Then how do they know which one he's wrong about? We were all nervous, you know that. Maybe one of us took two plates instead of one, and when she got to the dining room there she was with an extra, and she got rid of it by giving it to some guest that didn't have any."

"Then why didn't she say so?" I asked.

"Because she was scared. The way Nero Wolfe came at us was enough to scare anybody. And now she won't say so because she has signed a statement and she's even more scared."

I shook my head. "I'm sorry, but if you analyze that you'll see that it won't do. It's very tricky. You can do it the way I did this afternoon. Take twenty-four little pieces of paper, on twelve of them write the names of the guests, and arrange them as they sat at the table. On the other twelve pieces write the names of the twelve girls. Then try to manipulate the twelve girl pieces so that one of them either took in two plates at once, and did not give either of them to Pyle, or went back for a second plate, and did not give either the first one or the second one to Pyle. It can't be done. For if either of those things happened there wouldn't have been one mix-up, there would have been two. Since there was only one mix-up, Pyle couldn't possibly have been served by a girl who neither brought in two plates at once nor went back for a second one. So the idea that a girl *innocently* brought in two plates is out."

"I don't believe it," Nora said flatly.

"It's not a question of believing." I was still sympathetic. "You might as well say you don't believe two plus two is four. I'll show you. May I have some paper? Any old kind."

She went to a table and brought some, and I took my pen and wrote the twenty-four names, spacing them, and tore the paper into twenty-four pieces. Then I knelt on a rug and arranged the twelve guest pieces in a rectangle as they had sat at table—not that that mattered, since they could have been in a straight line or a circle, but it was plainer that way. The girls gathered around. Nora knelt facing me, Lucy rolled over closer and propped on her elbows, Carol came and squatted beside me, Peggy plopped down at the other side, and Helen stood back of Nora.

"Okay," I said, "show me." I took "Quinn" and put it back of "Leacraft." "There's no argument about that, Marjorie Quinn brought the first plate and gave it to Leacraft. Remember there was just one mix-up, started by Peggy when she saw Pyle had been served and gave hers to Nero Wolfe. Try having any girl bring in a second plate—or bring in two at once if you still think that might have happened—without either serving Pyle or starting a second mix-up."

My memory has had a long stiff training under the strains and pressures Wolfe has put on it, but I wouldn't undertake to report all the combinations they tried, huddled around me on the floor, even if I thought you cared. They stuck to it for half an hour or more. The most persistent was Peggy Choate, the redhead. After the others had given up she stayed with it, frowning and biting her lip, propped first on one hand and then the other. Finally she said, "Nuts," stretched an arm to make a jumble of all the pieces of paper, guests and girls, got up, and returned to her chair. I did likewise.

"It's just a trick," said Carol Annis, perched on the couch again.

"I still don't believe it," Nora Jaret declared. "I do not believe that one of us deliberately poisoned a man—one of us sitting here." Her big brown eyes were at me. "Good lord, look at us! Point at her! Point her out! I dare you to!"

That, of course, was what I was there for—not exactly to point her out, but at least to get a hint. I had had a vague idea that one might come from watching them maneuver the pieces of paper, but it hadn't. Nor from anything any of them had said. I had been expecting Helen Iacono to introduce the subject of Vincent Pyle's *modus operandi* with girls, but apparently she had decided it was up to me. She hadn't spoken more than twenty words since we arrived.

"If I could point her out," I said, "I wouldn't be bothering

the rest of you. Neither would the cops if *they* could point
her out. Sooner or later, of course, they will, but it begins to
look as if they'll have to get at it from the other end. Motive.
They'll have to find out which one of you had a motive, and
they will—sooner or later—and on that maybe I can help. I
don't mean help them, I mean help you—not the one who
killed him, the rest of you. That thought occurred to me
after I learned that Helen Iacono had admitted that she had
gone out with Pyle a few times last winter. What if she had
said she hadn't? When the police found out she had lied, and
they would have, she would have been in for it. It wouldn't
have proved she had killed him, but the going would have
been mighty rough. I understand that the rest of you have
all denied that you ever had anything to do with Pyle. Is
that right? Miss Annis?"

"Certainly." Her chin was up. "Of course I had met him.
Everybody in show business has. Once when he came backstage at the Coronet, and once at a party somewhere, and one
other time but I don't remember where."

"Miss Morgan?"

She was smiling at me, a crooked smile. "Do you call this
helping us?" she demanded.

"It might lead to that after I know how you stand. After all,
the cops have your statement."

She shrugged. "I've been around longer than Carol, so I
had seen him to speak to more than she had. Once I danced
with him at the Flamingo, two years ago. That was the
closest I had ever been to him."

"Miss Choate?"

"I never had the honor. I only came to New York last
fall. From Montana. He had been pointed out to me from a
distance, but he never chased me."

"Miss Jaret?"

"He was Broadway," she said. "I'm TV."

"Don't the twain ever meet?"

"Oh, sure. All the time at Sardi's. That's the only place I
ever saw the great Pyle, and I wasn't with him."

I started to cross my legs, but the wobbly chair leg reacted,
and I thought better of it. "So there you are," I said, "you're
all committed. If one of you poisoned him, and though I hate
to say it I don't see any way out of that, that one is lying.
But if any of the others are lying, if you saw more of him
than you admit, you had better get from under quick. If you
don't want to tell the cops tell me, tell me now, and I'll pass
it on and say I wormed it out of you. Believe me, you'll
regret it if you don't."

"Archie Goodwin, a girl's best friend," Lucy said. "My bosom pal."

No one else said anything.

"Actually," I asserted, "I *am* your friend, all of you but one. I have a friendly feeling for all pretty girls, especially those who work, and I admire and respect you for being willing to make an honest fifty bucks by coming there yesterday to carry plates of grub to a bunch of finickers. I *am* your friend, Lucy, if you're not the murderer, and if you are no one is."

I leaned forward, forgetting the wobbly chair leg, but it didn't object. It was about time to put a crimp in Helen's personal project. "Another thing. It's quite possible that one of you *did* see her returning to the kitchen for another plate, and you haven't said so because you don't want to squeal on her. If so, spill it now. The longer this hangs on the hotter it will get. When it gets so the pressure is too much for you and you decide you have got to tell it, it will be too late. Tomorrow may be too late. If you go to the cops with it tomorrow they probably won't believe you; they'll figure that you did it yourself and you're trying to squirm out. If you don't want to tell me here and now, in front of her, come with me down to Nero Wolfe's office and we'll talk it over."

They were exchanging glances, and they were not friendly glances. When I had arrived probably not one of them, excluding the murderer, had believed that a poisoner was present, but now they all did, or at least they thought she might be; and when that feeling takes hold it's good-by to friendliness. It would have been convenient if I could have detected fear in one of the glances, but fear and suspicion and uneasiness are too much alike on faces to tell them apart.

"You *are* a help," Carol Annis said bitterly. "Now you've got us hating each other. Now everybody suspects everybody."

I had quit being nice and sympathetic. "It's about time," I told her. I glanced at my wrist. "It's not midnight yet. If I've made you all realize that this is no Broadway production, or TV either, and the longer the pay-off is postponed the tougher it will be for everybody, I *have* helped." I stood up. "Let's go. I don't say Mr. Wolfe can do it by just snapping his fingers, but he might surprise you. He has often surprised me."

"All right," Nora said. She arose. "Come on. This is getting too damn painful. Come on."

I don't pretend that that was what I had been heading for. I admit that I had just been carried along by my tongue. If I arrived with that gang at midnight and Wolfe had gone to bed, he would almost certainly refuse to play. Even if he were still up, he might refuse to work, just to teach me a lesson, since I had not stuck to my instructions. Those thoughts were at me as Peggy Choate bounced up and Carol Annis started to leave the couch.

But they were wasted. That tussle with Wolfe never came off. A door at the end of the room which had been standing ajar suddenly swung open, and there in its frame was a two-legged figure with shoulders almost as broad as the doorway, and I was squinting at Sergeant Purley Stebbins of Manhattan Homicide West. He moved forward, croaking, "I'm surprised at you, Goodwin. These ladies ought to get some sleep."

VI

Of course I was a monkey. If it had been Stebbins who had made a monkey of me I suppose I would have leaped for a window and dived through. Hitting the pavement from a fourth-story window should be enough to finish a monkey, and life wouldn't be worth living if I had been bamboozled by Purley Stebbins. But obviously it hadn't been him; it had been Peggy Choate or Nora Jaret, or both; Purley had merely accepted an invitation to come and listen in.

So I kept my face. To say I was jaunty would be stretching it, but I didn't scream or tear my hair. "Greetings," I said heartily. "And welcome. I've been wondering why you didn't join us instead of skulking in there in the dark."

"I'll bet you have." He had come to arm's length and stopped. He turned. "You can relax, ladies." Back to me: "You're under arrest for obstructing justice. Come along."

"In a minute. You've got all night." I moved my head. "Of course Peggy and Nora knew this hero was in there, but I'd—"

"I said come along!" he barked.

"And I said in a minute. I intend to ask a couple of questions. I wouldn't dream of resisting arrest, but I've got leg cramp from kneeling too long and if you're in a hurry you'll have to carry me." I moved my eyes. "I'd like to know if you all knew. Did you, Miss Iacono?"

"Of course not."

"Miss Morgan?"

"No."

"Miss Annis?"

"No, I didn't, but I think you did." She tossed her head and the corn silk fluttered. "That was contemptible. Saying you wanted to help us, so we would talk, with a policeman listening."

"And then he arrests me?"

"That's just an act."

"I wish it were. Ask your friends Peggy and Nora if I knew—only I suppose you wouldn't believe them. *They* knew, and they didn't tell you. You'd better all think over everything you said. Okay, Sergeant, the leg cramp's gone."

He actually started a hand for my elbow, but I was moving and it wasn't there. I opened the door to the hall. Of course he had me go first down the three flights; no cop in his senses would descend stairs in front of a dangerous criminal in custody. When we emerged to the sidewalk and he told me to turn left I asked him, "Why not cuffs?"

"Clown if you want to," he croaked.

He flagged a taxi on Amsterdam Avenue, and when we were in and rolling I spoke. "I've been thinking, about laws and liberties and so on. Take false arrest, for instance. And take obstructing justice. If a man is arrested for obstructing justice, and it turns out that he didn't obstruct any justice, does that make the arrest false? I wish I knew more about law. I guess I'll have to ask a lawyer. Nathaniel Parker would know."

It was the mention of Parker, the lawyer Wolfe uses when the occasion calls for one, that got him. He had seen Parker in action.

"They heard you," he said, "and I heard you, and I took some notes. You interfered in a homicide investigation. You quoted the police to them, you said so. You told them what the police think, and what they're doing and are going to do. You played a game with them with those pieces of paper to show them exactly how it figures. You tried to get them to tell you things instead of telling the police, and you were going to take them to Nero Wolfe so he could pry it out of them. And you haven't even got the excuse that Wolfe is representing a client. He hasn't got a client."

"Wrong. He has."

"Like hell he has. Name her."

"Not her, him. Fritz Brenner. He is seeing red because food cooked by him was poisoned and killed a man. It's convenient to have the client living right in the house. You admit that a licensed detective has a right to investigate on behalf of a client."

"I admit nothing."

"That's sensible," I said approvingly. "You shouldn't. When you're on the stand, being sued for false arrest, it would be bad to have it thrown up to you, and it would be two against one because the hackie could testify. Can you hear us, driver?"

"Sure I can hear you," he sang out. "It's very interesting."

"So watch your tongue," I told Purley. "You could get hooked for a year's pay. As for quoting the police, I merely said that they think it was one of those five, and when Cramer told Mr. Wolfe that he didn't say it was confidential. As for telling them what the police think, same comment. As for playing that game with them, why not? As for trying to get them to tell me things, I won't comment on that at all because I don't want to be rude. That must have been a slip of the tongue. If you ask me why I didn't balk there at the apartment and bring up these points then and there, what was the use? You had spoiled the party. They wouldn't have come downtown with me. Also I am saving a buck of Mr. Wolfe's money, since you had arrested me and therefore the taxi fare is on the city of New York. Am I still under arrest?"

"You're damn right you are."

"That may be ill-advised. You heard him, driver?"

"Sure I heard him."

"Good. Try to remember it."

We were on Ninth Avenue, stopped at Forty-second Street for a light. When the light changed and we moved, Purley told the hackie to pull over to the curb, and he obeyed. At that time of night there were plenty of gaps. Purley took something from a pocket and showed it to the hackie, and said, "Go get yourself a Coke and come back in ten minutes," and he climbed out and went. Purley turned his head to glare at me.

"I'll pay for the Coke," I offered.

He ignored it. "Lieutenant Rowcliff," he said, "is expecting us at Twentieth Street."

"Fine. Even under arrest, one will get you five that I can make him start stuttering in ten minutes."

"You're not under arrest."

I leaned forward to look at the meter. "Ninety cents. From here on we'll split it."

"Goddamn it, quit clowning! If you think I'm crawling you're wrong. I just don't see any percentage in it. If I deliver you in custody I know damn well what you'll do. You'll clam up. We won't get a peep out of you, and in the morning you'll make a phone call and Parker will come. What will that get us?"

I could have said, "A suit for false arrest," but it wouldn't have been diplomatic, so I made it, "Only the pleasure of my company."

There was one point of resemblance between Purley and Carol Annis, just one: no sense of humor. "But," he said, "Lieutenant Rowcliff is expecting you, and you're a material witness in a homicide case, and you were up there working on the suspects."

"You could arrest me as a material witness," I suggested helpfully.

He uttered a word that I was glad the hackie wasn't there to hear, and added, "You'd clam up and in the morning you'd be out on bail. I know it's after midnight, but the lieutenant is expecting you."

He's a proud man, Purley is, and I wouldn't go so far as to say that he has nothing to be proud of. He's not a bad cop, as cops go. It was a temptation to keep him dangling for a while, to see how long it would take him to bring himself to the point of coming right out and asking for it, but it was late and I needed some sleep.

"You realize," I said, "that it's a waste of time and energy. You can tell him everything we said, and if he tried to go into other aspects with me I'll only start making cracks and he'll start stuttering. It's perfectly useless."

"Yeah, I know, but—"

"But the lieutenant expects me."

He nodded. "It was him Nora Jaret told about it, and he sent me. The inspector wasn't around."

"Okay. In the interest of justice. I'll give him an hour. That's understood? Exactly one hour."

"It's not understood with me." He was emphatic. "When we get there you're his and he's welcome to you. I don't know if he can stand you for an hour."

VII

At noon the next day, Thursday, Fritz stood at the end of Wolfe's desk, consulting with him on a major point of policy: whether to switch to another source of supply for water cress. The quality had been below par, which for them means perfection, for nearly a week. I was at my desk, yawning. It had been after two o'clock when I got home from my chat with Lieutenant Rowcliff, and with nine hours' sleep in two nights I was way behind.

The hour since Wolfe had come down at eleven o'clock from his morning session with the orchids had been spent, most of it, by me reporting and Wolfe listening. My visit with

Rowcliff needed only a couple of sentences, since the only detail of any importance was that it had taken me eight minutes to get him stuttering, but Wolfe wanted my conversation with the girls verbatim, and also my impressions and conclusions. I told him my basic conclusion was that the only way she could be nailed, barring a stroke of luck, would be by a few dozen men sticking to the routine—her getting the poison and her connection with Pyle.

"And," I added, "her connection with Pyle may be hopeless. In fact, it probably is. If it's Helen Iacono, what she told us is no help. If what she told us is true she had no reason to kill him, and if it isn't true how are you going to prove it? If it's one of the others she is certainly no half-wit, and there may be absolutely nothing to link her up. Being very careful with visitors to your penthouse is fine as long as you're alive, but it has its drawbacks if one of them feeds you arsenic. It may save her neck."

He was regarding me without enthusiasm. "You are saying in effect that it must be left to the police. I don't have a few dozen men. I can expose her only by a stroke of luck."

"Right. Or a stroke of genius. That's your department. I make no conclusions about genius."

"Then why the devil were you going to bring them to me at midnight? Don't answer. I know. To badger me."

"No, sir. I told you. I had got nowhere with them. I had got them looking at each other out of the corners of their eyes, but that was all. I kept on talking, and suddenly I heard myself inviting them to come home with me. I was giving them the excuse that I wanted them to discuss it with you, but that may have been just a cover for certain instincts that a man is entitled to. They are very attractive girls—all but one."

"Which one?"

"I don't know. That's what we're working on."

He probably would have harped on it if Fritz hadn't entered to present the water-cress problem. As they wrestled with it, dealing with it from all angles, I swiveled my back to them so I could do my yawning in private. Finally they got it settled, deciding to give the present source one more week and then switch if the quality didn't improve; and then I heard Fritz say, "There's another matter, sir. Felix phoned me this morning. He and Zoltan would like an appointment with you after lunch, and I would like to be present. They suggested half past two, if that will suit your convenience."

"What is it?" Wolfe demanded. "Something wrong at the restaurant?"

"No, sir. Concerning the misfortune of Tuesday evening."

"What about it?"

"It would be better for them to tell you. It is their concern."

I swiveled for a view of Fritz's face. Had Felix and Zoltan been holding out on us? Fritz's expression didn't tell me, but it did tell Wolfe something: that it would be unwise for him to insist on knowing the nature of Felix's and Zoltan's concern because Fritz had said all he intended to. There is no one more obliging than Fritz, but also there is no one more immovable when he has taken a stand. So Wolfe merely said that half past two would be convenient. When Fritz had left I offered to go to the kitchen and see if I could pry it out of him, but Wolfe said no, apparently it wasn't urgent.

As it turned out, it wasn't. Wolfe and I were still in the dining room, with coffee, when the doorbell rang at 2:25 and Fritz answered it, and when we crossed the hall to the office Felix was in the red leather chair, Zoltan was in one of the yellow ones, and Fritz, was standing. Fritz had removed his apron and put on a jacket, which was quite proper. People do not attend business conferences in aprons.

When we had exchanged greetings, and Fritz had been told to sit down and had done so, and Wolfe and I had gone to our desks, Felix spoke. "You won't mind, Mr. Wolfe, if I ask a question? Before I say why we requested an appointment?"

Wolfe told him no, go ahead.

"Because," Felix said, "we would like to know this first. We are under the impression that the police are making no progress. They haven't said so, they tell us nothing, but we have the impression. Is it true?"

"It was true at two o'clock this morning, twelve hours ago. They may have learned something by now, but I doubt it."

"Do you think they will soon make progress? That they will soon be successful?"

"I don't know. I can only conjecture. Archie thinks that unless they have a stroke of luck the inquiry will be long and laborious, and even then may fail. I'm inclined to agree with him."

Felix nodded. "That is what we fear—Zoltan and I and others at the restaurant. It is causing a most regrettable atmosphere. A few of our most desirable patrons make jokes, but most of them do not, and some of them do not come. We do not blame them. For the maître d'hôtel and one of our chefs to assist at a dinner where a guest is served poison —that is not pleasant. If the—"

"Confound it, Felix! I have avowed my responsibility. I have apologized. Are you here for the gloomy satisfaction of reproaching me?"

"No, sir." He was shocked. "Of course not. We came to say that if the poisoner is not soon discovered, and then the affair will be forgotten, the effect on the restaurant may be serious. And if the police are making no progress that may happen, so we appeal to you. We wish to engage your professional services. We know that with you there would be no question. You would solve it quickly and completely. We know it wouldn't be proper to pay you from restaurant funds, since you are the trustee, so we'll pay you with our own money. There was a meeting of the staff last night, and all will contribute, in a proper ratio. We appeal to you."

Zoltan stretched out a hand, arm's length. "We appeal to you," he said.

"Pfui," Wolfe grunted.

He had my sympathy. Not only was their matter-of-fact confidence in his prowess highly flattering, but also their appealing instead of demanding, since he had got them into it, was extremely touching. But a man with a long-standing reputation for being hard and blunt simply can't afford the softer feelings, no matter what the provocation. It called for great self-control.

Felix and Zoltan exchanged looks. "He said 'pfui,' " Zoltan told Felix.

"I heard him," Felix snapped. "I have ears."

Fritz spoke. "I wished to be present," he said, "so I could add my appeal to theirs. I offered to contribute, but they said no."

Wolfe took them in, his eyes going right to left and back again. "This is preposterous," he declared. "I said 'pfui' not in disgust but in astonishment. I am solely to blame for this mess, but you offer to pay me to clean it up. Preposterous! You should know that I have already bestirred myself. Archie?"

"Yes, sir. At least you have bestirred me."

He skipped it. "And," he told them, "your coming is opportune. Before lunch I was sitting here considering the situation, and I concluded that the only way to manage the affair with dispatch is to get the wretch to betray herself; and I conceived a plan. For it I need your cooperation. Yours, Zoltan. Your help is essential. Will you give it? I appeal to you."

Zoltan upturned his palms and raised his shoulders. "But yes! But how?"

"It is complicated. Also it will require great dexterity and aplomb. How are you on the telephone? Some people are not themselves, not entirely at ease, when they are phoning. A few are even discomfited. Are you?"

"No." He reflected. "I don't think so. No."

"If you are it won't work. The plan requires that you telephone five of those women this afternoon. You will first call Miss Iacono, tell her who you are, and ask her to meet you somewhere—in some obscure restaurant. You will say that on Tuesday evening, when you told me that you had not seen one of them return for a second plate, you were upset and flustered by what had happened, and later, when the police questioned you, you were afraid to contradict yourself and tell the truth. But now that the notoriety is harming the restaurant you feel that you may have to reveal the fact that you did see her return for a second plate, but that before—"

"But I didn't!" Zoltan cried. "I told—"

"Tais-toi!" Felix snapped at him.

Wolfe resumed. "—but that before you do so you wish to discuss it with her. You will say that one reason you have kept silent is that you have been unable to believe that anyone as attractive and charming as she is could be guilty of such a crime. A parenthesis. I should have said at the beginning that you must not try to parrot my words. I am giving you only the substance; the words must be your own, those you would naturally use. You understand that?"

"Yes, sir." Zoltan's hands were clasped tight.

"So don't try to memorize my words. Your purpose is to get her to agree to meet you. She will of course assume that you intend to blackmail her, but you will not say so. You will try to give her the impression, in everything you say and in your tone of voice, that you will not demand money from her, but will expect her favors. In short, that you desire her. I can't tell you how to convey that impression; I must leave that to you. The only requisite is that she must be convinced that if she refuses to meet you, you will go at once to the police and tell them the truth."

"Then you know," Zoltan said. "Then she is guilty."

"Not at all. I haven't the slightest idea who is guilty. When you have finished with her you will phone the other four and repeat the performance—Miss Choate, Miss Annis, Miss—"

"My God, Mr. Wolfe! That's impossible!"

"Not impossible, merely difficult. You alone can do it, for they know your voice. I considerd having Archie do it, imitating your voice, but it would be too risky. You said you would help, but there's no use trying it if the bare idea appalls you. Will you undertake it?"

"I don't . . . I would . . ."

"He will," Felix said. "He is like that. He only needs to

swallow it. He will do it well. But I must ask, can he be expected to get them all to agree to meet him? The guilty one, yes, but the others?"

"Certainly not. There is much to discuss and arrange. The innocent ones will react variously according to their tempers. One or more of them will probably inform the police, and I must provide for that contingency with Mr. Cramer." To Zoltan: "Since it is possible that one of the innocent ones will agree to meet you, for some unimaginable reason, you will have to give them different hours for the appointments. There are many details to settle, but that is mere routine. The key is you. You must of course rehearse, and into a telephone transmitter. There are several stations on the house phone. You will go to Archie's room and speak from there. We will listen at the other stations: Archie in the plant rooms, I in my room, Fritz in the kitchen, and Felix here. Archie will handle the other end of the conversation; he is much better qualified than I to improvise the responses of young women. Do you want me to repeat the substance of what you are to say before rehearsal?"

Zoltan opened his mouth and closed it again. "Yes," he said.

VIII

Sergeant Purley Stebbins shifted his fanny for the nth time in two hours. "She's not coming," he muttered. "It's nearly eight o'clock." His chair was about half big enough for his personal dimensions.

We were squeezed in a corner of the kitchen of John Piotti's little restaurant on 14th Street between Second and Third Avenues. On the midget table between us were two notebooks, his and mine and a small metal case. Of the three cords extending from the case, the two in front went to the earphones we had on, and the one at the back ran down the wall, through the floor, along the basement ceiling toward the front, back up through the floor, and on through a table top, where it was connected to a microphone hidden in a bowl of artificial flowers. The installation, a rush order, had cost Wolfe $191.67. Permission to have it made had cost him nothing because he had once got John Piotti out of a difficulty and hadn't soaked him beyond reason.

"We'll have to hang on," I said. "You never can tell with a redhead."

The exposed page of my notebook was blank, but Purley had written on his. As follows:

Helen Iacono	6:00 p.m.
Peggy Choate	7:30 p.m.
Carol Annis	9:00 p.m.
Lucy Morgan	10:30 p.m.
Nora Jaret	12:00 p.m.

It was in my head. If I had had to write it down I would certainly have made one "p.m." do, but policemen are trained to do things right.

"Anyhow," Purley said, "we know damn well who it is."

"Don't count your poisoners," I said, "before they're hatched." It was pretty feeble, but I was tired and still short on sleep.

I hoped to heaven he was right, since otherwise the operation was a flop. So far everything had been fine. After half an hour of rehearsing Zoltan had been wonderful. He had made the five calls from the extension in my room, and when he was through I told him his name should be in lights on a Broadway marquee. The toughest job had been getting Inspector Cramer to agree to Wolfe's terms, but he had no good answer to Wolfe's argument that if he insisted on changing the rules Zoltan wouldn't play. So Purley was in the kitchen with me, Cramer was with Wolfe in the office, prepared to stay for dinner, Zoltan was at the restaurant table with the hidden mike, and two homicide dicks, one male and one female, were at another table twenty feet away. One of the most elaborate charades Wolfe had ever staged.

Purley was right when he said we knew who it was, but I was right too—she hadn't been hatched yet. The reactions to Zoltan's calls had settled it. Helen Iacono had been indignant and after a couple of minutes had hung up on him, and had immediately phoned the District Attorney's office. Peggy Choate had let him finish his spiel and then called him a liar, but she had not said definitely that she wouldn't meet him, and the DA or police hadn't heard from her. Carol Annis, after he had spoken his lines, had used only ten words: "Where can I meet you?" and, after he had told her where and when: "All right, I'll be there." Lucy Morgan had coaxed him along, trying to get him to fill it all in on the phone, had finally said she would keep the appointment, and then had rushed downtown and rung our doorbell, told me her tale, demanded that I accompany her to the rendezvous, and insisted on seeing Wolfe. I had to promise to go to get rid of her. Nora Jaret had called him assorted names, from liar on up, or on down, and had told him she had a friend listening in on an extension, which was almost certainly a lie. Neither we nor the law had had a peep from her.

So it was Carol Annis with the corn-silk hair, that was plain enough, but there was no salt on her tail. If she was really smart and really tough she might decide to sit tight and not come, figuring that when they came at her with Zoltan's story she would say he was either mistaken or lying, and we would be up a stump. If she was dumb and only fairly tough she might scram. Of course they would find her and haul her back, but if she said Zoltan was lying and she had run because she thought she was being framed, again we would be up a stump. But if she was both smart and tough but not quite enough of either, she would turn up at nine o'clock and join Zoltan. From there on it would be up to him, but that had been rehearsed too, and after his performance on the phone I thought he would deliver.

At half past eight Purley said, "She's not coming," and removed his earphone.

"I never thought she would," I said. The "she" was of course Peggy Choate, whose hour had been seven-thirty. "I said you never can tell with a redhead merely to make conversation."

Purley signaled to Piotti, who had been hovering around most of the time, and he brought us a pot of coffee and two fresh cups. The minutes were snails, barely moving. When we had emptied the cups I poured more. At 8:48 Purley put his earphone back on. At 8:56 I asked, "Shall I do a count down?"

"You'd clown in the hot seat," he muttered, so hoarse that it was barely words. He always gets hoarser as the tension grows; that's the only sign.

It was four minutes past nine when the phone brought me the sound of a chair scraping, then faintly Zoltan's voice saying good evening, and then a female voice, but I couldn't get the words.

"Not loud enough," Purley whispered hoarsely.

"Shut up." I had my pen out. "They're standing up."

There came the sound of chairs scraping, and other little sounds, and then:

Zoltan: Will you have a drink?

Carol: No. I don't want anything.

Zoltan: Won't you eat something?

Carol: I don't feel . . . maybe I will.

Purley and I exchanged glances. That was promising. That sounded as if we might get more than conversation.

Another female voice, belonging to Mrs. Piotti: We have good Osso Buco, madame. Very good. A specialty.

Carol: No, not meat.

Zoltan: A sweet perhaps?

Carol: No.

Zoltan: It is more friendly if we eat. The spaghetti with anchovy sauce is excellent. I had some.

Carol: You had some?

I bit my lip, but he handled it fine.

Zoltan: I've been here half an hour, I wanted so much to see you. I thought I should order something, and I tried that. I might even eat another portion.

Carol: You should know good food. All right.

Mrs. Piotti: Two spaghetti anchovy. Wine? A very good Chianti?

Carol: No. Coffee.

Pause.

Zoltan: You are more lovely without a veil, but the veil is good too. It makes me want to see behind it. Of course I—

Carol: You have seen behind it, Mr. Mahany.

Zoltan: Ah! You know my name?

Carol: It was in the paper.

Zoltan: I am not sorry that you know it, I want you to know my name, but it will be nicer if you call me Zoltan.

Carol: I might some day. It will depend. I certainly won't call you Zoltan if you go on thinking what you said on the phone. You're mistaken, Mr. Mahany. You didn't see me go back for another plate, because I didn't. I can't believe you would tell a vicious lie about me, so I just think you're mistaken.

Mrs. Piotti, in the kitchen for the spaghetti, came to the corner to stoop and hiss into my free ear, "She's wearing a veil."

Zoltan: I am not mistaken, my dear. That is useless. I know. How could I be mistaken when the first moment I saw you I felt . . . but I will not try to tell you how I felt. If any of the others had come and taken another plate I would have stopped her, but not you. Before you I was dumb. So it is useless.

Needing only one hand for my pen, I used the free one to blow a kiss to Purley.

Carol: I see. So you're sure.

Zoltan: I am, my dear. Very sure.

Carol: But you haven't told the police.

Zoltan: Of course not. As I told you.

Carol: Have you told Nero Wolfe or Archie Goodwin?

Zoltan: I have told no one. How could I tell anyone? Mr. Wolfe is sure that the one who returned for another plate is the one who killed that man, gave him poison, and

Mr. Wolfe is always right. So it is terrible for me. Could I
tell anyone that I know you killed a man? You? How could
I? That is why I had to see you, to talk with you. If you
weren't wearing that veil I could look into your beautiful
eyes. I think I know what I would see there. I would see
suffering and sorrow. I saw that in your eyes Tuesday evening. I know he made you suffer. I know you wouldn't kill
a man unless you had to. That is why—

The voice stopped. That was understandable, since Mrs.
Piotti had gone through the door with the spaghetti and coffee
and had had time to reach their table. Assorted sounds came
as she served them. Purley muttered, "He's overdoing it,"
and I muttered back, "No. He's perfect." Piotti came over
and stood looking down at my notebook. It wasn't until after
Mrs. Piotti was back in the kitchen that Carol's voice came.

Carol: That's why I am wearing the veil, Zoltan, because
I know it's in my eyes. You're right. I had to. He did make me
suffer. He ruined my life.

Zoltan: No, my dear. Your life is not ruined. No! No
matter what he did. Was he . . . did he . . .

I was biting my lip again. Why didn't he give them the
signal? The food had been served and presumably they
were eating. He had been told that it would be pointless to
try to get her to give him any details of her relations with
Pyle, since they would almost certainly be lies. Why didn't
he give the signal? Her voice was coming:

Carol: He promised to marry me. I'm only twenty-two
years old, Zoltan. I didn't think I would ever let a man
touch me again, but the way you . . . I don't know. I'm
glad you know I killed him because it will be better now,
to know that somebody knows. To know that *you* know. Yes,
I had to kill him, I *had* to, because if I didn't I would
have had to kill myself. Some day I may tell you what a
fool I was, how I—Oh!

Zoltan: What? What's the matter?

Carol: My bag. I left it in my car. Out front. And I didn't
lock the car. A blue Plymouth hardtop. Would you . . . I'll
go. . . .

Zoltan: I'll get it.

The sound came of his chair scraping, then faintly his
footsteps, and then silence. But the silence was broken in
ten seconds, whereas it would have taken him at least a minute to go for the purse and return. What broke it was a
male voice saying, "I'm an officer of the law, Miss Annis,"
and a noise from Carol. Purley, shedding his earphone,
jumped up and went, and I followed, notebook in hand.

It was quite a tableau. The male dick stood with a hand

on Carol's shoulder. Carol sat stiff, her chin up, staring straight ahead. The female dick, not much older than Carol, stood facing her from across the table, holding with both hands, at breast level, a plate of spaghetti. She spoke to Purley. "She put something in it and then stuck something in her dress. I saw her in my mirror."

I moved in. After all, I was in charge, under the terms Cramer had agreed to. "Thank you, Miss Annis," I said. "You were a help. On a signal from Zoltan they were going to start a commotion to give him an excuse to leave the table, but you saved them the trouble. I thought you'd like to know. Come on, Zoltan. All over. According to plan."

He had entered and stopped three paces off, a blue handbag under his arm. As he moved toward us Purley put out a hand. "I'll take that."

IX

Cramer was in the red leather chair. Carol Annis was in a yellow one facing Wolfe's desk, with Purley on one side of her and his female colleague on the other. The male colleague had been sent to the laboratory with the plate of spaghetti and a roll of paper that had been fished from inside Carol's dress. Fritz, Felix, and Zoltan were on the couch near the end of my desk.

"I will not pretend, Miss Annis," Wolfe was saying. "One reason that I persuaded Mr. Cramer to have you brought here first on your way to limbo was that I needed to appease my rancor. You had injured and humiliated not only me, but also one of my most valued friends, Fritz Brenner, and two other men whom I esteem, and I had arranged the situation that gave you your opportunity; and I wished them to witness your own humiliation, contrived by me, in my presence."

"That's enough of that," Cramer growled.

Wolfe ignored him. "I admit the puerility of that reason, Miss Annis, but in candor I wanted to acknowledge it. A better reason was that I wished to ask you a few questions. You took such prodigious risks that it is hard to believe in your sanity, and it would give me no satisfaction to work vengeance on a madwoman. What would you have done if Felix's eyes had been on you when you entered with the plate of poison and went to Mr. Pyle? Or if, when you returned to the kitchen for a second plate, Zoltan had challenged you? What would you have done?"

No answer. Apparently she was holding her gaze straight at Wolfe, but from my angle it was hard to tell because she still had the veil on. Asked by Cramer to remove it, she had refused. When the female dick had extracted the roll of paper from inside Carol's dress she had asked Cramer if she should pull the veil off and Cramer had said no. No rough stuff.

There was no question about Wolfe's gaze at her. He was forward in his chair, his palms flat on his desk. He persisted. "Will you answer me, Miss Annis?"

She wouldn't.

"Are you a lunatic, Miss Annis?"

She wasn't saying.

Wolfe's head jerked to me. "Is she deranged, Archie?"

That was unnecessary. When we're alone I don't particularly mind his insinuations that I presume to be an authority on women, but there was company present. I gave him a look and snapped, "No comment."

He returned to her. "Then that must wait. I leave to the police such matters as your procurement of the poison and your relations with Mr. Pyle, mentioning only that you cannot now deny possession of arsenic, since you used it a second time this evening. It will unquestionably be found in the spaghetti and in the roll of paper you concealed in your dress; and so, manifestly, if you are mad you are also ruthless and malevolent. You may have been intolerably provoked by Mr. Pyle, but not by Zoltan. He presented himself not as a nemesis or a leech, but as a bewitched and befuddled champion. He offered his homage and compassion, making no demands, and your counter-offer was death. I would myself—"

"You lie," Carol said. It was her first word. "And he lied. He was going to lie about me. He didn't see me go back for a second plate, but he was going to say he did. And you lie. He did make demands. He threatened me."

Wolfe's brows went up. "Then you haven't been told?"

"Told what?"

"That you were overheard. That is the other question I had for you. I have no apology for contriving the trap, but you deserve to know you are in its jaws. All that you and Zoltan said was heard by two men at the other end of a wire in another room, and they recorded it—Mr. Stebbins of the police, now seated at your left, and Mr. Goodwin."

"You lie," she said.

"No, Miss Annis. This isn't the trap; it has already sprung. You have it, Mr. Stebbins?"

Purley nodded. He hates to answer questions from Wolfe.

"Archie?"

"Yes, sir."

"Did Zoltan threaten her or make demands?"

"No, sir. He followed instructions."

He returned to Carol. "Now you know. I wanted to make sure of that. To finish, since you may have had a just and weighty grievance against Mr. Pyle, I would myself prefer to see you made to account for your attempt to kill Zoltan, but that is not in my discretion. In any case, my rancor is appeased, and I hold—"

"That's enough," Cramer blurted, leaving his chair. "I didn't agree to let you preach at her all night. Bring her along, Sergeant."

As Purley arose a voice came. "May I say something?" It was Fritz. Heads turned as he left the couch and moved, detouring around Zoltan's feet and Purley's bulk to get to Carol, and turning to stand looking down at her.

"On account of what Mr. Wolfe said," he told her. "He said you injured me, and that is true. It is also true that I wanted him to find you. I can't speak for Felix, and you tried to kill Zoltan and I can't speak for him, but I can speak for myself. I forgive you."

"You lie," Carol said.

METHOD THREE FOR MURDER

I

When I first set eyes on Mira Holt, as I opened the front door and she was coming up the seven steps to the stoop, she was a problem, though only a minor one compared to what followed.

At the moment I was unemployed. During the years I have worked for Nero Wolfe and lived under his roof, I have quit and been fired about the same number of times, say thirty or forty. Mostly we have been merely letting off steam, but sometimes we have meant it, more or less, and that Monday evening in September I was really fed up. The main dish at dinner had been pork stewed in beer, which both Wolfe and Fritz know I can get along without, and we had left the dining room and crossed the hall to the office, and Fritz had brought coffee and Wolfe had poured it, and I had said, "By the way, I told Anderson I'd phone and confirm his appointment for tomorrow morning."

And Wolfe had said, "No. Cancel it." He picked up the book he was on, John Gunther's *Inside Russia Today*.

I sat in my working chair and looked across his desk at him. Since he weighs a seventh of a ton he always looks big, but when he's being obnoxious he looks even bigger. "Do you suppose it's possible," I asked, "that that pork has a bloating effect?"

"No indeed," he said, and opened the book.

If I had been a camel and the book had been a straw you could have heard my spine crack. He knew darned well he shouldn't have opened it until we had finished with coffee. I put my cup down. "I am aware," I said, "that you are sitting pretty. The bank balance is fat enough for months of paying Fritz and Theodore and me, and buying pork and beer in car lots, and adding more orchids to the ten thousand you've already got. I'll even grant that a private detective has a right to refuse to take a case with or without a reason. But as I told you before dinner, this Anderson is known to me, and he asked me as a personal favor to get him fifteen minutes with you, and I told him to come at eleven o'clock tomorrow morning. If you're determined not to work because your tax bracket is already too high, okay, all you have to do is tell him no. He'll be here at eleven."

He was holding the book open and his eyes were on it, but he spoke. "You know quite well, Archie, that I must be consulted on appointments. Did you owe this man a favor?"

"I do now that he asked for one and I said yes."

"Did you owe him one before?"

"No."

"Then you are committed but I am not. Since I wouldn't take the job it would waste his time and mine. Phone him not to come. Tell him I have other engagements."

So I quit. I admit that on some other occasions my quitting had been merely a threat, to jolt him into seeing reason, but not that time. When a mule plants its feet a certain way there's no use trying to budge it. I swiveled, got my memo pad, wrote on it, yanked the sheet off, got up and crossed to his desk, and handed him the sheet.

"That's Anderson's number," I told him. "If you're too busy to phone him not to come, Fritz can. I'm through. I'll stay with friends tonight and come tomorrow for my stuff."

His eyes had left the book to glare at me. "Pfui," he said.

"I agree," I said. "Absolutely." I turned and marched out. I do not say that as I got my hat from the rack in the hall my course was clearly mapped for the next twenty years, or even twenty hours. Wolfe owned the house but not everything in it, for the furniture in my room on the third floor had been bought and paid for by me. That would have to wait until I found a place to move it to, but I would get my clothes and other items tomorrow, and would I come for them before eleven o'clock and learn from Fritz whether a visitor named Anderson was expected, or would it be better strategy to come in the afternoon and learn if Anderson had been admitted and given his fifteen minutes? Facing that problem as I pulled the door open, I was immediately confronted by another one. A female was coming up the seven steps to the stoop.

II

I couldn't greet her and ask her business, since it was a cinch she would say she wanted to see Nero Wolfe and I couldn't carry on with a job I no longer held by returning to the office to ask Wolfe if he would receive a caller. Anyway I wouldn't. I couldn't step aside and let her enter by the door I had opened with no questions asked, since there was a possibility that she was one of the various people who had it in for Wolfe, and while I might have considered shooting him myself I didn't want to get him plugged by a total stranger. So I crossed the sill, pulled the door shut, sidestepped to pass her, and was starting down the steps when my sleeve was caught and jerked.

"Hey," she said, "aren't you Archie Goodwin?"

My eyes slanted down to hers. "You're guessing," I said.

"I am not. I've seen you at the Flamingo. You're not very polite, shutting the door in my face." She spoke in jerks, as if she wasn't sure she had enough breath. "I want to see Nero Wolfe."

"This is his house. Ring the bell."

"But I want to see you too. Let me in. Take me in."

My eyes had adjusted enough to the poor light to see that she was young, attractive, and hypped. She had on a cap with a beak. In normal circumstances it would have been a pleasure to escort her into the front room and go and badger Wolfe into seeing her, but as things stood I didn't even consider it. "I'm sorry," I said, "but I don't work here any more. I just quit. I am now on my way to bum a bed for the night. You'll have to ring the bell, but I should warn you that in Mr. Wolfe's present mood there's not a chance. You might as well skip it. If your trouble is urgent you ought to—"

"I'm not in trouble."

"Good. You're lucky."

She touched my sleeve. "I don't believe it. That you've quit."

"I do. Would I say so if I hadn't? Running the risk that you're a journalist and tomorrow there will be a front-page spread, 'Archie Goodwin, the famous private detective, has severed his connection with Nero Wolfe, also a detective, and it is thought—' "

"Shut up!" She was close to me, gripping my arm. She let loose and backed up a step. "I beg your pardon. I seem to be . . . you think Nero Wolfe wouldn't see me?"

"I don't think. I know."

"Anyway I want to see you too. For what I want I guess you would be better than him. I want some advice—no, not advice exactly, I want to consult you. I'll pay cash, fifty dollars. Can't we go inside?"

Naturally I was uplifted. Since I had left Wolfe, and since there was no other outfit in New York I would work for, my only possible program was to set up for myself, and before I even got down to the sidewalk here was a pretty girl offering me fifty bucks just for consultation.

"I'm afraid not," I told her, "since I no longer belong here. If that's your taxi waiting that will do fine, especially

with the driver gone." A glance had shown me that there
was no one behind the wheel of the cab at the curb. Probably, having been told to wait for her, he had beat it to
Al's diner at the corner of Tenth Avenue, which was pop-
ular with hackies.

She shook her head. "I don't—" she began, and let it hang.
She glanced around. "Why not here? It shouldn't take very
long—I just want you to help me win a bet." She moved,
descended two steps, and sat on the landing, swaying a little
as she bent. "Have a seat."

We were still on Wolfe's premises, but he rarely used the
outdoors part, and after she paid me I could slip a buck
under the door for rent. I sat down beside her, not crowding.
I had often sat there watching the neighborhood kids at
stoop ball.

"Do I pay in advance?" she asked.

"No, thanks, I'll trust you. What's the bet about?"

"Well . . ." She was squinting at me in the dim light. "I
had an argument with a friend of mine. She said there were
ninety-three women cab drivers in New York, and she
thought it was dangerous because sometimes things happen
in cabs that it takes a man to handle, and I said things like
that can happen anywhere just as well as in cabs, and we
had an argument, and she bet me fifty dollars she could prove
that something dangerous could happen in a cab that couldn't
happen anywhere else. She thought up some things, but I
made her admit they could happen other places too, and then
she said what if a woman cab driver left her empty cab to go
into a building for something, and when she came back there
was a dead woman in the cab? She claimed that won the bet,
and the trouble was I didn't know enough about what
you're supposed to do when you find a dead body. That's
what I want you to tell me. I'm sure she's wrong. And I'll pay
you the fifty dollars."

I was squinting back at her. "You don't look it," I stated.

"I don't look what?"

"Loony. Two things. First, the same thing could happen if
she were driving a private car instead of a cab, and why didn't
you tell her that? Second, where's the danger? She merely
finds a phone and notifies the police. It would be a nuisance,
but you said dangerous."

"Oh. Of course." She bit her lip. "I left something out.
It's not her cab. She has a friend who is a cab driver, and
she wanted to see what driving a cab was like, and her friend
let her take it. So she can't notify the police because her friend
broke some law when she let her take the cab, and she broke
one too, driving a cab without a license, so it wouldn't have

been the same if she had been driving a private car. And the only way I can win the bet is to prove that it wouldn't be dangerous. She doesn't know how the dead woman got in the cab or anything about it. All she has to do is get the body out of the cab, but that might be dangerous unless she did it just right, and that's what I want you to tell me so I won't make some awful mistake—I mean when I tell my friend why it wouldn't be dangerous. Things like where would she go to— to take it out of the cab, and would she have to wait until late at night, and how would she make sure there were no traces left in the cab." She bit her lip again, and her fingers were curled to make fists. "Things like that."

"I see." I had stopped squinting. "What's your name?"

She shook her head. "You don't have to know. I'm just consulting you." She stuck her fingers in the pocket of her jacket, a grayish number with pointed lapels that had seen wear, came out with a purse, and opened it.

I reached to snap it shut. "That can wait. I certainly wouldn't take your money without knowing your name. Of course you can make one up."

"Why should I?" She gestured. "All right. My name is Mira Holt. Mira with an I." She opened the purse again.

"Hold it," I told her. "A couple of questions. The dead woman she finds in the cab—does she recognize her?"

"No, how could she?"

"She could if she knew her when she was alive."

"She didn't."

"Good. That helps. You say she left her empty cab to go into a building for something. For what?"

"Oh, just anything. I don't know. That doesn't matter."

"It might, but if you don't know you can't tell me. I want to make it clear, Miss Holt, that I accept without question all that you *have* told me. Since I am a trained detective I am chronically suspicious, but you are so frank and intelligent and pleasing to look at that I wouldn't dream of doubting you. A man who was sap enough to size you up wrong might even suspect you of feeding him a phony, and go and take a look in that taxi, but not me. I don't even ask you where the driver is, because I assume he has gone to the corner for a ham on rye and a cuppa coffee. In short, I trust you fully. That's understood?"

Her lips were tight. She was probably frowning, but the beak of her cap screened her brow. "I guess so." She wasn't at all sure. "But maybe—if that's how you feel—maybe it would be better just to—"

"No. It's better like this. Much better. About this situation your friend thought up and claims she won the bet, it has many aspects. You say you didn't know enough about what you're supposed to do when you find a dead body. First and foremost, you're supposed to notify the police immediately. That goes for everybody, but it's a must for a private detective—me, for instance—if he wants to keep his license. Is that clear?"

"Yes." She nodded. "I see."

"Also you're not supposed to touch the body or anything near it. Also you're not supposed to leave it unguarded, but that's not so important because you may have to in order to call a cop. As for your idea that all she has to do is get the body out of the cab, and where would she go to ditch it, and would she have to wait until late at night, and so on, I admit it has possibilities and I could make a lot of practical suggestions. But you have to show that it could be done without danger, and that's too big an order. That's what licks you. Forget it. However, your friend hasn't won the bet. She was to produce a situation showing that a woman cab driver runs special risks as a hackie, and in this case the danger comes from the fact that she was *not* driving the cab. So your friend—"

"That's no help. You know very well—"

"Shut up. I beg your pardon."

Her fingers were curled into fists again. "You said you could make some practical suggestions."

"I was carried away. The idea of disposing of a dead body is fascinating as long as it's only an idea. By the way, I took one thing for granted that I shouldn't have—that your friend specified that the woman had died by violence. If she could have died of natural causes—"

"No. She had been stabbed. There was a knife, the handle of a knife. . . ."

"Then it's impossible. A hackie letting someone else drive his cab is a misdemeanor, and so is driving a cab without a license, but driving off with a dead body with a knife sticking in it, and dumping it somewhere, and not reporting it—that's a felony. Good for at least a year and probably more."

She opened a fist to grip my arm, leaning to me. "But not if she did it right! Not if no one ever knew! I told you one thing wrong—she *did* recognize her! She *did* know her when she was alive! So she can't—"

"Hold it," I growled. "Give me some money quick. Pay me. A dollar bill, five—don't sit and stare. See that police car? If it goes on by—no, it's stopping—pay me!"

She was going to panic. She started up, but my hand on her shoulder stopped her and held her down. She opened the purse and took out folded bills without fumbling, and I

took them and put them in my pocket. "Staring is okay," I
told her, not too loud. "People stare at police cars. Stay put
and keep your mouth shut. I'm going to take a look. Naturally I'm curious."

That was perfectly true. I *was* curious. The prowl car had
stopped alongside the taxi, and a cop, not the one who was
driving, had got out and circled around to the door of the
taxi on his side and was opening it as I reached the sidewalk.
When you have a reputation for cheek you should live up to
it, so I crossed to the door on my side and pulled it open.
The seat was empty, but in front of it was a spread of
brown canvas held up by whatever was under it. The cop,
lifting a corner of the canvas, snarled at me, "Back up, you,"
and I retreated half a step, but he hadn't said to close the
door, so I had a good view when he pulled the canvas off.
More light would have helped, but there was enough to see
that it was a woman, or had been, and that the knife whose
handle was perpendicular to her ribs was all the way in.

"My God," I said with feeling.

"Shut that door!" the cop barked. "No, don't touch it!"

"I already have."

"I saw you. Beat it! No! What's your name?"

"Goodwin. Archie Goodwin. This is Nero Wolfe's house,
and—"

"I know it is. And I know about you. Is this your cab?"

"Certainly not. I'm not a hackie."

"I know you're not. I mean—" He stopped. Apparently
he had realized that the function of a prowl cop on finding
a corpse is not to argue with onlookers. His head jerked
around. "Climb out, Bill. DOA. I'll call in." The cop behind
the wheel wiggled out, and the one in command wiggled in,
and I mounted the stoop and sat down beside my client,
noting that she had removed the cap and apparently had
stashed it.

I kept my voice low, though it wasn't necessary since the
cop was talking on his radio. "In about eight minutes," I
said, "experts will begin arriving. They will not be strangers
to me. Since as far as I know you merely came to get me to
tell you how to win a bet, when they start asking questions
I'll be glad to answer them if you want to leave it to me. I've
had practice answering questions."

She was gripping my arm again. "You looked in. You
saw—"

"Shut up, and I don't beg your pardon. You talk too much.
Even if I still lived and worked here we wouldn't go inside
because it wouldn't be natural, with cops in a prowl car finding a corpse in a taxi parked at the curb—oh, I haven't men-

tioned that, that there's a dead woman in the taxi. I mention it now because naturally I would, and naturally I would stick around to watch developments. I'm talking to keep you from talking, since naturally we would talk. Not only have I had practice answering questions, but I know some of the rules. There are only three methods that are any good in the long run. You have strong fingers."

"I'm sorry." Her grip relaxed a little, but she held on. "What are the three methods?"

"One. Button your lip. Answer nothing whatever. Two. Tell the truth straight through. The works. Three. Tell a simple basic lie with no trimmings, and stick to it. If you try a fancy lie, or a mixture of truth and lies, or part of the truth but try to save some, you're sunk. Of course I'm just talking to pass the time. In the present situation, as far as I know, there is no reason why you shouldn't just tell the truth."

"You said to leave it to you."

"Yes, but they won't. There are very few people in their jurisdiction they wouldn't rather leave it to than me, on account of certain—here they come. We can stop talking. Naturally we would watch."

An official car I had seen before rolled to a stop behind the prowl car, and Inspector Cramer of Homicide West climbed out.

III

If you are surprised that an inspector had come in response to a report that a corpse had been found, I wasn't. The report had of course given the location, in front of 918 West 35th Street, and that address held memories, most of them sour, for the personnel at Homicide West, from Cramer down. A violent death that was in any way connected with Nero Wolfe made them itch, and presumably the report had included the item that Archie Goodwin was present and had stuck his nose in.

My client and I watched the routine activities from our grandstand seat. They were swift, efficient, and thorough. Traffic was detoured at the corner of Ninth Avenue. A section of the street and sidewalk was roped off to enclose the taxi. Floodlights were focused on the taxi and surroundings. A photographer took shots from various angles. Pedestrians from both directions were shunted across the street, where a crowd gathered behind the rope. Some twenty city employees, in uniform and out, were on the scene in less than half an hour after the cop had made the radio call—five of them

known to me by name and four others by sight. The second
floodlight had just been turned on when Cramer came around
the front of the taxi, crossed to the steps and mounted the
first three, and faced me. Since I was sitting, that made our
eyes level.

"All right," he said. "Let's go in. I might as well have you
and Wolfe together, and this woman too. That may simplify
it. Open the door."

"On the contrary," I said, not moving, "it would complicate
it. Mr. Wolfe is in the office reading a book and knows nothing of all the excitement, and cares less. If I went in and told
him you wanted to see him, and what about, you know what
he would say and so do I. Nothing doing."

"Who came here in that taxi?"

"I don't know. I know nothing whatever about the taxi.
When I came out it was there at the curb."

"When did you come out?"

"Twenty minutes past nine."

"Why did you come out?"

"To find a place to spend the night. I have quit my job, so
if you're determined to see Mr. Wolfe you'll have to ring the
bell."

"You're telling me you've *quit?*"

"Right. I don't work here any more."

"By God. I thought you and Wolfe had tried all the
wrinkles there are, but this is a new one. Do you expect me to
buy it?"

"It's not a wrinkle. I meant it. I wouldn't sign a pledge
never to sleep here again, that depends on Mr. Wolfe's handling of a certain problem, but when I left the house I meant
it. The problem has no connection with that taxi or what's in
it."

"Did this woman leave the house with you?"

"No. When I opened the door, coming out, she was coming
up the stoop. She said she wanted to see Nero Wolfe, and
when I told her I no longer worked for him, and anyway he
probably wouldn't see her, she said she guessed that for what
she wanted I would be better than him. She offered to pay me
fifty dollars for consultation on how to win a bet she had
made, and we sat here to consult. We had been here fifteen
or twenty minutes when the prowl car came along and stopped
by the taxi, which had been standing there when I left the
house, and naturally I was curious and went to take a look.
The cop asked me my name and I told him. When he went to
his radio to report I came back to my client, but we didn't
do much consulting on account of the commotion. That's the
crop."

"Had you ever seen this woman before?"

"No."

"What was the bet she wanted to consult about?"

"That's her affair. She's here. Ask her."

"Did she come in that taxi?"

"Not to my knowledge. Ask her."

"Did you see her get out of the taxi?"

"No. She was halfway up the stoop when I opened the door."

"Did you see anyone get out of the taxi? Or near it?"

"No."

"What's her name?"

"Ask her."

His head moved. "Is your name Judith Bram?"

That was no news for me, since my view through the open door had included the framed picture of the hackie and her name. As well as I had been able to tell in the dim light, the picture was not of my client.

"No," she said.

"What is it?"

"Mira Holt. Mira with an I." Her voice was clear and steady.

"Did you drive that taxi here?"

"No."

"Did you come here in it?"

"No."

So she had picked method three, a simple basic lie.

"Did you have an appointment to see Nero Wolfe?"

"No."

"Where do you live?"

"Seven-fourteen East Eighty-first Street."

"What is your occupation?"

"Modeling. Mostly fashion modeling."

"Are you married?"

"Yes, but I don't live with my husband."

"What's your husband's name?"

She opened her mouth and closed it again. "Waldo Kearns. I use my own name."

"Are you divorced?"

"No."

"Was that taxi here when you arrived?"

"I don't know. I didn't notice, but I suppose it was because it didn't come after we sat down."

"How did you come here?"

"I don't think that matters."

"I'll decide if it matters. How did you come?"

She shook her head. "No. For instance, if somebody drove

me here, or near here, you would ask him, and I might not want you to. No."

So she also knew what "no trimmings" meant.

"I advise you," Cramer advised her, "to tell me how you came."

"I would rather not."

"What was the bet you wanted to consult about?"

"That doesn't matter either. It was a private bet with a friend." Her head turned. "You're a detective, Mr. Goodwin, so you ought to know, do I have to tell him about my private affairs just because I was sitting here with you?"

"Of course not," I assured her. "Not unless he shows some connection between your private affairs and his public affairs, and he hasn't. It's entirely up to you whether—"

"What the devil is all this?" Nero Wolfe bellowed.

I twisted around and so did my client. The door was wide open and he was standing on the threshold, his bulk towering above us. "What's going on?" he demanded.

Since I was merely an ex-employee and Cramer was an inspector I thought it fitting to let him reply, but he didn't. Apparently he was too flabbergasted at seeing Wolfe actually stick his nose outdoors. Wolfe advanced a step. "Archie. I asked a question."

I had stood up. "Yes, sir, I heard you. Miss Holt, this is Mr. Wolfe. Miss Mira Holt. When I left the house she was coming up the steps. I had never seen her before. When I told her I was no longer in your employ she said I would be better than you and asked to consult me. She has paid me. We sat down to confer. There was an empty taxi parked at the curb, no driver in it. A police car came along and stopped, and a cop found a dead body, female, in the taxi under a piece of canvas. I was there looking in when he removed the canvas. I came back up the stoop to sit with my client. We recessed our conference to watch the proceedings. Officers arrived promptly, including Inspector Cramer. When he got around to it he came and questioned us. I knew nothing about the taxi or its contents and said so. She told him she had not driven the taxi here and hadn't come in it. She gave him her name and address and occupation, but refused to answer questions about her private affairs—for instance, what she was consulting me about. I was telling her that was entirely up to her when you appeared."

Wolfe grunted. "Why didn't you bring Miss Holt inside?"

"Because it's not my house. Or my office."

"Nonsense. There is the front room. If you wish to stand on ceremony, I invite you to use it for consultation with your client. Sitting here in this hubbub is absurd. Have you any further information for Mr. Cramer?"

"No."

"Have you, Miss Holt?"

She was on her feet beside me. "I didn't have any," she said. "I haven't got any."

"Then get away from this turmoil. Come in."

Cramer found his tongue. "Just a minute." He had come on up to the stoop and was at my elbow, focused on Wolfe. "This is all very neat. Too damn neat. Goodwin says he quit his job. Did he?"

"Yes."

"Why?"

"Pfui. That's egregious, Mr. Cramer, and you know it."

"Did it have anything to do with Miss Holt or what she was coming to consult about?"

"No."

"Or with the fact that a taxi was parked at your door with a dead body in it?"

"No."

"Did you know Miss Holt was coming?"

"No. Nor, patently, did Mr. Goodwin."

"Did you know the taxi was out here?"

"No. I am bearing with you, sir. You persist beyond reason. If Mr. Goodwin or I were involved in the circumstance that brought you here, or Miss Holt, would he have sat here with her, supine, awaiting your assault? You know him, and you know me. Come, Archie. Bring your client." He turned.

I told Cramer, "I'll be glad to type up statements and bring them down," touched Mira Holt's arm, and followed her inside, Wolfe having preceded us.

When I had shut the door and the lock had clicked Wolfe spoke. "Since there's no telephone in the front room and you may have occasion to use one, perhaps the office would be better. I will go to my room."

"Thank you," I said politely. "But it might be still better for us to leave the back way. You may not want us here when I explain the situation. Miss Holt drove that taxi here. A friend of hers named Judith Bram is one of the ninety-three female hackies in New York, and she let Miss Holt take her cab—or maybe Miss Holt took it without Miss Bram's knowledge. She left—"

"No," Mira said. "Judy let me take it."

"Possible," I conceded. "You're a pretty good liar. Let me finish. She left it, empty, in front of a building and went in the building for something, and when she came back there was a dead body in it, a woman, with a knife between its ribs. Either it was covered with a canvas, or she—"

"I covered it," Mira said. "It was under that panel by the driver's seat."

"She's level-headed," I told Wolfe. "Somewhat. She couldn't notify the police, because not only had she and her friend violated the law, but also she had recognized the dead woman. She knew her. She decided to come and consult you and me. I met her on the stoop. She told me a cockeyed tale about a bet she had made with a friend which I'll skip. I said *somewhat* level-headed. I let her see that I knew she was feeding me soap but kept her from blurting it out. So I told Cramer no lies, but she did, and did a good job. But the lies won't keep long. It's barely possible that Judith Bram will deny that she let someone take her cab, but sooner or later—"

"I tried to phone her," Mira said, "but she didn't answer. I was going to tell her to say that someone stole it."

"Quit interrupting me. Did you ever hear of fingerprints? Did you see them working on that cab? So I have a client who is in a double-breasted jam. I'll know more about it after she tells me things. The point is, did she kill that woman? If I thought she did I would bow out quick—I would already have bowed out because it would have been hopeless. But she didn't. One will get you ten that she didn't. If she had—"

That interruption wasn't words; it was her lips against mine and her palms covering my ears. If she had been Wolfe's client I would have shoved her off quick, since that sort of demonstration only ruffles him, but she was mine and there was no point in hurting her feelings. I even patted her shoulder. When she was through I resumed.

"If she had killed her she would not have driven here with the corpse for a passenger to tell you, or even me, a goofy tale about a bet with a friend. Not a chance. She would have dumped the corpse somewhere. Make it twenty to one. Add to that my observation of her while we sat there on the stoop, and it's thirty to one. Therefore I am keeping the fee she paid me, and I'm—by the way." I reached in my pocket for the bills she had given me, unfolded them, and counted. Three twenties, three tens, and a five. Returning two twenties and a ten to my pocket, I offered her the rest. "Your change. I'm keeping fifty."

She hesitated, then took it. "I'll pay you more. Of course. What are you going to do?"

"I'll know better after you answer some questions. One that shouldn't wait: what did you do with the cap?"

"I have it." She patted her front.

"Good." I returned to Wolfe. "So we'll be going. Thank you again for your offer of hospitality, but Cramer may be ringing the bell any minute. We'll go out the rear, Miss Holt. This way."

"No." Wolfe snapped it. "This is preposterous. Give me half of that fifty dollars."

I raised a brow. "For what?"

"To pay me. You have helped me with many problems; surely I can help you with one. I am not being quixotic. I do not accept your headstrong decision that our long association has ended, but even if it has, your repute is inextricably involved with mine. Your client is in a pickle. I have never tried to do a job without your help; why should you try to do one without mine?"

I wanted to grin at him, but he might have misunderstood. "Okay," I said, and got a twenty from the pocket where I had put the fee, and a five from my wallet, and handed them to him. He took them, turned, and headed for the office, and Mira and I followed.

IV

Where to sit was a delicate question—not for Wolfe, who of course went to his oversized custom-built chair behind his desk, nor for the client, since Wolfe wiggled a finger to indicate the red leather chair that would put her facing him, but for me. The desk at right angles to Wolfe's was no longer mine. I had a hand on one of the yellow chairs, to move it up, when Wolfe growled, "Confound it, don't be frivolous. We have a job to do."

I went and sat where I had belonged, and asked him, "Do I proceed?"

"Certainly."

I looked at her. In good light, with the cap off, she was very lookable, even in a pickle. "I would like," I said, "to be corroborated. Did you kill that woman?"

"No. *No!*"

"Okay. Out with it. This time, method two, the truth. Judith Bram is a friend of yours?"

"Yes."

"Did she let you take her cab?"

"Yes."

"Why?"

"I asked her to."

"Why did you ask her to?"

"Because . . . it's a long story."

"Make it as short as you can. We may not have much time."

She was on the edge of the chair, which would have held two of her. "I have known Judy three years. She was a model too, but she didn't like it. She's very unconventional. She had money she had inherited, and she bought a cab and a license about a year ago. She cruises when she feels like it, but she has some regular customers who think it's chic to ride in a cab with a girl driver, and my husband is one of them. He often—"

"Your husband?" Wolfe demanded. *"Miss* Holt?"

"They don't live together," I told him. "Not divorced, but she uses her own name. Fashion model. Go ahead but keep it short."

She obeyed. "My husband's name is Waldo Kearns. He paints pictures but doesn't sell any. He has money. He often calls Judy to take him somewhere, and he called last night when I was with her and told her to come for him at eight o'clock this evening, and I asked Judy to let me go instead of her. I have been trying to see him for months, to have a talk with him, and he refuses to see me. He doesn't answer my letters. I want a divorce and he doesn't. I think the reason he doesn't is that—"

"Skip it. Get on."

"Well . . . Judy said I could take the cab, and today at seven o'clock I went to her place and she brought it from the garage, and she gave me her cap and jacket, and I drove it to—"

"Where is her place?"

"Bowdoin Street. Number seventeen. In the Village."

"I know. You got in the cab there?"

"Yes. I drove it to Ferrell Street. It's west of Varick, below—"

"I know where it is."

"Then you know it's a dead end. Close to the end is an alley that goes between walls to a little house. That's my husband's. I lived there with him about a year. I got there a little before eight, and turned around and parked in front of the alley. Judy had said she always waited for him there. He didn't come. I didn't want to go to the house, because as soon as he saw me he would shut the door on me, but when he hadn't come at half past eight I got out and went—"

"You're sure of the time?"

"Yes. I looked at my watch. Of course."

"What does it say now?"

She lifted her wrist. "Two minutes after eleven."

"Right. You went through the alley?"

"Yes, to the house. There's a brass knocker on the door,

no bell. I knocked with it, but nobody came. I knocked several times. I could hear the radio or television going inside, I could just barely hear it, so I knocked loud. He couldn't have recognized me through a window because it was too dark and I had the cap pulled down. Of course it could have been Morton, his man as he calls him, playing the radio, but I don't think so because he would have heard the knocker and come to the door. I finally gave up and went back to the cab, and as I was getting in I saw her. At first I thought it was a trick he had played, but when I looked closer I saw the knife, and then I recognized her, and she was dead. If I hadn't turned around and gripped the wheel as hard as I could I think I would have fainted. I never have fainted. I sat there—"

"Who was it?"

"It was Phoebe Arden. She was the reason my husband didn't want a divorce. I'm sure she was, or anyway one of the reasons. I think he thought that as long as he was still married to me he couldn't expect him to marry her, and neither could anyone else. But I wasn't thinking about that while I sat there, I was thinking what to do. I knew the right thing was to call the police, but I was driving Judy's cab, and, what was worse, I would have to admit I knew who she was, and they would find out about her and my husband. I don't know how long I sat there."

"It must have been quite a while. You left the cab to go to the house at eight-thirty. How long were you gone?"

"I don't know. I knocked several times, and looked in at the windows, and then knocked some more." She considered. "At least ten minutes."

"Then you were back at the cab at eight-forty, and from there to here wouldn't take more than ten minutes, and you got here at nine-twenty. Did you sit there half an hour?"

"No. I decided to get her—to get it out of the cab. I found that canvas under the panel. I thought the best place would be somewhere along the river front, and I drove there but didn't see a good place, and men tried to stop me twice, and once when I stopped for a light a man opened the door and when I told him I was making a delivery he almost climbed in anyway. Then I thought I would just leave the cab somewhere, anywhere, and I went to a phone booth to call Judy and tell her to say the cab had been stolen, but there was no answer. Then I thought of Nero Wolfe and you, and I drove here. I didn't have much time to make that up about the bet, just on my way here. I knew it wasn't much good while I was telling it."

"So did I." I was frowning at her. "I want you to realize

one thing. I believe you when you say you didn't kill her, but it doesn't follow that I swallow you whole. For instance, the divorce situation. If the fact is that your husband wanted one so he could marry Phoebe Arden, and you balked, that would make it different."

"No." She was frowning back. "I've told you the truth, every word. I lied to you out there, but if I lied to you now I'd be a fool."

"You sure would. How good a friend of yours is Judy Bram?"

"She's my best friend. She's a little wild, but I like her. I love her."

"Are you sure she rates it?"

"Yes."

"You'd better cross your fingers." I turned to Wolfe. "Since you're helping on this, and I fully appreciate it, our minds should meet. Do you accept it that she didn't kill her?"

"As a working hypothesis, yes."

"Then isn't it likely that she was killed by someone who knew that Miss Holt would be driving the cab? Since Kearns didn't show, taking her away from the cab, and the radio or television was on in the house?"

"Likely, but far from certain. It could have been impromptu. Or the embarrassment could have been meant for Miss Bram, not for Miss Holt."

I returned to Mira. "How close are Judy Bram and your husband?"

"Close?" The frown was getting chronic. "They aren't close. If you mean intimate, I doubt if Judy has ever allowed any man to be intimate. My husband may have tried. I suppose he has."

"Could Judy have had any reason to kill Phoebe Arden?"

"Good lord, no."

"Isn't it possible that Judy, unknown to you, had got an idea that she would like to break the ice with your husband, and Phoebe Arden was in the way?"

"I suppose it is, if you want to say that anything is possible, but I don't believe it."

"You heard what I asked Mr. Wolfe and what he answered. I still like it that whoever killed her knew that you were going to drive the cab there. It's certainly possible that Judy Bram told someone."

"Yes, it's possible, but I don't believe it. Judy wouldn't. She just wouldn't."

"It's also possible that you told someone. Did you?"

Her lips twitched. Twice. Two seconds. "No," she said.

"You're lying. I haven't time to be polite. You're lying. Whom did you tell?"

"I'm not going to say. The person I told couldn't possibly have . . . have done anything. Some things are *not* possible."

"Who was it?"

"No, Mr. Goodwin. Really."

I got the twenty and ten from my pocket and twenty from my wallet, got up, and went to her. "Here's your fifty bucks," I said. "Count me out. You can leave the back way."

"But I tell you he couldn't!"

"Then he won't get hurt. I won't bite him. But I've got to know everything you do or it's no good."

Her lips twitched again. "You would really do that? Just give me up?"

"I sure would. I will. With regrets and best wishes."

She breathed. "I phoned a friend of mine last evening and told him. His name is Gilbert Irving."

"Is he more than a friend?"

"No. He is married and so am I. We're friends, that's all."

"Does he know your husband?"

"Yes. They've known each other for years, but they've never been close."

"Did he know Phoebe Arden?"

"He had met her. He didn't *know* her."

"Why did you tell him about your plan to drive the cab?"

"Because I wanted to know what he thought of it. He is very—a very intelligent man."

"What did he think of it?"

"He thought it was foolish. Not foolish exactly, useless. He thought my husband would refuse to listen to me. Honestly, Mr. Goodwin, this *is* foolish. There is absolutely no—"

The doorbell rang. I had taken three steps before I remembered that I no longer worked there; then, not wishing to be frivolous, I continued to the hall and took a look through the one-way glass panel of the front door. A man and a woman were there on the stoop. A glance was enough to recognize Inspector Cramer, but it took closer inspection for the woman, and I moved down the hall. Even then I wasn't positive, since the light had been dim on the picture of the female hackie in the taxi, but I was sure enough. It was Judith Bram.

v

It was up to me, since it was my case and Wolfe was merely helping, but he had many times asked for my opinion and it wouldn't hurt to reciprocate, so I stepped to the office door and said, "Cramer and Judy Bram. Shall I—"

"Judy!" Mira cried. "She's here?"

I ignored her. "Shall I scoot with Miss Holt and leave them to you?"

He closed his eyes. In three seconds he opened them. "I would say no. The decision is yours."

"Then we stick. I want to meet Judy anyhow. Sit tight, Miss Holt. Never drop a simple basic lie until it drops you."

As I turned the bell rang again. I went to the front, put the chain bolt on, opened the door the two inches the chain allowed, and spoke through the crack. "Do you want me, Inspector?"

"I want in. Open up."

"Glad to for you, but not for strangers. Who is the lady?"

"Her name is Judith Bram. She's the owner and driver—"

"I want to see Mira Holt!" the lady said, meaning it. "Open the door!"

I removed the chain, but didn't have to swing the door because she saved me the trouble. She came with it and darted down the hall. Seeing that Cramer, after her, would brush me, I stiffened to make the brush a bump, and he wobbled and lost a step, giving me time to shut the door and reach the office at his heels. When we entered Judy was sitting on the arm of the red leather chair with her arm across Mira's shoulders, jabbering. Cramer grabbed her arm and barked at her, but she ignored him.

"—and I said yes, the cab might have still been there in front when you left, but I was sure you wouldn't take it, and anyway—"

Cramer yanked her up and around, and as she came she swung with her free hand and smacked him in the face. There was too much of him to be staggered by it, but the sound effect was fine. She jerked loose and glared at him. Her big, brown, well-spaced eyes were ideal for glaring. I had a feeling that I had seen her before, but I hadn't. It was just an old memory: a seventh-grade classmate out in Ohio whom I had been impelled to kiss, and she had socked me on the ear with her arithmetic. She is now married, with five children.

"That's not advisable, Miss Bram," Cramer stated. "Striking a police officer." He moved, got a yellow chair, and swung it around. "Here. Sit down."

"I'll sit where I please." She perched again on the red leather arm. "Is it advisable for a police officer to manhandle a citizen? When I got a hack license I informed myself about laws. Am I under arrest?"

"No."

"Then don't touch me." Her head swung around. "You're Nero Wolfe? You're even bigger." She didn't say bigger than what. "I'm Judy Bram. Are you representing my friend Mira Holt?"

His eyes on her were half closed. " 'Representing' is not the word, Miss Bram. I'm a detective, not a lawyer. Miss Holt has hired Mr. Goodwin, and he has hired me as his assistant. You call her your friend. Are you her friend?"

"Yes. And I want to know. She left my place around half past seven, and about an hour later I went out to keep a date. I had left my cab out front and it wasn't there, but I supposed—"

"Hold it," Cramer snapped. He was on the yellow chair, and I was at my desk. "I'll do the talking—"

She merely raised her voice. "—I supposed a man from the garage had come and got it, I have that arrangement—"

"Shut up!" Cramer roared. "Or I'll shut you up!"

"How?" she asked.

It was a question. He had several choices: clamp his paw on her mouth, or pick her up and carry her out, or call in a couple of big strong men from out front, or hit her with a blunt instrument, or shoot her. All had drawbacks.

"Permit me," Wolfe said. "I suggest, Mr. Cramer, that you have bungled it. The notion of suddenly confronting Miss Holt with Miss Bram was of course tempting, but your appraisal of Miss Bram's temperament was faulty. Now you're stuck. You won't get the contradictions you're after. Miss Holt would be a simpleton to supply particulars until she knows what Miss Bram has said. As you well know, that does not necessarily imply culpability for either of them."

Cramer rasped, "You're telling Miss Holt not to answer any questions."

"Am I? If so, unwittingly. Now, of course, you have made it plain. It would appear that you have only two alternatives: either let Miss Bram finish her account, or remove her."

"There's a third one I like better. I'll remove Miss Holt." Cramer got up. "Come on, Miss Holt. I'm taking you down for questioning in connection with the murder of Phoebe Arden."

"Is she under arrest?" Judy demanded.

"No. But if she doesn't talk she will be. As a material witness."

"Can he do that, Mr. Wolfe?"

"Yes."

"Without a warrant?"

"In the circumstances, yes."

"Come on, Miss Holt," Cramer growled.

I was sitting with my jaw set. Wolfe would rather miss a meal than let Cramer or any other cop take a client of his

from that office into custody, and over the years I had seen
and heard him pull some fancy maneuvers to prevent it. But
this was my client, and he wasn't batting an eye. I admit
that it would have had to be something extra fancy, and it
was up to me, not him, but I had split the fee with him.
So I sat with my jaw set while Mira left the chair and Judy
jabbered and Cramer touched Mira's arm and they headed
for the door. Then I came to, scribbled on my memo pad—
formerly my memo pad—tore the sheet off, and made for
the hall. Cramer had his hand on the knob.

"Here's the phone number," I told her. "Twenty-four-hour
service. Don't forget method three."

She took the slip, said, "I won't," and crossed the sill, with
Cramer right behind. I noted that the floodlights and the taxi
were still there before I shut the door.

Back in the office, Wolfe was leaning back with his eyes
closed and Judy Bram was standing scowling at him. She
switched the scowl to me and demanded, "Why don't you
put him to bed?"

"Too heavy. How many people did you tell that Mira was
going to drive your cab to her husband's house?"

She eyed me, straight, for two breaths, then went to the
red leather chair and sat. I took the yellow one, to be closer.

"I thought you were working for her," she said.

"I am."

"You don't sound like it. She didn't drive my cab."

I shook my head. "Come on down. Would I be working
for her if she hadn't opened up? You told her yesterday that
Kearns had phoned you to call for him at eight o'clock today,
and she asked you to let her go instead of you. She wanted
to have a talk with him about a divorce. How many people
did you tell about it?"

"Nobody. If she opened up what's the rest of it?"

"Ask her when you see her. Did you kill Phoebe Arden?"

From the flash in her eye she would have smacked me if I
had been close enough. "Oh, for God's sake," she said. "Get
a club. Drag me by the hair."

"Later maybe." I leaned to her. "Look, Miss Bram. Give
your temperament a rest and use your brain. I am working
for Mira Holt. I know exactly where she was and what she
did, every minute, from seven o'clock this evening on, but I'm
not going to tell you. Of course you know that the dead body
of a woman named Phoebe Arden was found in your cab. I
am certain that Mira didn't kill her, but she is probably going
to be charged. I am not certain that the murderer tried to
get her tagged for it, but it looks like it. I would be a fathead

to tell the murderer about her movements. Wouldn't I? Answer with your brain."

"Yes." She was meeting my eyes.

"Okay. Give me one good reason why I should cross you off. One you would accept if you were in my place. Mira has, naturally, but why should I?"

"Because there's not the slightest—" She stopped. "No. You don't know that. All right. But don't try twisting my arm. I know some tricks."

"I'll keep my distance if you will. Did you kill Phoebe Arden?"

"No."

"Do you know who did?"

"No."

"Have you any suspicions? Any ideas?"

"Yes. Or I would have if I knew anything—where and when it happened. Did Phoebe come out to the cab with Waldo Kearns?"

"No. Kearns didn't show up. Mira never saw him."

"But Phoebe came?"

"Not alive. When Mira saw her she was dead. In the cab."

"Then my idea is Waldo. The sophisticated ape. You know, you're not any too bright. If I killed her in my own cab while Mira was driving it, I already know everything you do and more. Why not tell me?"

I looked at Wolfe, who had opened his eyes off and on. He grunted. "You told her to use her brain," he muttered.

I returned to Judy. "You certainly would know this: Mira got there before eight o'clock and parked in front. When Kearns hadn't showed at eight-thirty she went to the house and spent ten minutes knocking and looking in windows. When she returned to the cab the dead body was in it. She never saw Kearns."

"But my God." Her brows were up. She turned her hands over. "All she had to do was dump it out!"

"She hasn't got your temperament. She—"

"She drove *here* with it? To consult with *you?*"

"She might have done worse. In fact, she tried to. She phoned *you*, and got no answer. What's your idea about Kearns?"

"He killed Phoebe."

"Then that's settled. Why?"

"I don't know. He tried to shake her and she hung on. Or she cheated on him. Or she had a bad cold and he was afraid he would catch it. He put the body in the cab to fix Mira. He hates her because she told him the truth about himself once."

"Did you know Phoebe well? Who and what was she?"

"Well enough. She was a widow at thirty, roaming around. I might have killed her, at that. About a year ago she started scattering remarks about me, and I broke her neck. Almost. She spent a week in a hospital."

"Did it cure her? I mean of remark-scattering?"

"Yes."

"We might as well finish with you. You told Mr. Wolfe Mira left your place around half past seven and about an hour later you went out to keep a date. So you might have left at a quarter after eight."

"I might, but I didn't. I walked to Mitchell Hall on Fourteenth Street to make a speech at a cab drivers' meeting, and I got there at five minutes to nine. After the meeting I walked back home, and two cops were there waiting for me. They were dumb enough to ask me first where my cab was, and I said I supposed it was in the garage. When they said no, it was parked on Thirty-fifth Street, and asked me to come and identify it, naturally I went. I also identified a dead body, which they hadn't mentioned. Is that Inspector Cramer dumb?"

"No."

"I thought not. When he asked me if I knew Mira Holt of course I said yes, and when he asked when I last saw her I told him. Since I had no idea what had happened I thought that was safest, but I said I hadn't told her she could take the cab and I knew she wouldn't take it without asking me. Does that finish with me?"

"It's a good start. How well do you know Gilbert Irving?"

That fazed her. Her mouth opened and she gawked with her big, brown, well-spaced eyes. "Are my ears working?" she demanded. "Did you say Gilbert Irving?"

"That's right."

"Who let him in?"

"Mira mentioned him. How well do you know him?"

"Too well. I dream about a lion standing on a rock about to spring at me, and I suspect it's him. If my subconscious is yearning for him it had better go soak its head, because first he's married and his wife has claws, and second, when he looks at Mira or hears her voice he has to lean against something to keep from trembling. Did she tell you that?"

"No. Who is he? What does he do?"

"Something in Wall Street, but he doesn't look it. Why did Mira mention him?"

"Because I made her. She phoned him last evening and

told him she was going to drive your cab and why. She wanted to know what he thought of it. I want to know what motive he might have for killing Phoebe Arden."

She opened her mouth to reply, then decided to laugh instead. It was a real laugh, no giggle.

I raised a brow. "Your subconscious taking over?" I inquired.

"No." She sobered. "I couldn't help it. It struck me, of course Gil killed her. He couldn't bear the thought of Mira's husband being unfaithful to her, it was an insult to her womanhood, so he killed Phoebe. Do you blame me for laughing?"

"No. I'll laugh too when I get around to it. Does anything else strike you? A motive for him you wouldn't laugh at?"

"Of course not. It's ridiculous. You're just floundering around. Have you finished with me?"

I looked at Wolfe. His eyes were closed. "For now, yes," I told her, "unless Mr. Wolfe thinks I skipped something."

"How can he? You can talk in your sleep, but you can't think." She stood up. "What are you going to do?"

"Find a murderer and stick pins in him. Or her."

"Not sitting here you aren't. Don't bother, I know the way out. Why don't you go and tackle Wally Kearns? I'll go with you."

"Thanks, I'll manage."

"Where did he take Mira?"

"Either to Homicide West, two-thirty West Twentieth, or to the District Attorney's office, one-fifty-five Leonard. Try Twentieth Street first."

"I will." She turned and was off. I followed, to let her out, but she was a fast walker and I would have had to trot to catch up. When I reached the door she had it open. I stepped out to the stoop and watched her descend to the sidewalk and turn west. The floodlights and ropes and police cars were gone, and so was Judy's cab. My wrist watch said five minutes past midnight as I went in and shut the door. I returned to the office and found Wolfe on his feet with his eyes open.

"I assumed," I said, "that if you wanted something from her I hadn't got you would say so."

"Naturally."

"Have you any comments?"

"No. It's bedtime."

"Yeah. Since you're with me on this, which I appreciate, perhaps I'd better sleep here. If you don't mind."

"Certainly. You own your bed. I have a suggestion. I

presume you intend to have a look at that place in the morning, and to see Mr. Kearns. It might be well for me to see him too."

"I agree. Thank you for suggesting it. If they haven't got him downtown I'll have him here at eleven o'clock." I made it eleven because that was his earliest hour for an appointment, when he came down from his two-hour session up in the plant rooms with the orchids.

"Make it a quarter past eleven," he said. "I will be engaged until then with Mr. Anderson."

I opened my mouth and closed it again. "Didn't you phone him not to come?"

"On the contrary, I phoned him to come. On reflection I saw that I had been hasty. In my employ, as my agent, you had made a commitment, and I was bound by it. I should not have repudiated it. I should have honored it, and then dismissed you if I considered your disregard of the rules intolerable."

"I see. I can understand that you'd rather fire me than have me quit."

"I said 'if.' "

I lifted my shoulders and dropped them. "It's a little complicated. If I have quit you can't fire me. If I haven't quit I am still on your payroll, and it would be unethical for me to have Miss Holt as my client. It would also be wrong for you to accept pay from me for helping me with the kind of work you are paying me to do. If you return the twenty-five to me and I return the fifty to Miss Holt, I will be deserting an innocent fellow being in a jam whom I have accepted as a client, and that would be inexcusable. It looks to me as if we have got ourselves in a fix that is absolutely hopeless, and I can't see—"

"Confound it," he roared, "go to bed!" and marched out.

VI

By 8:15 Tuesday morning I was pretty well convinced that Mira Holt was in the coop, since I had got it from three different sources. At 7:20 Judy Bram phoned to say that Mira was under arrest and what was I going to do. I said it wouldn't be practical to tell a suspect my plans, and she hung up on me. At 7:40 Lon Cohen of the *Gazette* phoned to ask if it was true that I had quit my job with Nero Wolfe, and if so what was I doing there, and was Mira Holt my client, and if so what was she doing in the can, and had she killed Phoebe Arden or not. Since Lon had often been useful and might be again, I explained fully, off the record, why I couldn't explain. And at eight o'clock the radio said that Mira Holt was being held as a material witness in the murder of Phoebe Arden.

Neither Lon nor the radio supplied any items that helped, nor did the morning papers. The *Star* had a picture of the taxi parked in front of Wolfe's house, but I had seen that for myself. It also had a description of the clothes Phoebe Arden had died in, but what I needed was a description of the clothes the murderer had killed in. And it gave the specifications of the knife—an ordinary kitchen knife with a five-inch blade and a plastic handle—but if the answer was going to come from any routine operation like tracing the knife or lifting prints from the handle, it would be Cramer's army who would get it, not me.

I made one phone call, to Anderson, to ask him to postpone his appointment because Wolfe was busy on a case, and he said sure, it wasn't urgent; and, since Fritz takes Wolfe's breakfast to his room and I seldom see him before he comes down to the office at eleven, I put a note on his desk. I wanted to make another call, to Nathaniel Parker, the lawyer, but vetoed it. For getting Mira out on bail he would have charged about ten times what she had paid me, and there was no big hurry. It would teach her not to drive a hack without a license.

At a quarter past eight I left the house and went to Ninth Avenue for a taxi, and at half past I dismissed it at the corner of Carmine and Ferrell, and walked down Ferrell Street to its dead end. There were only two alternatives for what had happened during the period—call it ten minutes—when Mira had been away from the cab: either the murderer, having already killed Phoebe Arden, had carried or dragged the body to the cab and hoisted it in, or he had got in the cab with her and killed her there. I preferred the latter, since you can walk to a cab with a live woman in much less time than you can carry her to it dead, and also since, even in a secluded spot like that and even after dark, there is much less risk of being noticed. But in either case they had to come from some place nearby.

The first place to consider was Kearns' house, but it only took five minutes to cross it off. The alley that led to it was walled on both sides, Mira had been parked at its mouth, and there was no other way to get from the house to the street. On the left of the alley was a walled-in lumber yard, and on the right was a dingy old two-story warehouse. On inspection neither of them seemed an ideal spot for cover, but across the street was a beaut. It was an open lot cluttered with blocks of stone scattered and piled around, some rough

and some chiseled and polished. A whole company could
have hid there, let alone one murderer and one victim. As
you know, I was already on record that Mira hadn't killed
her, but it was nice to see that stoneyard. If there had been
no place to hide in easy distance . . . Three men were there,
two discussing a stone and one chiseling, but they wouldn't
be there at eight in the evening. I recrossed the street and
entered the alley, and walked through.

By gum, Kearns had a garden, a sizable patch, say forty
by sixty, with flowers in bloom and a little pool with a
fountain, and a flagstone path leading to the door of a two-
story brick house painted white. I hadn't known there was
anything like it in Manhattan, and I thought I knew Manhattan. A man in a gray shirt and blue jeans was kneeling
among the flowers, and half way up the path I stopped and
asked him, "Are you Waldo Kearns?"

"Do I look it?" he demanded.

"Yes and no. Are you Morton?"

"That's my name. What's yours?"

"Goodwin." I headed for the house, but he called, "Nobody there," and I turned.

"Where's Mr. Kearns?"

"I don't know. He went out a while ago."

"When will he be back?"

"I couldn't say."

I looked disappointed. "I should have phoned. I want to
buy a picture. I came last evening around half past eight
and knocked, but nothing doing. I knocked loud because I
heard the radio or TV going."

"It was the TV. I was watching it. I heard you knock. I
don't open the door at night when he's not here. There's some
tough ones around this neighborhood."

"I don't blame you. I suppose I just missed him. What time
did he leave last evening?"

"What difference does it make when he left if he wasn't
here?"

Perfectly logical, not only for him but for me. If Kearns
hadn't been there when Mira arrived in the cab it didn't
matter when he had left. I would have liked to ask Morton
one more question, whether anyone had left with him, but
from the look in his eye he would have used some more
logic on me, so I skipped it, said I'd try again, and went.

There was no use hanging around because if Kearns had
gone to call at the District Attorney's office by request,
which was highly probable, there was no telling when he
would be back. I had got Gilbert Irving's business address
from the phone book, on Wall Street, but there was no use

going there at that early hour. However, I had also got his home address, on East 78th Street, and I might catch him before he left, so I hoofed it along Ferrell Street back to civilization and flagged a taxi.

It was 9:15 when I climbed out in front of the number on 78th Street, a tenement palace with a marquee and a doorman. In the lobby another uniformed sentry sprang into action, and I told him, "Mr. Gilbert Irving. Tell him a friend of Miss Holt." He went and used a phone, returned and said, "Fourteen B," and watched me like a hawk as I walked to the elevator and entered. When I got out at the fourteenth floor the elevator man stood and watched until I had pushed the button and the door had opened and I had been invited in.

The inviter was no maid or butler. She might have passed for a maid in uniform, but not in the long, flowing, patterned-silk number which she probably called a breakfast gown. Without any suggestions about my hat she said, "This way, please," and led me across the hall, through an arch into a room half as big as Kearns' garden, and over to chairs near a corner. She sat on one of them and indicated another for me.

I stood. "Perhaps the man downstairs didn't understand me," I suggested. "I asked for Mr. Irving."

"I know," she said. "He isn't here. I am his wife. We are friends of Miss Holt, and we're disturbed about the terrible —about her difficulty. You're a friend of hers?" Her voice was a surprise because it didn't fit. She was slender and not very tall, with a round little face and a little curved mouth, but her deep strong voice was what you would expect from a female sergeant. Nothing about her suggested the claws Judy Bram had mentioned, but they could have been drawn in.

"A new friend," I said. "I've known her twelve hours. If you've read the morning paper you may have noted that she was sitting on the stoop of Nero Wolfe's house with a man named Archie Goodwin when a cop found the body in the taxi. I'm Goodwin, and she has hired me to find out things."

She adjusted the gown to cover a leg better. "According to the radio she has hired Nero Wolfe. She was arrested in his house."

"That's a technical point. We're both working on it. I'm seeing people who might have some information, and Mr. Irving is on my list. Is he at his office?"

"I suppose so. He left earlier than usual." The leg was safe, no exposure above the ankle, but she adjusted the gown again. "What kind of information? Perhaps I could help?"

I couldn't very well ask if her husband had told her that

Mira had told him she was going to drive Judy's cab. But she wanted to help. I sat down. "Almost anything might be useful, Mrs. Irving. Were you and your husband also friends of Phoebe Arden?"

"I was. My husband knew her, of course, but you couldn't say they were friends."

"Were they enemies?"

"Oh, no. It was just that they didn't hit it off."

"When did you see her last?"

"Four days ago, last Friday, at a cocktail party at Waldo Kearns' house. I was thinking about it when you came. She was so gay. She was a gay person."

"You hadn't seen her since?"

"No." She was going to add something, but checked it.

It was so obvious that I asked, "But you had heard from her? A letter or a phone call?"

"How did you know that?" she demanded.

"I didn't. Most detective work is guessing. Was it a letter?"

"No." She hesitated. "I would like to help, Mr. Goodwin, but I doubt if it's important, and I certainly don't want any notoriety."

"Of course not, Mrs. Irving." I was sympathetic. "If you mean, if you tell me something will I tell the police, absolutely not. They have arrested my client."

"Well." She crossed her legs, glancing down to see that nothing was revealed. "I phoned Phoebe yesterday afternoon. My husband and I had tickets for the theater last evening, but about three o'clock he phoned me that a business associate from the West Coast had arrived unexpectedly, and he had to take him to dinner. So I phoned Phoebe and we arranged to meet at Morsini's at a quarter to seven for dinner and then go to the theater. I was there on time, but she didn't come. At a quarter past seven I called her number, but there was no answer. I don't like to eat alone at a place like Morsini's, so I waited a little longer and then left word for her and went to Schrafft's. She didn't come. I thought she might come to the theater, the Majestic, and I waited in the lobby until after nine, and then I left a ticket for her at the box office and went in. I would tell the police about it if I thought it was important, but it doesn't really *tell* anything except that she was at home when I phoned around three o'clock. Does it?"

"Sure it does. Did she agree definitely to meet you at Morsini's or was it tentative?"

"It was definite. Quite definite."

"Then it was certainly something that happened after three o'clock that kept her from meeting you. It was probably something that happened after six-thirty or she would have phoned you—if she was still alive. Have you any idea at all what it might have been?"

"None whatever. I can't guess."

"Have you any ideas about who might have killed her?"

"No. I can't guess that either."

"Do you think Mira Holt killed her?"

"Good heavens, no. Not Mira. Even if she had—"

"Even if she had what?"

"Nothing. Mira wouldn't kill anybody. They don't think that, do they?"

Over the years at least a thousand people have asked me what the police think, and I appreciate the compliment though I rarely deserve it. Life would be much simpler if I always knew what the police think at any given moment. It's hard enough to know what I think. After another ten minutes with her I decided that I thought that Mrs. Irving had nothing more to contribute, so I thanked her and departed. She came with me to the hall, and even picked up my hat from the chair where I had dropped it. I had yet to get a glimpse of her legs.

It was ten minutes to ten when I emerged to the sidewalk and turned left for Lexington Avenue and the subway, and a quarter past when I entered the marble lobby of a towering beehive on Wall Street and consulted the building directory. Gilbert Irving's firm had the whole thirtieth floor, and I found the proper bank of elevators, entered one, and was hoisted straight up three hundred feet for nothing. In a paneled chamber with a thick conservative carpet a handsome conservative creature at a desk bigger than Wolfe's told me in a voice like silk that Mr. Irving was not in and that she knew not when he would arrive or where he was. If I cared to wait?

I didn't. I left, got myself dropped back down the three hundred feet, and went to another subway, this time the west side; and, leaving at Christopher, walked to Ferrell Street and on to its dead end and through the alley. Morton, still at work in the garden, greeted me with reserve but not coldly, said Kearns had not returned and there had been no word from him, and, as I was turning to go, suddenly stood up and asked, "Did you say you wanted to *buy* a picture?"

I said that was my idea but naturally I wanted to see it first, left him wagging his head, walked the length of Ferrell Street the fourth time that day, found a taxi, and gave the driver the address which might or might not still be mine. As we turned into 35th Street from Eighth Avenue, at five minutes past eleven, there was another taxi just ahead of us, and

it stopped at the curb in front of the brownstone. I handed
my driver a bill, hopped out, and had mounted the stoop
by the time the man from the other cab had crossed the
sidewalk. I had never seen him or a picture of him, or heard
him described, but I knew him. I don't know whether
it was his floppy black hat or shoestring tie, or neat little
ears or face like a squirrel, but I knew him. I had the door
open when he reached the stoop.

"I would like to see Mr. Nero Wolfe," he said. "I'm Waldo
Kearns."

VII

Since Wolfe had suggested that I should bring Kearns
there so we could look at him together, I would just as
soon have let him think that I had filled the order, but of
course that wouldn't do. So when, having taken the floppy
black hat and put it on the shelf in the hall, I escorted him
to the office and pronounced his name, I added, "I met
Mr. Kearns out front. He arrived just as I did."

Wolfe, behind his desk, had been pouring beer when we
entered. He put the bottle down. "Then you haven't talked
with him?"

"No, sir."

He turned to Kearns, in the red leather chair. "Will you
have beer, sir?"

"Heavens, no." Kearns was emphatic. "I didn't come for
amenities. My business is urgent. I am extremely displeased
with the counsel you have given my wife. You must have
hypnotized her. She refuses to see me. She refuses to accept
the services of my lawyer, even to arrange bail for her. I
demand an explanation. I intend to hold you to account
for alienating the affection of my wife."

"Affections," Wolfe said.

"What?"

"Affections. In that context the plural is used." He lifted
the glass and drank, and licked his lips.

Kearns stared at him. "I didn't come here," he said, "to
have my grammar corrected."

"Not grammar. Diction."

Kearns pounded the chair arm. "What have you to say?"

"It would be futile for me to say anything whatever
until you have regained your senses, if you have any. If you
think your wife had affection for you until she met me
twelve hours ago, you're an ass. If you know she hadn't your
threat is fatuous. In either case what can you expect but
contempt?"

"I expect an explanation! I expect the truth! I expect you to tell me why my wife refuses to see me!"

"I can't tell you what I don't know. I don't even know that she has, since in your present state I question the accuracy of your reporting. When and where did she refuse?"

"This morning. Just now, in the District Attorney's office. She won't even talk to my lawyer. She told him she was waiting to hear from you and Goodwin." His head jerked to me. "You're Goodwin?"

I admitted it. His head jerked back. "It's humiliating! It's degrading! My wife under arrest! Mrs. Waldo Kearns in jail! Dishonor to my name and to me! And you're to blame!"

Wolfe took a breath. "I doubt if it's worth the trouble," he said, "but I'm willing to try. I presume what you're after is an account of our conversation with your wife last evening. I might consider supplying it, but first I would have to be satisfied of your *bona fides*. Will you answer some questions?"

"It depends on what they are."

"Probably you have already answered them, to the police. Has your wife wanted a divorce and have you refused to consent?"

"Yes. I regard the marriage contract as a sacred covenant."

"Have you refused to discuss it with her in recent months?"

"The police didn't ask me that."

"I ask it. I need to establish not only your *bona fides*, Mr. Kearns, but also your wife's. It shouldn't embarrass you to answer that."

"It doesn't embarrass me. You can't embarrass me. It would have been useless to discuss it with her since I wouldn't consider it."

"So you wouldn't see her?"

"Naturally. That was all she would talk about."

"Have you been contributing to her support since she left you?"

"She didn't leave me. We agreed to try living separately. She wouldn't let me contribute to her support. I offered to. I wanted to."

"The police certainly asked you if you killed Phoebe Arden. Did you?"

"No. Why in God's name would I kill her?"

"I don't know. Miss Judith Bram suggested that she may have had a bad cold and you were afraid you would catch it, but that seems farfetched. By the way——"

"Judy? Judy Bram said that? I don't believe it!"

"But she did. In this room last evening, in the chair you now occupy. She also called you a sophisticated ape."

"You're lying!"

"No. I'm not above lying, or below it, but the truth will do now. Also—"

"You're lying. You've never seen Judy Bram. You're merely repeating something my wife said."

"That's interesting, Mr. Kearns, and even suggestive. You are willing to believe that your wife called you a sophisticated ape, but not that Miss Bram did. When I do lie I try not to be clumsy. Miss Bram was here last evening, with Mr. Goodwin and me, for half an hour or more; and that brings me to a ticklish point. I must ask you about a detail that the police don't know about. Certainly they asked about your movements last evening, but they didn't know that you had arranged with Judith Bram to call for you in her cab at eight o'clock. Unless you told them?"

Kearns sat still, and for him it is worth mentioning. With many people sitting still is nothing remarkable, but with him it was. His sitting, like his face, reminded me of a squirrel; he kept moving or twitching something—a hand, a shoulder, a foot, even his head. Now he was motionless all over.

"Say that again," he commanded.

Wolfe obeyed. "Have you told the police that you had arranged with Miss Bram to call for you in her cab at eight o'clock last evening?"

"No. Why should I tell them something that isn't true?"

"You shouldn't, ideally, but people often do. I do occasionally. However, that's irrelevant, since it would have been the truth. Evidently Miss Bram hasn't told the police, but she told me. I mention it to ensure that you'll tell *me* the truth when you recount your movements last evening."

"If she told you that she lied."

"Oh, come, Mr. Kearns." Wolfe was disgusted. "It is established that her cab stood at the mouth of the alley leading to your house for more than half an hour, having come at your bidding. If you omitted that detail in your statement to the police I may have to supply it. Haven't you spoken with Miss Bram since?"

"No." He was still motionless. "Her phone doesn't answer. She's not at home. I went there." He passed his tongue across his lower lip. I admit I have never seen a squirrel do that. "I couldn't tell the police her cab was there last evening because I didn't know it was. I wasn't there."

"Where were you? Consider that I know you had ordered the cab for eight o'clock and hadn't canceled the order."

"I've told the police where I was."

"Then your memory has been jogged."

"It didn't need jogging. I was at the studio of a man named Prosch, Carl Prosch. I went there to meet Miss Arden and look at a picture she was going to buy. I got there at a quarter to eight and left at nine o'clock. She hadn't come, and—"

"If you please. Miss Phoebe Arden?"

"Yes. She phoned me at half past seven and said she had about decided to buy a painting, a still life, from Prosch, and was going to his studio to look at it again, and asked me to meet her there to help her decide. I was a little surprised because she knows what I think of daubers like Prosch, but I said I would go. His studio is on Carmine Street, in walking distance from my house, and I walked. She hadn't arrived, and I had only been there two or three minutes when she phoned and asked to speak to me. She said she had been delayed and would get there as soon as she could, and asked me to wait for her. My thought was that I would wait until midnight rather than have her buy a still life by Prosch, but I didn't say so. I didn't wait until midnight, but I waited until nine o'clock. I discussed painting with Prosch a while, until he became insufferable, and then went down to the street and waited there. She never came. I walked back home."

Wolfe grunted. "Can there be any doubt that it was Miss Arden on the phone? Both times?"

"Not the slightest. I couldn't possibly mistake her voice."

"What time was it when you left Mr. Prosch and went down to the street?"

"About half past eight. I told the police I couldn't be exact about that, but I could about when I started home. It was exactly nine o'clock." Kearns' hands moved. Back to normal. "Now I'll hear what you have to say."

"In a moment. Miss Bram was to come at eight o'clock. Why didn't you phone her?"

"Because I thought I would be back. Probably a little late, but she would wait. I didn't phone her after Miss Arden phoned that she was delayed because she would be gone."

"Where was she to drive you?"

"To Long Island. A party. What does that matter?" He was himself again. "You talk now, and I want the truth!"

Wolfe picked up his glass, emptied it, and put it down. "Possibly you are entitled to it, Mr. Kearns. Unquestionably a man of your standing would feel keenly the ignominy of having a wife in jail—the woman to whom you have given your name, though she doesn't use it. You may know that she came to this house at twenty minutes past nine last evening."

"I know nothing. I told you she won't see me."

"So you did. She arrived just as Mr. Goodwin was leaving the house on an errand and they met on the stoop. No

doubt you know that Mr. Goodwin is permanently in my
employ as my confidential assistant—permanently, that is,
in the sense that neither of us has any present intention of
ending it or changing its terms."

Kearns was fidgeting again. I was not. He spoke. "The
paper said he had left your employ. It didn't say on account
of my wife, but of course it was."

"Bosh." Wolfe's head turned. "Archie?"

"Bosh," I agreed. "The idea of quitting on account of Miss
Holt never entered my head."

Kearns hit the chair arm. "Mrs. Kearns!"

"Okay," I conceded. "Mrs. Waldo Kearns."

"So," Wolfe said, "your wife's first contact was with Mr.
Goodwin. They sat on the stoop and talked. You know, of
course, that Miss Bram's cab was there at the curb with Miss
Arden's body in it."

"Yes. What did my wife say?"

"I'll come to that. Police came along in a car and discovered the body, and reported it, and soon there was an
army. A policeman named Cramer talked with Mr. Goodwin
and your wife, I went to the door and invited them to enter
—not Mr. Cramer—and they did so. We talked for half an
hour or so, when Mr. Cramer came with Miss Bram, and
they were admitted. Mr. Cramer, annoyed by the loquacity of
Miss Bram, and wishing to speak with your wife privately,
took her away. You demanded the truth, sir, and you have
it. I add one item, also true: since your wife had engaged
Mr. Goodwin's services, and through him mine also, what
she told us was confidential and can't be divulged. Now
for—"

Kearns bounced out of the chair, and as he did so the
doorbell rang. Since a man who might have stuck a knife in
a woman might be capable of other forms of violence, I
was going to leave it to Fritz, but Wolfe shot me a glance
and I went to the hall for a look. On the stoop was a tall guy
with a bony face and a strong jaw. Behind me Kearns was
yapping but had drawn no weapon. I went to the front and
opened the door.

"To see Mr. Wolfe," he said. "My name is Gilbert Irving."

The temptation was too strong. Only twelve hours ago I
had seen a confrontation backfire for Cramer, when he had
brought Judy Bram in to face Mira, but this time the temperament was already in the office, having a fit, and it would be
interesting to see the reaction, and possibly helpful. So I
told him to come in, took his Homburg and put it on the
shelf beside the floppy black number, and steered him to
the office.

Kearns was still on his feet yapping, but when Wolfe's eyes left him to direct a scowl at me he turned his head. I ignored the scowl. I had disregarded another rule by bringing in a visitor without consulting Wolfe, but as far as I was concerned Mira was still my client and it was my case. I merely pronounced names. "Mr. Gilbert Irving. Mr. Wolfe."

The reaction was interesting enough, though not helpful, since it was no news that Kearns and Irving were not pals. Perhaps Kearns didn't actually spit at him because it could have been merely that moisture came out with his snort. Two words followed immediately. "You bastard!"

Irving must have had lessons or practice, or both. His uppercut, with his right, was swift and sure, and had power. It caught Kearns right on the button and sent him straight up a good six inches before he swayed against the corner of Wolfe's desk.

VIII

To do him justice, Kearns handled it as well as could be expected, even better. He surprised me. He didn't utter a peep. The desk saved him from going down. He stayed propped against it for three seconds, straightened with his hand on it for support, moved his head backward and forward twice, decided his neck was still together, and moved. His first few steps were wobbly, but by the time he reached the door to the hall they were steadier, and he made the turn okay. I went to the hall and stood, as he got his hat from the shelf and let himself out, pulling the door shut without banging it, and re-entered the office as Irving was saying, "I should beg your pardon. I do. I'm sorry."

"You were provoked," Wolfe told him. He gestured at the red leather chair. "Be seated."

"Hold it." I was there. "I guess I should beg your pardon, Mr. Irving, for not telling you he was here, and now I just beg it again. I have to tell Mr. Wolfe something that can't wait. It won't take long." I went and opened the door to the front room. "If you'll step in here."

He didn't like the idea. "My business is pressing," he said.

"So is mine. If you please?"

"Your name is Archie Goodwin?"

"Yes."

He hesitated a second, and then came, and crossed the sill, and I closed the door. Since it and the wall were soundproofed, I didn't have to lower my voice to tell Wolfe, "I want to report. I saw his wife."

"Indeed. Will a summary do?"

"No." I sat. "It will for one detail, that eighty feet from where the cab was parked there is a stoneyard that would be perfect cover, you couldn't ask for better, but you must have my talk with Mrs. Irving verbatim."

"Go ahead."

I did so, starting with a description of her. It had been years since he had first told me that when I described a man he must see him and hear him, and I had learned the trick long ago. I also knew how to report conversations word for word—much longer ones than the little chat I had had with Mrs. Irving.

When I had finished he asked one question. "Was she lying?"

"I wouldn't bet either way. If so she is good. If it was a mixture I'd hate to have to sort it out."

"Very well." He closed his eyes. In a moment they opened. "Bring him."

I went and opened the door to the front room and told him to come, and he entered, crossed to the red leather chair, sat, and aimed his eyes at Wolfe. "I should explain," he said, "that I am here as a friend of Miss Mira Holt, but she didn't send me."

Wolfe nodded. "She mentioned your name last evening. She said you are an intelligent man."

"I'm afraid she flatters me." Evidently it was normal for him to sit still. "I have come to you for information, but I can't pretend I have any special right to it. I can only tell you why I want it. When I learned on the radio this morning that Miss Holt was in custody I started downtown to see her, to offer my help, but on the way I decided that it wouldn't be advisable because it might be misconstrued, since I am merely a friend. So I called on my lawyer instead. His name is John H. Darby. I explained the situation and asked him to see Miss Holt, and he arranged to see her and has talked with her, but she won't tell him anything. She even refused to authorize him to arrange bail for her. She says that Archie Goodwin and Nero Wolfe are representing her, and she will say nothing and do nothing without their advice."

I touched my lips with a fingertip, the lips that Mira had kissed. I was blowing the kiss back to her. Not only had she put my name first, but also she had improved on my suggestion by combining method three and method one. She was a client in a thousand. She had even turned down two offers to spring her.

"I'm not a lawyer," Wolfe said, "and neither is Mr. Goodwin."

"I'm aware of that. But you seem to have hypnotized Miss Holt. With no offense intended, I must ask, are you acting in her interest or in Waldo Kearns'?"

Wolfe grunted. "Hers. She hired us."

I put in, "You and Kearns agree. He thinks we hypnotized her too. Nuts."

He regarded me. "I prefer to deal with Mr. Wolfe. This is his office."

"You're dealing with both of us," Wolfe told him. "Professionally we are indiscrete. What information do you want?"

"I want to know why you are taking no steps to get her released and what action you intend to take in her interest. I also want you to advise her to accept the services of my lawyer. He is highly qualified."

Wolfe rested his palms on the chair arms. "You should know better, Mr. Irving; you're a man of affairs. Before I gave you an inch, let alone the mile you ask for, I would have to be satisfied that your interest runs with hers."

"Damn it, I'm her friend! Didn't she say I am? You said she mentioned me."

"She could be mistaken." Wolfe shook his head. "No. For instance, I don't even know what you have told the police."

"Nothing. They haven't asked me anything. Why should they?"

"Then you haven't told them that Miss Holt told you on the phone Sunday evening that she was going to drive Judith Bram's cab?"

It got him. He stared. He looked at me and back at Wolfe. "No," he said. "Even if she had, would I tell the police?"

"Do you deny that she did?"

"I neither deny it nor affirm it."

Wolfe upturned a palm. "How the devil can you expect candor from me? Do you want me to suspect that Miss Holt lied when she told us of that phone call?"

"When did she tell you?"

"Last evening. Here. Not under hypnosis."

He considered. "All right. She told me that."

"And whom did you tell?"

"No one."

"You're certain?"

"Of course I'm certain."

"Then it won't be easy to satisfy me. Assuming that Miss Holt fulfilled her intention and took the cab, and arrived with it at Mr. Kearns' address at eight o'clock, and combining that assumption with the fact that at twenty minutes past nine the cab was standing in front of my house with a dead body in it, where are you? Miss Bram states that she told no one of the arrangement. Miss Holt states that she told no one but you. Is it any wonder that I ask where you are? And, specifically, where you were last evening from eight o'clock on?"

"I see." Irving took a breath, and another. "It's utterly preposterous. You actually suspect me of being involved in the murder of Phoebe Arden."

"I do indeed."

"But it's preposterous! I had no concern whatever with Miss Arden. She meant nothing to me. Not only that, apparently whoever killed her managed to get Miss Holt involved —either managed it or permitted it. Would I do that?" He made his hands fists and raised them, shook them. "Damn it, I have to know what happened! You know. Miss Holt told you. I have to know!"

"There are things I have to know," Wolfe said drily. "I mentioned one: your movements last evening. We have it from your wife, but I prefer it from you. That's the rule, and a good one: get the best available evidence."

Irving was staring again. "My wife? You have seen my wife?"

"Mr. Goodwin has. He called at your home this morning to see you, and you had gone. Your wife wished to be helpful. You know, of course, what she told him."

"Did she tell him—" He stopped and started over. "Did she tell him about a phone call she made yesterday afternoon?"

Wolfe nodded. "And one she received. She received one from you and made one to Miss Arden."

Irving inclined his head forward to look at his right hand. Its fingers bent, slowly, to make a fist. Apparently something about the operation was unsatisfactory, for he repeated it several times, gazing at it. At length his head came up. "My lawyer wouldn't like this," he said, "but I'm going to tell you something. I have to if I expect you to tell me anything. If I told you what I told my wife you would check it, and it won't check. I know Miss Holt drove Judy Bram's cab there last evening. I know she got there at five minutes to eight and left at ten minutes to nine. I saw her."

"Indeed. Where were you?"

"I was in a cab parked on Carmine Street, around the corner from Ferrell Street. I suppose you know what her purpose was in driving Judy's cab?"

"Yes. To talk with her husband."

"I had tried to persuade her not to. Did she tell you that?"

"Yes."

"I didn't like it. There isn't much that Kearns isn't capable of. I don't mean violence; just some trick like getting her out of the cab and going off with it. I decided to be there, and I phoned my wife that I would have to spend the evening with a business associate. I was afraid if I took my car Miss Holt might recognize it, so I got a taxi with a driver I know. Carmine Street is one-way, and we parked where we would be ready to follow when she came out of Ferrell Street. We were there when she arrived, at five minutes to eight. When she came back, nearly an hour later, she was alone. There was no one in the cab. I supposed Kearns had refused to let her drive him, and I was glad of it."

"What then?"

"I went to my club. If you want to check I'll give you the cab driver's name and address. I rang Judy Bram's number, and I rang Miss Holt's number three or four times, but there was no answer. I supposed they were out somewhere together. And this morning I heard the radio and saw the paper." He breathed. "I hope to heaven I won't have to regret telling you this. If it contradicts anything she told you she's right and I'm wrong. I could be lying, you know, for my own protection."

I was thinking, if so you're an expert.

Wolfe's eyes, at him, were half closed. "It was dark. How could you know there was no one in the cab?"

"There's a light at that corner. I have good eyes and so has the driver. She was going slow, for the turn."

"You didn't follow her?"

"No. There was no point in following her if Kearns wasn't with her."

"What would you say if I told you that Miss Holt saw you in your parked taxi as she drove by?"

"I wouldn't believe it. When she drove by arriving I was flat on the seat. It was dark but I didn't risk her seeing me. When she left she didn't drive by. Carmine Street is one-way."

Wolfe leaned back and shut his eyes, and his lips began to work. Irving started to say something, and I snapped at him, "Hold it." Wolfe pushed his lips out and pulled them in, out and in, out and in. . . . He was earning the twenty-five bucks I had paid him. I had no idea how, but when he starts that lip operation the sparks are flying inside his skull.

Irving tried again. "But I want—"

"Hold it."

"But I don't—"

"Shut up!"

He sat regarding me, not warmly.

Wolfe opened his eyes and straightened. "Mr. Irving." He was curt. "You will get what you camè here for, but not forthwith. Possibly within the hour, probably somewhat later. Tell me where I can reach you, or you may—"

"Damn it, no! I want—"

"If you please. Confound it, I've been yelped at enough today. Or you may wait here. That room has comfortable chairs—or one at least. Mr. Goodwin and I have work to do."

"I don't intend—"

"Your intentions have no interest or point. Where can we reach you?"

Irving looked at me and saw nothing hopeful. He arose. "I'll wait here," he said, and headed for the front room.

IX

Having turned my head to see that Irving shut the door, I turned it back again. "Fine," I said. "We're going to work."

"I'm a dunce," he said. "So are you."

"It's possible," I conceded. "Can you prove it?"

"It's manifest. Why did that policeman stop his car to look inside that cab?"

"Cops do. That's what a prowl car is for. They saw it parked with the hackie gone, and while that's nothing strange they thought it was worth a look. Also it was parked in front of your house. He knew it was your house. He said so."

"Nevertheless, we are dunces not to have questioned it. I want to know if that policeman had been prompted. At once."

"It's a point," I admitted. "The papers haven't mentioned it. I doubt if Cramer would—"

"No."

"I could try Lon Cohen."

"Do so."

I swiveled and dialed the *Gazette* number, and got Lon. Wolfe lifted his receiver to listen in. I told Lon I wanted something for nothing. He said I always did and usually got it, but if what I was after this time was an ad under "Situations Wanted" I would have to pay.

"That was just a dirty rumor," I said. "I am permanently in Mr. Wolfe's employ—permanently, that is, in the sense that I may still be here tomorrow. On our present job we're shy a detail. If you'll supply it I'll give you something for the front page if and when. We don't know whether the cop who stopped to uncover Phoebe Arden's body in the taxi had been steered or was just nosy. Do you?"

"Yes, but I'm not supposed to. The DA is saving it. He may release it this afternoon. If he does I'll call you."

"We need it now. Not for publication, and we wouldn't dream of quoting you. We're just curious."

"I'll bet you are. I wish I got paid as much for being curious as Wolfe does. Okay. It was a dialed phone call to Canal six, two thousand. Probably a man, but it could have been a woman trying to sound like a man or the reverse. It said there was a taxi standing in front of nine-eighteen West Thirty-fifth Street with a dead woman in it. As you know, that address has been heard from before. The sergeant radioed a prowl car."

"Has the call been traced?"

"How? Modern improvements. But you'd better ask the DA."

"A good idea. I will. Many thanks and I won't forget the front page." I hung up and swiveled. "I'll be damned. Where can we buy dunce caps? For a passerby to see it he would have had to open the door and lift the canvas."

Wolfe's lips were tight. "We should have done that hours ago."

"Lon may not have known hours ago."

"True. Even so. Get Mr. Cramer."

I swiveled and dialed. It wasn't as simple as getting Lon Cohen had been. Cramer was in conference and couldn't be disturbed. I was hacking away at it when Wolfe took his phone and said, "This is Nero Wolfe. I have something that will not wait. Ask Mr. Cramer if he prefers that I deal with the District Attorney."

In two minutes there was a bark. "What do you want?"

"Mr. Cramer?" He knew darned well it was.

"Yes. I'm busy."

"So am I. Is it true that Miss Holt refuses to talk without advice from Mr. Goodwin or me?"

"Yes it is, and I was just telling Stebbins to get Goodwin down here. And then I'm going—"

"If you please. Mr. Goodwin and I have decided that it is now desirable for Miss Holt to answer any questions you care to ask—or that it will be after we have had a brief talk with her. Since I must be present and I transact business only in my own office, it will be pointless for you to send for him. If you want her to talk bring her here."

"You're too late, Wolfe. I don't need her to tell me that

she drove that cab to your address. I already know it. Her prints are on the steering wheel and the door, and other places. You're too late."

"Has she admitted it?"

"No, but she will."

"I doubt it. She's rather inflexible. I regret having called you to the phone to no purpose. May I make a request? Don't keep Mr. Goodwin longer than necessary. I am about to conclude a matter in which he has an interest and would like him present. I wanted Miss Holt here too, but since I'm too late I'll have to manage without her."

Silence. Prolonged.

"Are you there, Mr. Cramer?"

"Yes. So you're going to conclude a matter."

"I am. Soon afterwards Miss Holt and Mr. Goodwin and I will talk not by your sufferance but at our will."

"Are you saying that you know who killed Phoebe Arden?"

"'Know' implies certitude. I have formed a conclusion and intend to verify it. It shouldn't take long. But I'm keeping you. Could you do without Mr. Goodwin until, say, four o'clock? It's half past twelve. By then we should have finished."

Another silence, not quite so long. "I'll be there in fifteen minutes," Cramer said.

"With Miss Holt?"

"Yes."

"Satisfactory. But not in fifteen minutes. I must get Judith Bram and Waldo Kearns. Do you know where they are?"

"Kearns is at his home. He said he would be if we wanted him again. Judith Bram is here. I'll bring her along, and I'll send for Kearns. Now."

"No. People have to eat. Will you lunch with us? And Miss Holt?"

"I will not. Did you ever skip a meal in your life?"

"Many times when I was younger, by necessity. Then I suggest that you arrive with Miss Holt at two o'clock, and arrange for Miss Bram and Mr. Kearns to come at two-thirty. Will that be convenient?"

"By God. *Convenient!*"

A click. He was off. We hung up. I said, "Probably Irving eats too."

"Yes. Bring him."

I went and got him. He marched to Wolfe's desk and demanded, "Well?"

Wolfe's head slanted back. "I forgot, sir, when I said possibly within the hour, that lunch would interfere. It will be a little longer. I have spoken with Inspector Cramer, and he will arrive with Miss Holt at two o'clock. We shall expect you and your wife to join us at two-thirty."

His jaw was working. "Miss Holt will be here?"

"Yes."

"Why my wife?"

"Because she has something to contribute. As you know, she had an appointment with Miss Arden which Miss Arden did not keep. That will be germane."

"Germane to what?"

"To our discussion."

"I don't want a discussion. I certainly don't want one with a police inspector. I told you what I want."

"And you'll get it, sir, but the method and manner are in my discretion. I give you my assurance without qualification that I am acting solely in the interest of Miss Holt, that I expect to free her of any suspicion of complicity in the murder of Phoebe Arden, and that I shall not disclose what you have told me of your movements last evening without your prior permission. Confound it, do I owe you anything?"

"No." His jaw was still working. "I'd rather not bring my wife."

"We'll need her. If you prefer, I'll arrange for Inspector Cramer to send for her."

"No." He breathed. He looked at me and back at Wolfe. "All right. We'll be here." He wheeled and went.

x

Five of the yellow chairs were in place facing Wolfe's desk, three in front and two behind, and Mira was in the one nearest to Cramer. I had intended the one at my end for her, but Cramer had vetoed it, and since she was his prisoner I hadn't insisted. Of course he was in the red leather chair, and the uninvited guest he had brought along, Sergeant Purley Stebbins, was seated at his right, with his broad, burly shoulders touching the wall.

Mira looked fine, considering. Her eyes were a little heavy and the lids were swollen, and her jacket could have stood washing and ironing, and the corners of her mouth pointed down, but I thought she looked fine. Wolfe, seated behind his desk, was glowering at her, but the glower wasn't meant for her. It was merely that he had had to tell Fritz to advance the lunch hour fifteen minutes, and then had had to hurry through the corn fritters and sausage cakes and wild-thyme honey from Greece and cheese and blackberry pie with not enough time to enjoy it properly.

"Was it bad?" he asked her.

"Not too bad," she said. "I didn't get too much sleep. The worst was when the morning passed and I didn't hear from you." Her head turned. "Or you, Mr. Goodwin."

I nodded. "I was busy earning my fee. I wasn't worried about you because you had promised you wouldn't forget method three."

"I kept my promise."

"I know you did. I'll buy you a drink any time you're thirsty."

"Get on," Cramer growled.

"Have you been told," Wolfe asked her, "that others will join us shortly?"

"No," she said. "Here? Who?"

"Miss Bram, Mr. Kearns, and Mr. and Mrs. Gilbert Irving." Her eyes widened. "Why Mr. and Mrs. Irving?"

"That will appear after they arrive. I thought you should know that they're coming. They'll soon be here, and we have two points to cover. First I need a question answered. When you drove away from Ferrell Street last evening, and meandered in search of a place to dispose of the corpse—don't interrupt me—and finally drove here, did you at any time suspect that you were being followed by another car?"

Her mouth was hanging open. "But you—" she stammered. Her head jerked to me. "Did you know he was—what good did it do to keep my promise?"

"A lot," I told her. "Yes, I knew he was. Everything is under control. Believe me, I would rather lose an arm than lose the right to ask you to promise me something. We know what we're doing. Shall I repeat the question?"

"But—"

"No buts. Leave it to us. Shall I repeat the question?"

"Yes."

I did so, omitting the "don't interrupt me."

"No," she said.

"Proceed," Wolfe told me.

I knew it would have been better to have her closer. She was six yards away. "This one is more complicated and more important. During that drive, from Ferrell Street to here, are you certain that another car was *not* following you? There are various ways of making sure of that. Did you use any of them?"

"No. I never thought of that. I was looking for a place—"

"I know you were. All we want is this: if I told you that a car was following you, all the way, what would you say?"

"I would want to know who it was."

I wanted to go and pat her on the head, but it might

have been misconstrued. "Okay," I said. "That's one point.
The other one is simple. Tell Inspector Cramer what you
told us last night, including the phone call to Gilbert Irving
to tell him that you were going to drive Judy's cab." I looked
at my wrist. "You only have fifteen minutes, so reel it off."

"I won't," she said. "Not until you tell me why you're
doing this."

"Then I'll tell him. You'll know why after the others get
here. I'll tell you this: someone tried to frame you for murder and this is payday. Anyway there's not much left, now
that the inspector knows you drove the cab here with the
corpse in it. Would we have spilled that if we didn't have a
good hold? Go ahead."

Wolfe put in, "Don't interrupt with questions, Mr. Cramer.
They can wait. Yes, Miss Holt?"

She still didn't like it, not a bit, but she delivered, starting
with Sunday evening. She left gaps. She didn't say that Judy
had given her permission to take the cab, merely that she had
taken it, and she didn't mention the phone call to Irving; but
since I had already mentioned it that didn't matter. The
main thing was what had happened after she got to Ferrell
Street with the cab, and she covered that completely; and
when she got to where she and I had sat on the stoop and
talked, Cramer began cutting in with questions. I will not
say that he was more interested in tagging me for obstructing
justice than he was in solving a murder case, since I don't
like to brag, but it sounded like it. He was firing away at
her, and Sergeant Stebbins was scrawling in his notebook,
when the doorbell rang and I went to answer it. It was Waldo
Kearns. When I took him to the office he went to Mira, without so much as a glance for the three men, and put out a
hand.

"My dear wife," he said.

"Don't be ridiculous," Mira said.

I can't report whether he handled that as well as he had
handled the uppercut by Irving because the bell rang again
and I had to leave them, to admit Judy Bram. She had an
escort, a Homicide dick I only knew by sight, and he thought
he was going to enter with her and I didn't, and while we
were discussing it she slipped in and left it to us. We were
still chatting when a taxi stopped out front and Mr. and Mrs.
Irving got out and headed for the steps. The dick had to give
them room to pass, and I was able to shut the door on him
without flattening his nose. Since it was quite possible that
Irving's appearance would start something I entered the office
on their heels.

Nothing happened. Mira merely shot him a glance and he

returned it. Kearns didn't even glance at him. The newcomers
stood while Wolfe pronounced their names for Cramer and
Stebbins and told them who Cramer and Stebbins were, and
then went to the two chairs still vacant, the two nearest my
desk. Mrs. Irving took the one in front, with Judy between her
and Mira, and her husband took the one back of her, which
put him only a long arm's length from Waldo Kearns.

As Wolfe's eyes moved from right to left, stopping at
Mira, and back again, Cramer spoke. "You understand that
this is not an official inquiry. Sergeant Stebbins and I are
looking on. You also understand that Mira Holt is under arrest
as a material witness. If she had been charged with murder
she wouldn't be here."

"Why isn't she out on bail?" Judy Bram demanded. "I want
to know why—"

"That will do," Wolfe snapped. "You're here to listen, Miss
Bram, and if you don't hold your tongue Mr. Goodwin will
drag you out. If necessary Mr. Stebbins will help."

"But why—"

"No! One more word and out you go."

She set her teeth on her lip and glared at him. He glared
back, decided she was squelched, and left her.

"I am acting," he said, "jointly with Mr. Goodwin, on
behalf of Miss Holt. At our persuasion she has just told Mr.
Cramer of her movements last evening. I'll sketch them
briefly. Shortly after seven-thirty she took Miss Bram's cab
and drove it to Ferrell Street and parked at the mouth of
the alley leading to Mr. Kearns' house. She expected him to
appear but he didn't. At eight-thirty she left the cab, went
through the alley to the house, knocked several times, and
looked in windows. Getting no response, she returned to the
cab, having been gone about ten minutes. There was a dead
body in the cab, a woman, and she recognized her. It was
Phoebe Arden. I will not—"

"You fat fool!" Judy blurted. "You're a fine—"

"Archie!" he commanded.

I stood up. She clamped her teeth on her lip. I sat down.

"I will not," Wolfe said, "go into her thought processes,
but confine myself to her actions. She covered the body with
a piece of canvas and drove away. Her intention was to dispose of her cargo in some likely spot, and she drove around
in search of one, but found none. I omit details—for instance,
that she rang the number of Miss Bram from a phone booth
and got no answer. She decided she must have counsel, drove
to my house, met Mr. Goodwin on the stoop, and gave him a
rigmarole about a bet she had made. Since he is vulnerable

to the attractions of personable young women, he swallowed
it."

I swallowed *that*. I had to, with Cramer sitting there.

"Now," Wolfe said, "a crucial fact. I learned it myself
less than three hours ago. Only a few minutes after Miss
Holt and Mr. Goodwin met on the stoop someone phoned
police headquarters to say that a taxi standing in front of this
address had a dead woman in it. That is—"

"Where did you get that?" Cramer demanded.

Wolfe snorted. "Pfui. Not from you or Mr. Stebbins. That
is proof, to me conclusive, that the murderer of Phoebe Arden
had no wish or need for her to die. Phoebe Arden was killed
only because her corpse was needed as a tool for the destruction of another person—a design so cold-blooded and
malign that even I am impressed. Whether she was killed
in the cab, or at a nearby spot and the body taken to the cab,
is immaterial. The former is more likely, and I assume it.
What did the murderer do? He, or she—we lack a neuter
pronoun—he entered the cab with Phoebe Arden the moment Miss Holt disappeared in the alley, coming from their
hiding place in the stoneyard across the street. Having stabbed
his victim—or rather his tool—he walked up Ferrell Street
and around the corner to where his car was parked on Carmine Street. Before going to his car he stood near the corner
to see if Miss Holt, on returning to the cab, removed the
body before driving away. If she had, he would have found a
booth and phoned police headquarters immediately."

Cramer growled, "What if Kearns had come out with
Miss Holt?"

"He knew he wouldn't. I'll come to that. You are assuming that Kearns was not the murderer."

"I am assuming nothing."

"That's prudent. When Miss Holt turned the cab into
Carmine Street and drove on, he followed her. He followed
her throughout her search for a place to get rid of the corpse,
and on to her final destination, this house. Some of my particulars are assumption or conjecture, but not this one. He
must have done so, for when she stopped here he drove on
by, found a phone booth, and made the call to the police.
The only other possible source of the call was a passerby
who had seen the corpse in the cab as it stood at the curb,
and a passerby couldn't have seen it without opening the
door and lifting the canvas." His eyes went to Cramer. "Of
course that hadn't escaped you."

Cramer grunted.

Wolfe turned a hand over. "If his objective was the death
of Phoebe Arden, why didn't he kill her in the stoneyard—

they must have been there, since there is no other concealment near—and leave her there? Or if he did kill her there,
which is highly unlikely, why did he carry or drag the body
to the cab? And why, his objective reached, did he follow
the cab in its wanderings and at the first opportunity call the
police? I concede the possibility that he had a double objective, to destroy both Miss Arden and Miss Holt, but if so
Miss Holt must have been his main target. To kill Miss Arden,
once he had her in the stoneyard with a weapon at hand,
was simple and involved little risk; to use her body as a tool
for the destruction of Miss Holt was a complicated and daring operation, and the risks were great. I am convinced that
he had a single objective, to destroy Miss Holt."

"Then why?" Cramer demanded. "Why didn't he kill *her?*"

"I can only conjecture, but it is based on logic. Because it
was known that he had reason to wish Miss Holt dead, and
no matter how ingenious his plan and adroit its execution,
he would have been suspected and probably brought to account. I have misstated it. That's what he did. He devised a
plan so ingenious that he thought he would be safe."

Purley Stebbins got up, circled around the red leather
chair, and stood at Waldo Kearns' elbow.

"No, Mr. Stebbins," Wolfe said. "Our poor substitute for a
neuter pronoun is misleading. I'll abandon it. If you want to
guard a murderer stand by Mrs. Irving."

Knowing that was coming any second, I had my eye on
her. She was only four feet from me. She didn't move a
muscle, but her husband did. He put a hand to his forehead
and squeezed. I could see his knuckles go white. Mira's eyes
stayed fixed on Wolfe, but Judy and Kearns turned to look
at Mrs. Irving. Stebbins did too, but he didn't move.

Cramer spoke. "Who is Mrs. Irving?"

"She is present, sir."

"I know she is. Who is she?"

"She is the wife of the man whom Miss Holt called on the
phone Sunday evening to tell him that she was going to take
Miss Bram's cab, and why. Mr. Irving has stated that he told
no one of that call. Either he lied or his wife eavesdropped.
Mr. Irving. Might your wife have overheard that conversation on an extension?"

Irving's hand left his forehead. He lowered it slowly until
it touched his knee. I had him in profile. A muscle at the side
of his neck was twitching. "To say that she might," he said
slowly and precisely, as if he only had so many words and
didn't want to waste any, "isn't saying that she did. You have
made a shocking accusation. I hope—" He stopped, leaving

it to anybody's guess what he hoped. He blurted, "Ask her!"

"I shall. Did you, madam?"

"No." Her deep, strong voice needed more breath behind it. "Your accusation is not only shocking, it's absurd. I told Mr. Goodwin what I did last evening. Hasn't he told you?"

"He has. You told him that your husband had been prevented by a business emergency from keeping a dinner and theater engagement with you, and you had phoned Phoebe Arden to go in his stead, and she agreed. When she didn't appear at the restaurant you rang her number and got no answer, and then went to another restaurant to eat alone, presumably one where you are not known and plausibly would not be remembered. After waiting for her at the theater until after nine o'clock you left a ticket for her at the box office and went in to your seat. That sounds impressive, but actually it leaves you free for the period that counts, from half past seven until well after nine o'clock. Incidentally, it was a mistake to volunteer that account of your movements, so detailed and precise. When Mr. Goodwin reported it to me I marked you down as worthy of attention."

"I wasn't free at all," she said. "I told Mr. Goodwin I wanted to help, and—"

"Don't talk," her husband commanded the back of her head. "Let him talk." To Wolfe: "Unless you're through?"

"By no means. I'll put it directly to you, madam. This is how you really spent those hours. You did phone Phoebe Arden yesterday afternoon, but not to ask her to join you at dinner and the theater. You told her of Miss Holt's plan to drive Miss Bram's cab in an effort to have a talk with her husband, and you proposed a prank. Miss Arden would arrange that Mr. Kearns would fail to appear, and if he didn't, Miss Holt would certainly leave the cab to go to his house to inquire. Whereupon you and Miss Arden, from your concealment in the neighboring stoneyard, would go and enter the cab, and when Miss Holt returned she would find you there, to her discomfiture and even consternation."

"You can't prove any of this," Cramer growled.

"No one ever can, since Miss Arden is dead." Wolfe's eyes didn't leave Mrs. Irving. He went on, "I didn't know Miss Arden, so I can't say whether she agreed to your proposal from mere caprice or from an animus for Miss Holt, but she did agree, and went to her doom. The program went as planned, without a hitch. No doubt Miss Arden herself devised the stratagem by which Mr. Kearns was removed from the scene. But at this point I must confess that my case is not flawless. Certainly you would not have been so

witless as to let anyone have a hand in your deadly prank—
either a cab driver or your private chauffeur. Do you drive a
car?"

"Don't answer," Irving commanded her.

"Yes, she does," Judy Bram said, louder than necessary.

"Thank you, Miss Bram. Apparently you *can* speak to the
point. Then you and Miss Arden went in your car, and
parked it on Carmine Street—away from the corner in the
direction Miss Holt would take when, leaving, she made the
turn from Ferrell Street. You walked to the stoneyard and
chose your hiding spot, and when Miss Holt left the cab
you went and entered it. It is noteworthy that at that point
you were committed to nothing but a prank. If Miss Holt
had suddenly returned, or if anyone had come close enough
to observe, you would merely have abandoned your true objective—a disappointment, but no disaster. As it was, you
struck. I am not a moralizer, but I permit myself the comment that in my experience your performance is without
parallel for ruthlessness and savagery. It appears that Miss
Arden was not merely no enemy of yours; she was your
friend. She must have been, to join with you in your impish
prank; but you needed her corpse for a tool to gratify your
mortal hatred for Miss Holt. That was—"

"Her hatred for Miss Holt," Cramer said. "You assume
that too?"

"No indeed. That is established. Miss Bram. Speaking of
Gilbert Irving, you said that when he looks at Miss Holt or
hears her voice he has to lean against something to keep
from trembling. You didn't specify the emotion that so af-
fects him. Is it repugnance?"

"No. It's love. He wants her."

"Was his wife aware of it?"

"Yes. Lots of people were. You only had to see him look
at her."

"That is not true," Irving said. "I am merely Miss Holt's
friend, that's all, and I hope she is mine."

Judy's eyes darted at him and returned to Wolfe. "He's
only being a husband because he thinks he has to. He's being
a gentleman. A gentleman doesn't betray his wife. I was
wrong about you. I shouldn't have called you a fat fool. I
didn't know—"

Cramer cut in, to Wolfe. "All right, if that isn't established
it can be. But it's about all that's established. There's damn
little you can prove. Do you expect me to charge a woman
with murder on your guess?"

You don't often hear a sergeant disagree with an inspector
in public, but Purley Stebbins—no, I used the wrong word.

Not hear, see. Purley didn't say a word. All he did was leave his post at Kearns' elbow and circle around Irving to stand beside Mrs. Irving, between her and Judy Bram. Probably it didn't occur to him that he was disagreeing with his superior; he merely didn't like the possibility of Mrs. Irving's getting a knife from her handbag and sticking it in Judy's ribs.

"There's nothing at all I can prove," Wolfe said. "I have merely exposed the naked truth; it is for you, not me, to drape it and arm it with the evidence the law requires. For that you are well equipped; surely you need no suggestions from me; but, item, did Mrs. Irving get her car from the garage yesterday evening? What for? If to drive to a restaurant and then to a theater, in itself unlikely, where did she park it? Item, the knife. If she conceived her prank only after her husband phoned to cancel their engagement, which is highly probable, she hadn't time to contrive an elaborate and prudent plan for getting a weapon. She either bought one at a convenient shop, or she took one from her own kitchen; and if the latter her cook or maid will have missed it and can identify it. Her biggest mistake, of course, was leaving the knife in the body, even with the handle wiped clean; but she was in a hurry to leave, she was afraid blood would spurt on her, and she was confident that she would never be suspected of killing her good friend Phoebe Arden. Other items—"

Mrs. Irving was up, and as she arose her husband did too, and grabbed her arm from behind. He wasn't seizing a murderer; he was being a gentleman and stopping his wife from betraying herself. She jerked loose, but then Purley Stebbins had her other arm in his big paw.

"Take it easy," Purley said. "Just take it easy."

Mira's head dropped and her hands came up to cover her face, and she started to shake. Judy Bram put a hand on her shoulder and said, "Go right ahead, Mi, don't mind us. You've got it coming." Waldo Kearns was sitting still, perfectly still. I got up and went to the kitchen, to the extension, and dialed the *Gazette* number. I thought I ought to be as good at keeping a promise as Mira had been.

XI

Yesterday I drove Mira and Judy to Idlewild, where Mira was to board a plane for Reno. Judy and I had tossed a coin to decide whether the trip would be made in the Heron sedan which Wolfe owns and I drive, or in Judy's cab, and I had won. On the way back I remarked that I supposed Kearns

THE RODEO MURDER

I

Cal Barrow was standing at the tail end of the horse with
his arm extended and his fingers wrapped around the strands
of the rope that was looped over the horn of the cowboy
saddle. His gray-blue eyes—as much of them as the half-
closed lids left in view—were straight at me. His voice was
low and easy, and noise from the group out front was coming
through the open door, but I have good ears.

"Nothing to start a stampede," he said. "I just wanted to
ask you how I go about taking some hide off a toad in this
town." To give it as it actually sounded I would have to
make it, "Ah jist wanted to ask yuh how Ah go about takin'
some hide off a toad," but that's too complicated, and from
here on I'll leave the sound effects to you if you want to
bother.

I was sliding my fingertips up and down on the polished
stirrup strap so that observers, if any, would assume that we
were discussing the saddle. "I suppose," I said, "it's a two-
legged toad." Then, as a brown-haired cowgirl named Nan
Karlin, in a pink silk shirt opened at the throat and regula-
tion Levis, came through the arch and headed for the door to
the terrace, lifting the heels of her fancy boots to navigate
the Kashan rug that had set Lily Rowan back fourteen thousand bucks, I raised my voice a little so she wouldn't have
to strain her ears if she was curious. "Sure," I said, rubbing
the leather, "you could work it limber, but why don't they
make it limber?"

But I may be confusing you, since a Kashan carpet with
a garden pattern in seven colors is no place for a horse to
stand, so I had better explain. The horse was a sawhorse. The
saddle was to go to the winner in a roping contest that was
to start in an hour. The Kashan, 19x34, was on the floor of
the living room of Lily Rowan's penthouse, which was on
the roof of a ten-story building on 63rd Street between
Madison and Park Avenues, Manhattan. The time was three
o'clock Monday afternoon. The group out on the terrace had
just gone there for coffee after leaving the dining room, where
the high point of the meal had been two dozen young blue

103

grouse which had come from Montana on man-made wings, their own having stopped working. As we had moseyed through the living room on our way to the terrace Cal Barrow had got me aside to say he wanted to ask me something private, and we had detoured to inspect the saddle.

When Nan Karlin had passed and was outside, Cal Barrow didn't have to lower his voice again because he hadn't raised it. "Yeah, two legs," he said. (Make it "laigs.") "I got to ask somebody that knows this town and I was thinking this bozo Goodwin is the one to ask, he's in the detective business here and he ought to know. And my friend Harvey Greve tells me you're okay. I'm calling you Archie, am I?"

"So it was agreed at the table. First names all around."

"Suits me." He let go of the rope and gripped the edge of the cantle. "So I'll ask you. I'm a little worked up. Out where I live I wouldn't have to ask nobody, but here I'm no better'n a dogie. I been to Calgary and Pendleton, but I never come East before for this blowout. Huh. World Series Rodeo. From what I see so far you can have it."

He made it "roe-day-oh" with the accent on the "day." I nodded. "Madison Square Garden has no sky. But about this toad. We're supposed to go out with them for coffee. How much of his hide do you need?"

"I'll take a fair-sized patch." There was a glint in his eye. "Enough so he'll have to lick it till it gets a scab. The trouble is this blamed blowout, I don't want to stink it up my first time here, if it wasn't for that I'd just handle it. I'd get him to provoke me."

"Hasn't he already provoked you?"

"Yeah, but I'm leaving that out. I was thinking you might even like to show him and me something. Have you got a car?"

I said I had.

"Then when we get through here you might like to take him and me to show us some nice little spot like on the river bank. There must be a spot somewhere. It would be better if you was there anyhow because if I kinda lost control and got too rough you could stop me. When I'm worked up I might get my teeth on the bit."

"Or I could stop him if necessary."

The glint showed again. "I guess you don't mean that. I wouldn't like to think you mean that."

I grinned at him, Archie to Cal. "What the hell, how do I know? You haven't named him. What if it's Mel Fox? He's bigger than you are, and Saturday night at the Garden I saw him bulldog a steer in twenty-three seconds. It took you thirty-one."

"My steer was meaner. Mel said so himself. Anyway it's not him. It's Wade Eisler."

My brows went up. Wade Eisler couldn't bulldog a milk cow in twenty-three hours, but he had rounded up ten million dollars, more or less, and he was the chief backer of the World Series Rodeo. If it got out that one of the cowboy contestants had taken a piece of his hide it would indeed stink it up, and it was no wonder that Cal Barrow wanted a nice little spot on a river bank. I not only raised my brows; I puckered my lips.

"Ouch," I said. "You'd better let it lay, at least for a week, until the rodeo's over and the prizes awarded."

"No, sir. I sure would like to, but I got to get it done. Today. I don't rightly know how I held off when I got here and saw him here. It would be a real big favor, Mr. Goodwin. Here in your town. Will you do it?"

I was beginning to like him. Especially I liked his not shoving by overworking the "Archie." He was a little younger than me, but not much, so it wasn't respect for age; he just wasn't a fudger.

"How did he provoke you?" I asked.

"That's private. Didn't I say I'm leaving that out?"

"Yes, but I can leave it out too. I don't say I'll play if you tell me, but I certainly won't if you don't. Whether I play or not, you can count on me to leave it out—or keep it in. As a private detective I get lots of practice keeping things in."

The gray-blue eyes were glued on me. "You won't tell anyone?"

"Right."

"Whether you help me or not?"

"Right."

"He got a lady to go to his place last night by telling her he was having a party, and when they got there there wasn't any party, and he tried to handle her. Did you see the scratch on his cheek?"

"Yes, I noticed it."

"She's not very big, but she's plenty active. All she got was a little skin off her ear when her head hit a corner of a table."

"I noticed that too."

"So I figure he's due to lose a bigger—" He stopped short. He slapped the saddle. "Now, damn it, that's me every time. Now you know who she is. I was going to leave that out."

"I'll keep it in. She told you about it?"

"Yes, sir, she did. This morning."

"Did she tell anyone else?"

"No, sir, she wouldn't. I got no brand on her, nobody has, but maybe some day when she quiets down a little and I've got my own corral . . . You've seen her on a bronc."

I nodded. "I sure have. I was looking forward to seeing her off of one, closer up, but now of course I'll keep my distance. I don't want to lose any hide."

His hand left the saddle. "I guess you just say things. I got no claim. I'm a friend of hers and she knows it, that's all. A couple of years ago I was wrangling dudes down in Arizona and she was snapping sheets at the hotel, and we kinda made out together and I guess I come in handy now and then. I don't mind coming in handy as long as I can look ahead. Right now I'm a friend of hers and that suits me fine. She might be surprised to know how I—"

His eyes left me and I turned. Nero Wolfe was there, entering from the terrace. Somehow he always looks bigger away from home, I suppose because my eyes are so used to fitting his dimensions into the interiors of the old brownstone on West 35th. There he was, a mountain coming at us. As he approached he spoke. "If I may interrupt?" He allowed two seconds for objections, got none, and went on. "My apologies, Mr. Barrow." To me: "I have thanked Miss Rowan for a memorable meal and explained to her. To watch the performance I would have to stretch across that parapet and I am not built for it. If you drive me home now you can be back before four o'clock."

I glanced at my wrist. Ten after three. "More people are coming, and Lily has told them you'll be here. They'll be disappointed."

"Pfui. I have nothing to contribute to this frolic."

I wasn't surprised; in fact, I had been expecting it. He had got what he came for, so why stick around? What had brought him was the grouse. When, two years back, I had returned from a month's visit to Lily Rowan on a ranch she had bought in Montana, (where, incidentally, I had met Harvey Greve, Cal Barrow's friend), the only detail of my trip that had really interested Wolfe was one of the meals I described. At that time of year, late August, the young blue grouse are around ten weeks old and their main item of diet has been mountain huckleberries, and I had told Wolfe they were tastier than any bird Fritz had ever cooked, even quail or woodcock. Of course, since they're protected by law, they can cost up to five dollars a bite if you get caught.

Lily Rowan doesn't treat laws as her father did while he was piling up the seventeen million dollars he left her, but she can take them or leave them. So when she learned that Harvey Greve was coming to New York for the rodeo, and she decided to throw a party for some of the cast, and she thought it would be nice to feed them young blue grouse, the law was merely a hurdle to hop over. Since I'm a friend of hers and she knows it, that will do for that. I will add only a brief report of a scene in the office on the ground floor of the old brownstone. It was Wednesday noon. Wolfe, at his desk, was reading the *Times*. I, at my desk, finished a phone call, hung up, and swiveled.

"That's interesting," I said. "That was Lily Rowan. As I told you, I'm going to a roping contest at her place Monday afternoon. A cowboy is going to ride a horse along Sixty-third Street, and other cowboys are going to try to rope him from the terrace of her penthouse, a hundred feet up. Never done before. First prize will be a saddle with silver trimmings."

He grunted. "Interesting?"

"Not that. That's just games. But a few of them are coming earlier for lunch, at one o'clock, and I'm invited, and she just had a phone call from Montana. Twenty young blue grouse, maybe more, will arrive by plane Saturday afternoon, and Felix is going to come and cook them. I'm glad I'm going. It's too bad you and Lily don't get along—ever since she squirted perfume on you."

He put the paper down to glare. "She didn't squirt perfume on me."

I flipped a hand. "It was her perfume."

He picked up the paper, pretended to read a paragraph, and dropped it again. He passed his tongue over his lips. "I have no animus for Miss Rowan. But I will not solicit an invitation."

"Of course not. You wouldn't stoop. I don't—"

"But you may ask if I would accept one."

"Would you?"

"Yes."

"Good. She asked me to invite you, but I was afraid you'd decline and I'd hate to hurt her feelings. I'll tell her." I reached for the phone.

I report that incident so you'll understand why he got up and left after coffee. I not only wasn't surprised when he came and interrupted Cal Barrow and me, I was pleased, because Lily had bet me a sawbuck he wouldn't stay for coffee. Leaving him there with Cal, I went to the terrace.

In the early fall Lily's front terrace is usually sporting annual flowers along the parapet and by the wall of the penthouse, and a few evergreens in tubs scattered around, but for that day the parapet was bare, and instead of the evergreens, which would have interfered with rope whirling, there were

clumps of sagebrush two feet high in pots. The sagebrush had
come by rail, not by air, but even so the part of Lily that
had ordered it and paid for it is not my part. That will be no
news to her when she reads this.

I glanced around. Lily was in a group seated to the right,
with Wade Eisler on one side and Mel Fox on the other. In
dash she wasn't up to the two cowgirls there, Nan Karlin in
her pink silk shirt and Anna Casado, dark-skinned with black
hair and black eyes, in her yellow one, but she was the
hostess and not in competition. In situations that called for
dash she had plenty. The other four were standing by the
parapet at the left—Roger Dunning, the rodeo promoter,
not in costume; his wife Ellen, former cowgirl, also not in
costume; Harvey Greve in his brown shirt and red neck rag
and corduroy pants and boots; and Laura Jay. Having Laura
Jay in profile, I could see the bandage on her ear through the
strands of her hair, which was exactly the color of the
thyme honey that Wolfe gets from Greece. At the dinner
table she had told me that a horse had jerked his head
around and the bit had bruised her, but now I knew different.

Stepping across to tell Lily I was leaving but would be
back in time for the show, I took a side glance at Wade
Eisler's plump, round face. The scratch, which began an
inch below his left eye and slanted down nearly to the
corner of his mouth, hadn't gone very deep and it had had
some fifteen hours to calm down by Cal Barrow's account,
but it didn't improve his looks any, and there was ample room
for improvement. He was one of those New York characters
that get talked about and he had quite a reputation as a
smooth operator, but he certainly hadn't been smooth last
night—according to Laura Jay as relayed by Cal Barrow.
The cave-man approach to courtship may have its points if
that's the best you can do, but if I ever tried it I would have
more sense than to pick a girl who could rope and tie a frisky
calf in less than a minute.

After telling Lily I would be back in time for the show and
was looking forward to collecting the sawbuck, I returned to
the living room. Wolfe and Cal were admiring the saddle. I
told Cal I would think it over and let him know, went to
the foyer and got Wolfe's hat and stick, followed him down
the flight of stairs to the tenth floor, and rang for the elevator.
We walked the two blocks to the parking lot where I had left
the Heron sedan, which Wolfe had paid for but I had
selected. Of course a taxi would have been simpler, but he
hates things on wheels. To ride in a strange vehicle with a
stranger driving would be foolhardy; with me at the wheel
in a car of my choice it is merely imprudent.

Stopped by a red light on Park Avenue in the Fifties, I turned my head to say, "I'm taking the car back because I may need it. I may do a little errand for one of the cowboys. If so I probably won't be home for dinner."

"A professional errand?"

"No. Personal."

He grunted. "You have the afternoon, as agreed. If the errand is personal it is not my concern. But, knowing you as I do, I trust it is innocuous."

"So do I." The light changed and I fed gas.

II

It was ten minutes to four when I got back to the parking lot on 63rd Street. Walking west, I crossed Park Avenue and stopped for a look. Five cops were visible. One was talking to the driver of a car who wanted to turn the corner, two were standing at the curb talking, and two were holding off an assortment of pedestrians who wanted to get closer to three mounted cowboys. The cowboys were being spoken to by a man on foot, not in costume. As I moved to proceed one of the cops at the curb blocked me and spoke. "Do you live in this block, sir?"

I told him no, I was going to Miss Lily Rowan's party, and he let me pass. The New York Police Department likes to grant reasonable requests from citizens, especially when the request comes from a woman whose father was a Tammany district leader for thirty years. There were no parked cars on that side of the street, but twenty paces short of the building entrance a truck with cameras was hugging the curb, and there was another one farther on, near Madison Avenue.

When I had left with Wolfe Lily had had nine guests; now she had twenty or more. Three of the new arrivals were cowboys, making six with Cal Barrow, Harvey Greve, and Mel Fox; the rest were civilians. They were all on the terrace. The civilians were at the parapet, half at one end and half at the other, leaving the parapet clear for thirty feet in the middle. The cowboys, their ten-gallon hats on their heads and their ropes in their hands, were lined up facing a tall skinny man in a brown suit. At the man's elbow was Roger Dunning, the promoter. The man was speaking.

". . . and that's the way it's going to be. I'm the judge and what I say goes. I repeat that Greve hasn't done any practicing, and neither has Barrow or Fox. I have Miss Rowan's word for that, and I don't think you want to call her a liar. I've told you the order, but you don't move in until I call your name. Remember what I said, if you take a tumble off a

bronc it's four feet down; here it's a hundred feet down and
you won't get up and walk. Once again, *no hooligan stuff*.
There's not supposed to be any pedestrians on this side of
the street from four o'clock to five, but if one comes out of a
house and one of you drops a loop on him you won't sleep in
a hotel room tonight. We're here to have some fun, but don't
get funny." He looked at his watch. "Time to go. Fox, get—"

"I want to say something," Roger Dunning said.

"Sorry, Roger, no time. We promised to start on the dot.
Fox, get set. The rest of you scatter."

He went to the parapet, to the left, and picked up a green
flag on a stick that was there on a chair. Mel Fox stepped
to the middle of the clear stretch, straddled the parapet, and
started his noose going. The others went right and left to
find spots in the lines of guests. I found a spot on the right
that happened to be between Laura Jay and Anna Casado.
Leaning over to get a view of the street, I saw I was block-
ing Laura Jay and drew in a little. The three mounted cowboys and the man I had seen talking to them were grouped on
the pavement halfway to Park Avenue. The judge stuck his
arm out with the green flag and dipped it, the man down
with the mounted cowboys said something, and one of the
ponies was off on the jump, heading down the middle of the
lane between the curb on our side and the parked cars on the
other. Mel Fox, leaning out from his hips, moved his whirling loop back a little, and then brought it forward and let
it go. When it reached bottom it was a little too far out and
the cowboy on the pony was twenty feet ahead of it. The
instant it touched the pavement Fox started hauling it in; he
had thirty seconds until the flag started number two. He
had it up and a noose going in less than that, but the judge
went by his watch. The flag dipped, and here came the
second one. That was a little better; the rope touched the
pony's rump, but it was too far in. Fox hauled in again,
shifted his straddle a little, and started another whirl. That
time he nearly made it. Anna Casado, on my left, let out a
squeal as the rope, descending smoothly in a perfect circle,
brushed the edge of the cowboy's hat. The audience clapped,
and a man in a window across the street shouted "Bravo!"
Fox retrieved his rope, taking his time, dismounted from
the parapet, said something I didn't catch because of other
voices, and moved off as the judge called out, "Vince!"

A chunky little youngster in a purple shirt, Levis, and
working boots mounted the parapet. Saturday night I had
seen him stick it out bareback on one of the roughest broncs
I had ever seen—not speaking as an expert. He wasn't so
hot on a parapet. On his first try his loop turned straight

up, which could have been an air current, on his second it
draped over a parked car across the street, and on his
third it hit the asphalt ten feet ahead of the pony.

Harvey Greve was next. Naturally I was rooting for him,
since he had done me a lot of favors during the month I had
spent at Lily's ranch. Lily called something to him from the
other end of the parapet, and he gave her a nod as he
threw his leg over and started his loop. His first throw was
terrible; the noose buckled and flipped before it was
halfway down. His second was absolutely perfect; it cen-
tered around the cowboy like a smoke ring around a fingertip, and Harvey timed the jerk just right and had him. A yell
came from the audience as the cowboy tightened the reins
and the pony braked, skidding on the asphalt. He loosened
the loop with one hand and passed it over his head, and as
soon as it was free the judge sang out "Thirty seconds!" and
Harvey started hauling in. His third throw sailed down round
and flat, but it was too late by ten feet.

As the judge called Barrow's name and Cal stepped to the
parapet, Laura Jay, on my right, muttered, "He shouldn't try
it." She was probably muttering to herself, but my ear was
right there and I turned my head and asked her why. "Somebody stole his rope," she said.

"Stole it? When? How?"

"He don't know. It was in the closet with his hat and it
was gone. We looked all around. He's using the one that
was on that saddle and it's new and stiff, and he shouldn't—"

She stopped and I jerked my head around. The flag had
dipped and the target was coming. Considering that he was
using a strange rope, and a new one, Cal didn't do so bad. His
loops kept their shape clear down, but the first one was short,
the second was wide, and the third hit bottom before the
pony got there. Neither of the last two ropers, one named
Lopez and the other Holcomb, did as well. When Holcomb's
third noose curled on the curb below us the judge called,
"Second round starts in two minutes! Everybody stay put!"

There were to be three rounds, giving each contestant
a total of nine tries. Roger Dunning was stationed near the
judge, with a pad of paper and a pen in his hand, to keep
score in case the decision had to be made on form and how
close they came, but since Harvey Greve had got one that
wouldn't be necessary.

In the second round Fox got a rider and Lopez got a pony.
In the third round Holcomb got a rider and Harvey got
his second one. The winner and first world champion rope-
dropper or drop-roper from one hundred feet up: Harvey
Greve! He took the congratulations and the riding from the

other competitors with the grin I knew so well, and when he
got kissed by a friend of Lily's who was starring in a hit
on Broadway and knew how to kiss both on stage and off,
his face was nearly as pink as Nan Karlin's shirt. Anna Casado broke off a branch of sagebrush and stuck it under his
hatband. Lily herded us into the living room, where we
gathered around the sawhorse, and Roger Dunning was
starting a presentation speech when Cal Barrow stopped
him.

"Wait a minute, this goes with it," Cal said, and went and
hung the rope on the horn. He turned and sent the blue-
gray eyes right and then left. "I don't want to start no fuss
right now, but when I find out who took mine I'll want to
know." He moved to the rear of the crowd, and Dunning
put his hand on the seat of the saddle. Dunning had a long
and narrow bony face with a scar at the side of his jaw.

"This is a happy occasion," he said. "Thank God nothing
happened like one of you falling off. I wanted to have a net
down—"

"Louder!" Mel Fox called.

"You're just sore because you didn't win," Dunning told
him. "I wanted to have a net below but they wouldn't. This
magnificent saddle with genuine silver rivets and studs was
handmade by Morrison, and I don't have to tell you what
that means. It was donated by Miss Lily Rowan, and I
want to thank her for her generosity and hospitality on behalf of everybody concerned. I now declare Harvey Greve
the undisputed winner of the first and only roping contest
ever held in a Park Avenue penthouse—anyway just outside
the penthouse and we could see Park Avenue—and I award
him the prize, this magnificent saddle donated by Miss Lily
Rowan. Here it is, Harvey. It's all yours."

Applause and cheers. Someone called "Speech!" and others
took it up, as Harvey went and flattened his palm on
the sudadero. He faced the audience. "I tell you," he said,
"if I tried to make a speech you'd take this saddle away
from me. The only time I make a speech is when a cayuse
gets from under me and that's no kind for here. You all
know that was just luck out there, but I'm mighty glad I
won because I sure had my eye on this saddle. The lady that
kissed me, I didn't mind that atall, but I been working for
Miss Lily Rowan for more'n three years and she never kissed
me yet and this is her last chance."

They let out a whoop, and Lily ran to him, put her hands
on his shoulders, and planted one on each cheek, and he went
pink again. Two men in white jackets came through the
arch, with trays loaded with glasses of champagne. In the

alcove a man at the piano and two with fiddles started "Home on the Range." Lily had asked me a week ago what I thought of having the rug up and trying some barn dancing, and I had told her I doubted if many of the cowboys and girls would know how, and none of the others would. Better just let the East meet the West.

The best way to drink champagne, for me anyhow, is to gulp the first glass as a primer and sip from there on. Lily was busy being a hostess, so I waited to go and touch glasses with her until I had taken a couple of sips from my second. "Doggone it," I told her, "I'd a brung my rope and give it a whirl if I'd a known you was goin' tuh kiss the winner." She said, "Huh. If I ever kissed you in front of an audience the women would scream and the men would faint."

I moved around a while, being sociable, and wound up on a chair by a clump of sagebrush on the terrace, between Laura Jay and a civilian. Since I knew him well and didn't like him much, I didn't apologize for horning in. I asked her if Cal had found his rope, and she said she didn't think so, she hadn't seen him for the last half hour.

"Neither have I," I said. "He doesn't seem to be around. I wanted to ask him if he'd found it. I haven't seen Wade Eisler either. Have you?"

Her eyes met mine straight. "No. Why?"

"No special reason. I suppose you know I'm in the detective business."

"I know. You're with Nero Wolfe."

"I work for him. I'm not here on business, I'm a friend of Miss Rowan's, but I'm in the habit of noticing things, and I didn't see Wade Eisler at the parapet while they were roping, and I haven't seen him since. I know you better than I do the others, except Harvey Greve, because I sat next to you at lunch, so I just thought I'd ask."

"Don't ask me. Ask Miss Rowan."

"Oh, it's not that important. But I'm curious about Cal's rope. I don't see why—"

Cal Barrow was there. He had come from the rear and was suddenly there in front of me. He spoke, in his low easy voice. "Can I see you a minute, Archie?"

"Where have *you* been?" Laura demanded.

"I been around."

I stood up. "Find your rope?"

"I want to show you. You stay hitched, Laura." She had started up. "You hear me?" It was a command, and from her stare I guessed it was the first one he had ever given her. "Come along, Archie," he said, and moved.

He led me around the corner of the penthouse. On that side the terrace is only six feet wide, but in the rear there is space enough for a badminton court and then some. The tubs of evergreens that had been removed from the front were there, and Cal went on past them to the door of a shack which Lily used for storage. The grouse had been hung there Saturday afternoon. He opened the door and entered, and when I was in shut the door. The only light came from two small windows at the far end, so it was half dark coming in from broad daylight, and Cal said, "Look out, don't step on him."

I turned and reached for the light switch and flipped it, turned back, and stood and looked down at Wade Eisler. As I moved and squatted Cal said, "No use taking his pulse. He's dead."

He was. Thoroughly. The protruding tongue was purple and so were the lips and most of the face. The staring eyes were wide open. The rope had been wound around his throat so many times, a dozen or more, that his chin was pushed up. The rest of the rope was piled on his chest.

"That's my rope," Cal said. "I was looking for it and I found it. I was going to take it but I thought I better not."

"You thought right." I was on my feet. I faced him and got his eyes. "Did you do it?"

"No, sir."

I looked at my wrist: twelve minutes to six. "I'd like to believe you," I said, "and until further notice I do. The last I saw you in there you were taking a glass of champagne. More than half an hour ago. I haven't seen you since. That's a long time."

"I been hunting my rope. When I drank that one glass I asked Miss Rowan if she minded if I looked and she said no. We had already looked inside and out front. Then when I come in here and found him I sat on that box a while to think it over. I decided the best thing was to get you."

"Wasn't this door locked?"

"No, sir. It was shut but it wasn't locked."

That was possible. It was often left unlocked in the daytime. I looked around. The room held all kinds of stuff—stacks of luggage, chairs, card tables, old magazines on shelves—but at the front, where we were, there was a clear space. Everything seemed to be in place; there was no sign that Eisler had put up a fight, and you wouldn't suppose a man would stand with his hands in his pockets while someone got a noose around his neck and pulled it tight. If he had been conked first, what with? I stepped to a rack against the wall on the left and put a hand out, but pulled it back.

One of those three-foot stainless-steel rods, for staking plants, would have been just the thing, and the one on top was lying across the others. If I had had gloves and a glass with me, and there had been no rush, and Cal hadn't been there with his eyes boring at me, I would have given it a look.

I opened the door, using my handkerchief for the knob, and stepped out. There were six windows in the rear of the penthouse, but except for the two near the far corner, which belonged to the maid's room and bathroom, their view of the shack and the approach to it was blocked by the evergreens. That had been a break for the murderer; there had certainly been someone in the kitchen. I went back inside, shut the door, and told Cal, "Here's how it is. I have to get the cops here before anyone leaves if I want to keep my license. I don't owe Wade Eisler anything, but this will be a sweet mess for Miss Rowan and I'm a friend of hers, so I'm curious. When did you first miss the rope?"

He opened his mouth and closed it again. He shook his head. "I guess I made a mistake," he said. "I should have took that rope off and found it somewhere else."

"You should like hell. It would have been a cinch for the police lab to prove it had been around his neck. When did you first miss it?"

"But I had told you about last night and how I was worked up and you had promised to keep it in, and I figured I couldn't expect you to be square with me if I wasn't square with you, so I went and got you. Now the way you take it, I don't know."

"For God's sake." I wasn't as disgusted as I sounded. "What did you think, I'd bring you a bottle of champagne? Wait till you see how the cops take it. When did you first miss the rope?"

"I don't know just what time. It was a while after you left, maybe twenty minutes. With people coming and putting things in that closet I thought I'd get it and hang onto it."

"Had you put it in the closet yourself?"

"Yeah. On the shelf with my hat on top. The hat was there but the rope was gone."

"Did you tell someone right away?"

"I looked all over the closet and then I told Laura and she told Miss Rowan. Miss Rowan asked everybody and she helped Laura and me look some, but people started coming."

"At the time you missed the rope had anybody already come? Was anyone here besides those who ate lunch with us?"

"No, sir."

"You're sure?"

"I'm sure enough to put a no on it. They ain't much a man can be dead sure of. It might be someone came I didn't see, but I was right there and I'd have to—"

"Save it." I glanced at my watch: five minutes to six. "At the time you missed the rope where was Wade Eisler?"

"I don't know."

"When did you see him last?"

"I can't say exactly. I wasn't riding herd on him."

"Did you see him after you missed the rope? Take a second. This is important. Take ten."

He screwed up his lips and shut his eyes. He took the full ten seconds. His eyes opened. "No, sir, I didn't."

"Sure enough to put a no on it?"

"I already did."

"Okay. Do you know if anyone else was worked up about Wade Eisler?"

"I wouldn't say worked up. I guess nobody wanted him for a pet."

"As it looks now, someone who ate lunch with us killed him. Have you any idea who?"

"No, sir. I don't expect to have none."

"That's noble. Don't be *too* noble. There's plenty more, but it will have to wait. If I leave you here while I go in and tell Miss Rowan and call the cops will you stay put and keep your hands off of that rope?"

"No, sir. I'm going to see Laura. I'm going to tell her if they ask her anything she better leave it out about last night."

"You are not." I was emphatic. "You've got no brand on her, you said so. You may think you know how she'll take a going-over by experts, but you don't. Every move anybody makes from now on will get on the record, and if you go and call her away from that baboon she's sitting with, what does she say and what do you say when they ask you why? She'll either leave it out or she won't, and you'll only make it worse if you tell her to. If you won't promise you'll stick here I'll just open the door and yell for Miss Rowan, and she can call the cops."

His jaw was working. "You said you believed me."

"I do. If I change my mind I'll let you know first. What you told me and what you asked me to do, I said I'd keep it in and I will, provided you do too. We were discussing the saddle. Well?"

"I figure to keep everything in. But if I could just tell her—"

"No. She probably won't spill it, but if she does and says

she told you about it that won't break any bones. You left it out because you didn't want to cause her trouble. Everybody leaves things out when cops ask questions. Do I yell for Miss Rowan?"

"No. I'll stay hitched."

"Come outside and stand at the door. You've already touched the knob twice and that's enough. If anyone comes keep them off." Using my handkerchief again, I opened the door. He stepped out and I pulled the door shut as I crossed the sill. "Be seeing you," I said, and went.

I entered at the rear and glanced in at the kitchen on the chance that Lily was there. No. Nor the living room. The piano and fiddles were playing "These Fences Don't Belong." I found her on the terrace, caught her eye and gave her a sign, and she came. I headed for the dining room, and when she had followed me in I closed the door.

"One question," I said. "That's all there's time for. When did you last see Wade Eisler?"

She cocked her head and crinkled her eyes, remembering. I have mentioned a part of her that wasn't mine; this was a part of her that was mine. No what or why; I had asked her a question and she was digging up the answer. She took longer than Cal had. "It was soon after you left," she said. "He put his cup down and I asked him if he wanted more coffee and he said no. Someone did want some and the pot was nearly empty and I went to the kitchen for more. Felix and Robert were arguing about when the champagne should be put on ice, and I sent Freda to the terrace with the coffee and stayed there to calm them down. Who's worrying about Wade Eisler?"

"Nobody. How long did you stay in the kitchen?"

"Oh, ten minutes. Felix can be difficult."

"Eisler wasn't there when you went back?"

"I didn't notice. They had scattered. Some of them were in the living room. Then Laura Jay told me Cal Barrow's rope was gone and I helped them look, and then people came."

"When did you notice that Eisler wasn't around?"

"Some time later. Roger Dunning wanted someone to meet him and asked me where he was. I didn't know and didn't care. I supposed he had left without bothering to thank me for the meal. He would." She tossed her head. "That's four questions. What's the point?"

"Cal Barrow was looking for his rope and found Eisler's body on the floor of the shack with the rope around his neck. He came and got me. He's there guarding the door. Will you phone the police or do you want me to?" I glanced at my wrist: four minutes after six. "It's already been sixteen minutes since I saw him and that's enough."

"No," she said.

"Yes," I said.

"Wade Eisler hung himself?"

"No. He's not hanging, he's on the floor. Also after the noose was pulled tight the rope was wound around his neck a dozen times. He didn't do that."

"But how could—who would—*no!*"

"Yes. It would be me to hand you something like this, but at that I'm glad it is. I mean since it happened I'm glad I'm here. Do you want me to phone?"

She swallowed. "No, I will. It's my house." She touched my sleeve. "I'm *damn* glad you're here."

"Spring seven, three one hundred. I'll repeat that number: Spring seven—"

"You clown! All right, I needed it, that helped. I'll phone from the bedroom."

She moved, but I stopped her. "Do you want me to collect the guests and tell them the cops are coming?"

"Oh my God. Here in my house—but of course that's routine. That's etiquette—when you're having a party and someone finds a body you collect the guests and make an announcement and say you hope they'll come again and—"

"You're babbling."

"So I am." She went, and I had to step to get to the door ahead of her.

Since a prowl car was certainly in the neighborhood there wasn't much time, and I went to the terrace and sang out, "Everybody inside! Don't walk, run! Inside, everybody!" I entered the living room and mounted a chair. I wanted to see their faces. You seldom get anything helpful from faces, especially when there are more than twenty of them, but you always think you might. Those already inside approached, and those coming from the terrace joined them. I turned to the musicians and patted the air, and they broke off. Mel Fox said in a champagne-loud voice, "She's gone and got a saddle for me." Laughter. When you've been drinking champagne for an hour laughing comes easy.

I raised a hand and waggled it. "I've got bad news," I said. "I'm sorry, but here it is. A dead body has been found on the premises. The body of Wade Eisler. I have seen it. He was murdered. Miss Rowan is notifying the police and they will soon be here. She asked me to tell you. Of course nobody will leave."

What broke the silence was not a gasp but a giggle, from Nan Karlin. Then Roger Dunning demanded, "Where is he?"

and Laura Jay moved, darting to the door to the terrace and on out, and the faces I had wanted to see turned away as Lily appeared through the arch.

She came on. She raised her voice. "All right, I got you here and we're in for it. I don't go much by rules, but now I need one. What does the perfect hostess do when a guest murders another guest? I suppose I ought to apologize, but that doesn't seem . . ."

I had stepped down from the chair. It wasn't up to me to welcome the cops, it was Lily's house and she was there, and anyway it would only be a pair from a prowl car. The homicide specialists would come later. Circling the crowd, I made for a door at the other side of the room, passed through, and was in what Lily called the kennel because a guest's dog had once misused the rug there. There were book shelves, and a desk and safe and typewriter, and a phone. I went to the phone and dialed a number I could have dialed with my eyes shut. Since Wolfe's afternoon session up in the plant rooms with the orchids was from four to six, he would have gone down to the office and would answer it himself.

He did. "Yes?"

"Me. Calling from the library in Miss Rowan's apartment. Regarding Wade Eisler. The one with a pudgy face and a scratch on his cheek. I gathered from your expression when he called you Nero that you thought him objectionable."

"I did. I do."

"So did somebody else. His body had been found in a storage room here on the roof. Strangled with a rope. The police are on the way. I'm calling to say that I have no idea when I'll be home, and I thought you ought to know that you'll probably be hearing from Cramer. A man getting croaked a few hours after he ate lunch with you—try telling Cramer you know nothing about it."

"I shall. What do you know about it?"

"The same as you. Nothing."

"It's a confounded nuisance, but it was worth it. The grouse was superb. Give Miss Rowan my respects."

I said I would.

The kennel had a door to the side hall, and I left that way, went to the side terrace, and headed for the shack. As I expected, Cal was not alone. He stood with his back against the door, his arms folded. Laura Jay was against him, gripping his wrists, her head tilted back, talking fast in a voice so low I caught no words. I called sharply, "Break it up!" She whirled on a heel and a toe, her eyes daring me to come any closer. I went closer. "You damn fool," I said, reaching her. "Snap out of it. Beat it! Get!"

"She thinks I killed him," Cal said. "I been trying to tell her, but she won't—"

What stopped him was her hands pressed against his mouth. He got her wrists and pulled them away. "He knows about it," he said. "I told him."

"Cal! You didn't! You mustn't—"

I got her elbow and jerked her around. "If you want to make it good," I said, "put your arms around his neck and moan. When I poke you in the ribs that'll mean a cop's coming and you'll moan louder and then turn and let out a scream, and when he's close enough, say ten feet, you leap at him and start clawing his face. That'll distract him and Cal can run to the terrace and jump off. Have you got anything at all in your skull besides air? What do you say when they ask you why you dashed out to find Cal when I announced the news? That you wanted to be the first to congratulate him?"

Her teeth were clamped on her lip. She unclamped them. She twisted her neck to look at Cal, twisted back to look at me, and moved. One slow step, and then she was off, and just in time. As she passed the first evergreen the sound came of the back door of the penthouse closing, and heavy feet, and I turned to greet the company. It was a harness bull.

III

Even when I get my full ration of sleep, eight hours, I don't break through my personal morning fog until I have emptied my coffee cup, and when the eight is cut to five by events beyond my control, as it was that night, I have to grope my way to the bathroom. After getting home at five in the morning, and leaving a note for Fritz saying I would be down for breakfast at 10:45, I had set the alarm for ten o'clock. That had seemed sensible, but the trouble with an alarm clock is that what seems sensible when you set it seems absurd when it goes off. Before prying my eyes open I stayed flat a while, trying to find an alternative, and had to give up when I was conscious enough to realize that Wolfe would come down from the plant rooms at eleven. Forty minutes later I descended the two flights to the ground floor, entered the kitchen, told Fritz good morning, got my orange juice from the refrigerator, and sat at the table where my copy of the *Times* was on the rack. Fritz, who is as well acquainted with my morning fog as I am and never tries to talk through it, uncovered the sausage and lit the fire under the griddle for cakes.

The murder of Wade Eisler with a lasso at the penthouse of

Lily Rowan rated the front page even in the *Times*. There was no news in it for me, nothing that I didn't already know, after the five hours I had spent at the scene of the crime with Homicide personnel, three hours at the District Attorney's office, and three hours back at the penthouse with Lily, at her request. Cal Barrow was in custody as a material witness. The District Attorney couldn't say if he would be released in time for the Tuesday-evening rodeo performance. Archie Goodwin had told a *Times* reporter that he had not been at the penthouse in his professional capacity; he and Nero Wolfe had merely been guests. The police didn't know what the motive had been, or weren't telling. Wade Eisler, a bachelor, had been a well-known figure in sporting and theatrical circles. The *Times* didn't say that he had had a chronic and broad-minded taste for young women, but the tabloids certainly would. And so forth.

I was spreading honey on the third griddle cake when the sounds came of the elevator jolting to a stop and then Wolfe's footsteps in the hall crossing to the office. He wouldn't expect to find me there, since Fritz would have told him of my note when he took his breakfast tray up, so I took my time with the cake and honey and poured more coffee. As I was taking a sip the doorbell rang and I got up and went to the hall for a look. Through the one-way glass in the front door I saw a big broad frame and a big pink face that was all too familiar. The hall on the ground floor of the old brownstone is long and wide, with the walnut clothes rack, the elevator, the stairs, and the door to the dining room on one side, the doors to the front room and the office on the other, and the kitchen in the rear. I stepped to the office door, which was standing open, and said, "Good morning. Cramer."

Wolfe, in his oversized chair behind his desk, turned his head to scowl at me. "Good morning, I told him on the phone last evening that I have no information for him."

I had had two cups of coffee and the fog was gone. "Then I'll tell him to try next door."

"No." His lips tightened. "Confound him. That will only convince him that I'm hiding something. Let him in."

I went to the front, opened the door, and inquired, "Good lord, don't you ever sleep?"

I will never get to see Inspector Cramer at the top of his form, the form that has kept him in charge of Homicide for twenty years, because when I see him I am there and that throws him off. It's only partly me; it's chiefly that I make him think of Wolfe, and thinking of Wolfe is too much for him. When he has us together his face gets pinker and his voice gets gruffer, as it did that morning. He sat in the red leather chair near the end of Wolfe's desk, leaning forward, his elbows planted on the chair arms. He spoke. "I came to ask one question, why were you there yesterday? You told me on the phone last night that you went there to eat grouse, and Goodwin said the same. It's in his signed statement. Nuts. You could have had him bring the grouse here and had Fritz cook it."

Wolfe grunted. "When you are invited to someone's table to taste a rare bird you accept or decline. You don't ask that the bird be sent to you—unless you're a king."

"Which you think you are. You're named after one."

"I am not. Nero Claudius Caesar was an emperor, not a king, and I wasn't named after him. I was named after a mountain."

"Which you are. I still want to know why you were there with that bunch. You never leave your house on business, so it wasn't for a client. You went with Goodwin because he asked you to. Why did he ask you to? Why did you sit next to Wade Eisler at lunch? Why did Goodwin have a private talk with one of them, Cal Barrow, just before he drove you home? Why did Barrow go to him when he found the body? Why did Goodwin wait twenty minutes before he had Miss Rowan report it?"

Wolfe was leaning back, his eyes half closed, being patient. "You had Mr. Goodwin at your disposal all night. Weren't those points covered?"

Cramer snorted. "They were covered, all right. He knows how to cover. I'm not saying he knew or you knew Eisler's number was up. I don't say you know who did it or why. I do say there was some kind of trouble and Miss Rowan was involved in it, or at least she knew about it, and that's why Goodwin got you to go. You told me last night that you know nothing whatever about any of those people except Miss Rowan, and that your knowledge of her is superficial. I don't believe it."

"Mr. Cramer." Wolfe's eyes opened. "I lie only for advantage, never merely for convenience."

I cut in. "Excuse me." I was at my desk, at right angles to Wolfe's. Cramer turned to me. "I'd like to help if I can," I told him, "on account of Miss Rowan. I was backstage at the rodeo twice last week, and it's barely possible I heard or saw something that would open a crack. It would depend on how it stands. I know you're holding Cal Barrow. Has he been charged?"

"No. Material witness. It was his rope and he found the body."

"I am not concerned," Wolfe growled, "but I remark that that would rather justify holding the others."

"We haven't got your brains," Cramer growled back. To me: "What did you hear and see backstage at the rodeo?"

"I might remember something if I knew more about it. I know Eisler wasn't there when I returned at four o'clock, but I don't know who saw him last or when. Is everybody out except the ones who were there for lunch?"

"Yes. He was there when Miss Rowan left to go to the kitchen for coffee. That was at three-twenty, eight minutes after you left, as close as we can get it. No one remembers seeing him after that, so they say. No one noticed him leave the terrace, so they say. He got up from the lunch table at five minutes to three. He emptied his coffee cup at three-twenty. The stomach contents say that he died within twenty minutes of that. None of the other guests came until a quarter to four. So there's three cowboys: Harvey Greve, Cal Barrow, and Mel Fox. There's three cowgirls: Anna Casado, Nan Karlin, and Laura Jay. There's Roger Dunning and his wife. You and Wolfe weren't there. Miss Rowan was, but if you saw or heard anything that points at her you wouldn't remember it. Was she at the rodeo with you?"

"I don't remember. Skip it. You've got it down to twenty minutes, from three-twenty to three-forty. Wasn't anyone else missed during that period?"

"Not by anybody who says so. That's the hell of it. Nobody liked Eisler. Not a single one of them would give a bent nickel to see the murderer caught. Some of them might give a good nickel to see him get away with it. This might make you remember something you saw or heard: Sunday night he took a woman to his apartment, and it could have been one of the cowgirls. We haven't got a good description of her, but the fingerprint men are there now. Were you at the Garden Sunday night?"

I shook my head. "Wednesday and Saturday. What about prints in the shack?"

"None that are any good."

"Last night I mentioned that a steel rod in a rack was crosswise."

"Yeah. We might have noticed it ourselves in time. It had been wiped. He had been hit in the back of the head with it. You can read about it in the evening paper. Do you want to come down and look at it?"

"You don't have to take that tone." I was hurt. "I said I'd like to help and I meant it. You need help, you're up a stump, or you wouldn't be here. As for what I heard and saw at the rodeo, I didn't know there was going to be a murder. I'll have to sort it out. I'll see if I can dig up anything and let you know. I thought you might—"

"Why, goddam you!" He was on his feet. "String *me* along? I know damn well you know something! I'll see that you choke on it!" He took a step. "For the record, Goodwin. Have you knowledge of any facts that would help to identify the murderer of Wade Eisler?"

"No."

To Wolfe: "Have you?"

"No, sir."

"Have you any involvement of any kind with any of those people?"

"No, sir."

"Wait a minute," I put in. "To avoid a possible future misunderstanding." I got my case from my pocket, took out a slip of paper, and displayed it to Wolfe. "This is a check for five thousand dollars, payable to you, signed by Lily Rowan."

"What's it for?" he demanded. "She owes me nothing."

"She wants to. It's a retainer. She asked me to go back to her place after they finished with me at the DA's office last night, and I did so. She didn't like Wade Eisler any better than the next one, but two things were biting her. First, he was killed at her house by someone she had invited there. She calls that an abuse of hospitality and she thought you would. Don't you?"

"Yes."

"No argument there. Second, the daughter of District Attorney Bowen is a friend of hers. They were at school together. She has known Bowen for years. He has been a guest both at her apartment and her place in the country. And at midnight last night an assistant DA phoned her and told her to be at his office in the Criminal Courts Building at ten o'clock this morning, and she phoned Bowen, and he said he couldn't allow his personal friendships to interfere with the functions of his staff. She then phoned the assistant DA and told him she would call him today and tell him what time it would be convenient for her to see him at her apartment."

"There's too many like her," Cramer muttered.

"But she has a point," I objected. "She had told you all she knew and answered your questions and signed a statement, and why ten o'clock?" To Wolfe: "Anyway, here's her check. She wants you to get the murderer before the police do, and let her phone the DA and tell him to come for him—or she and I will deliver him to the DA's office, either way. Of course I told her you wouldn't take the job on those terms, but you might possibly consider investigating the abuse of hospitality by one of her guests. I also told her you charge high fees, but she already knew that. I bring this up now because you just told Cramer you're not involved, and if you take this retainer you *will* be involved. I told Miss Rowan you probably wouldn't take it because you're already in the ninety-per-cent bracket for the year and you hate to work."

He was glowering at me. He knew that I knew he wouldn't turn it down with Cramer there. "It will be a costly gratification of a pique," he said.

"I told her so. She can afford it."

"Her reason for hiring me is the most capricious in my experience. But I have not only eaten her bread and salt, I have eaten her grouse. I am in her debt. Mr. Cramer. I change my answer to your last question. I do have an involvement. My other answer holds. I have no information for you."

Cramer's jaw was clamped. "You know the law," he said, and wheeled and headed for the door.

When a visitor leaves the office it is my custom to precede him to the hall and the front door to let him out; but when it's Cramer and he's striding out in a huff I would have to hop on it to get ahead of him, which would be undignified, so I just follow to see that he doesn't take our hats from the shelf and tramp on them. When I emerged from the office Cramer was halfway down the hall, and after one glance I did hop on it. Out on the stoop, reaching a finger to the bell button, was Laura Jay.

I can outhop Cramer any day, but he was too far ahead and was opening the door when I reached it. Not wanting to give him an excuse to take me downtown, I didn't bump him. I braked. He said, "Good morning, Miss Jay. Come in."

I got Laura's eye and said, "Inspector Cramer is just leaving."

"I'm in no hurry," Cramer said, and backed up a step to give her room. "Come in, Miss Jay."

I saw it coming in her eyes—that is, I saw something was coming. They were at Cramer, not at me, but I saw the sudden sharp gleam of an idea, and then she acted on it. She came in all right, on the jump, through the air straight at Cramer, hands first reaching for his face. By instinct he should have jerked back, but experience is better than instinct. He ducked below her hands and came up against her with his arms around her, clamping her to him, leaving her nothing to paw but air. I got her wrists from the rear, pulled them to me, and crossed her arms behind her back.

"Okay," I said, "you can unwrap."

Cramer slipped his arms from under hers and backed away. "All right, Miss Jay," he said. "What's the idea?"

She tried to twist her head around. "Let me go," she demanded. "You're breaking my arm."

"Will you behave yourself?"

"Yes."

As I let go she started to tremble, but then she stiffened, pulling her shoulders back. "I guess I lost my head," she told Cramer. "I didn't expect to see you here. I do that sometimes, I just lose my head."

"It's a bad habit, Miss Jay. What time is your appointment with Nero Wolfe?"

"I haven't got an appointment."

"What do you want to see him about?"

"I don't want to see him. I came to see Archie Goodwin."

"What about?"

Before she could answer a voice came from behind Cramer. "Now what?" Wolfe was there, at the door to the office.

Cramer ignored him. "To see Goodwin about what?" he demanded.

"I think I know," I said. "It's a personal matter. Strictly personal."

"That's it," Laura said. "It's personal."

Cramer looked at me, and back at her. Of course the question was, if he took us downtown and turned us over to a couple of experts could they pry it out of us? He voted no. He spoke to me. "You heard me tell Wolfe he knows the law. So do you," and marched to the door, opened it, and was gone.

"Well?" Wolfe demanded.

I tried the door to make sure it was shut, and turned. "Miss Jay came to see me. I'll take her in the front room."

"No. The office." He turned and headed for the kitchen.

I allowed myself an inside grin. Thanks to my having produced the check with Lily's offer of a job in Cramer's presence, he was actually working. When Laura and I had entered the office he would emerge from the kitchen and station himself at the hole. On the office side the hole was covered by a picture of a waterfall, on the wall at eye level to the right of Wolfe's desk. On the other side, in a little alcove at the end of the hall, it was covered by a sliding panel, and with the panel pushed aside you could not only hear but also see through the waterfall. I had once stood there for three hours with a notebook, recording a conversation Wolfe was having with an embezzler.

Laura retrieved her handbag, a big gray leather one, from

the floor where it had dropped when she went for Cramer, and I escorted her to the office, took her jacket and put it on the couch, moved a chair for her to face my desk, swiveled my chair around, and sat. I looked at her. She was a wreck. I wouldn't have known her, especially since I had previously seen her all rigged out, and now she was in a plain gray dress with a black belt. Her cheeks sagged, her hair straggled, and her eyes were red and puffed. You wouldn't suppose a dashing cowgirl could get into such a state.

"First," I said, "why? Why did you go for him?"

She swallowed. "I just lost my head." She swallowed again. "I ought to thank you for helping me, when he asked what I came to see you for. I didn't know what to say."

"You're welcome. What do you say if I ask you?"

"I came to find out something. To find out if you told them what Cal told you yesterday. I know you must have because they've arrested him."

I shook my head. "They're holding him as a material witness because it was his rope and he found the body. I promised Cal I wouldn't repeat what he told me, and I haven't. If I did they'd have a motive for him, they couldn't ask for better, and they'd charge him with murder."

"You haven't told them? You swear you haven't?"

"I only swear on the witness stand and I'm not there yet. I have told no one, but I am now faced with a problem. Miss Rowan has hired Nero Wolfe to investigate the murder, and he will ask me for a full report of what happened there yesterday. I can't tell him what Cal told me because of my promise to Cal, and I'll have to tell him I am leaving something out, which he won't like. If Cal were available I would get his permission to tell Mr. Wolfe, but he isn't."

"Then you haven't even told Nero Wolfe?"

"No."

"Will you promise me you won't tell the police? That you'll never tell them no matter what happens?"

"Certainly not." I eyed her. "Use your head if you've found it again. Their charging Cal with murder doesn't depend only on me. They have found out that Eisler took a woman to his apartment Sunday night and they're going over it for fingerprints. If they find some of yours, and if they learn that you and Cal are good friends, as they will, he's in for it, and I would be a damn fool to wait till they get me on the stand under oath."

I turned a palm up. "You see, one trouble is, you and me talking, that you think Cal killed him and I know he didn't. You should be ashamed of yourself. You have known him two years and I only met him last week, but I know him better than you do. I can be fooled and have been, but when he got me aside yesterday and asked me how to go about taking some hide off a toad he was not getting set to commit a murder, and the murder of Wade Eisler was premeditated by whoever took Cal's rope. Not to mention how he looked and talked when he showed me the body. If I thought there was a chance that Cal killed him I wouldn't leave anything out when I report to Mr. Wolfe. But I can't promise to hang onto it no matter what happens."

"You can if you will," she said. "I don't think Cal killed him. I know he didn't. I did."

My eyes widened. "You did what? Killed Eisler?"

"Yes." She swallowed. "Don't you see how it is? Of course I've got to tell them I killed him, but when they arrest me Cal will say he killed him because I told him about Sunday night. But I'll say I *didn't* tell him about Sunday night, and it will be my word against his, and they'll think he's just trying to protect me. So it *does* depend on you. You've got to promise you won't tell them what Cal told you yesterday. Because I killed him, and why should you protect me? Why should you care what happens to me if I killed a man?"

I regarded her. "You know," I said, "at least you've answered my question, why you went for Cramer. You wanted to plant the idea that you're a holy terror. That wasn't so dumb, in fact it was half bright, but now listen to you. You might possibly sell it to the cops that you killed him, at least you could ball them up a while, but not me. When I went to the shack yesterday and found you there with Cal, the first thing he said was that you thought he had killed him. And now you—"

"Cal was wrong. How could I think he had killed him when I knew I had?"

"Nuts. I not only heard what he said, I saw his face, and I saw yours. You still think Cal killed him and you're acting like a half-wit."

Her head went down, her hands went up to cover her face, and she squeezed her breasts with her elbows. Her shoulders shook.

I sharpened my voice. "The very worst thing you could do would be to try telling the cops that you killed him. It would take them about ten minutes to trip you up, and then where would Cal be? But maybe you should tell them about Sunday night, but of course not that you told Cal about it. If they find your fingerprints in Eisler's apartment you'll have to account for them, and it will be better to give them the account before they ask for it. That won't be difficult; just tell them what happened."

"They won't find my fingerprints," she said, or I thought she did. Her voice was muffled by her hands, still over her face.

"Did you say they won't find your fingerprints?" I asked.

"Yes. I'm sure they won't."

I gawked at her. It wasn't so much the words as the tone— or not the tone, muffled as it was, but something. Call it a crazy hunch, and you never know exactly what starts a hunch. It was so wild that I almost skipped it, but it never pays to pass a hunch. "You can't be sure," I said. "You must have touched something. I've been to a party in that apartment. When you entered did you stop in the hall with the marble statues?"

"No. He . . . we went on through."

"To the living room. You stopped there?"

"Yes."

"Did he take you across to look at the birds in the cages? He always does. The cages are stainless steel, perfect for prints. Did you touch any of them?"

"No, I'm sure I didn't." She had dropped her hands and lifted her head.

"How close did you go to them?"

"Why . . . not very close. I'm sure I didn't touch them."

"So am I. I am also sure that you're a damn liar. There are no marble statues or bird cages in Eisler's apartment. You have never been there. What kind of a double-breasted fool are you, anyway? Do you go around telling lies just for the hell of it?"

Naturally I expected an effect, but not the one I got. She straightened up in her chair and gave me a straight look, direct and steady.

"I'm not a liar," she said. "I'm not a fool either, except about Cal Barrow. The kind of a life I've had a girl gets an attitude about men, or anyway I did. No monkey business. Keep your fences up and your cinch tight. Then I met Cal and I took another look, and after a while I guess you would say I was in love with him, but whatever you call it I know how I felt. I thought I knew how he felt too, but he never mentioned it, and of course I didn't. I only saw him now and then, he was mostly up north, and when I came to New York for this rodeo here he was. I thought he was glad to see me, and I let him know I was glad to see him, but still he didn't mention it, and when two weeks went by and pretty soon we would scatter I was trying to decide to mention it myself, and then Sunday night Nan told me about Wade Eisler, how he had—".

"Nan Karlin?"

"Yes. He had told her he was having a party at his apartment, and she went with him, and when they got there there wasn't any party, and he got rough, and she got rough too, and she got away."

"She told you this Sunday night?"

"Yes, when she got back to the hotel she came to my room. It's next to hers. Then there was this ear." She lifted a hand to push her hair back over her left ear. "I'm telling you the whole thing. I got careless with a bronc Sunday night and got bruised by a buckle, and I didn't want to admit to Cal that I didn't know how to keep clear around a horse. So when we met for breakfast yesterday morning I told him—you know what I told him. I guess I thought when he heard that, how a man had tried to bulldog me, he would see that it was time to mention something. I know I was a damn fool, I said I'm a fool when it comes to Cal Barrow, but I guess I don't know him as well as I thought I did. He never goes looking for trouble. I thought he would just ride herd on me, and that would be all right, I wanted him to. I never dreamt he would kill him."

"He didn't. How many times do I have to tell you he didn't? Who else did Nan tell about it?"

"She was going to tell Roger, Roger Dunning. She asked me if I thought she should tell Roger, and I said yes, because he had asked us to go easy with Eisler, not to sweat him unless we had to, so I thought he ought to know. Nan said she would tell him right away."

"Who else did she tell?"

"I guess not anybody. She made me promise not to tell Mel."

"Mel Fox?"

"Yes. She and Mel are going to tie up, and she was afraid he might do something. I'm sure she didn't tell him."

"Did you tell him?"

"Of course not. I promised Nan I wouldn't."

"Well." I lifted my hands and dropped them. "You're about the rarest specimen I've ever come across. I know something about geniuses, I work for one, but you're something new, an anti-genius. It wouldn't do any good to try to tell you—"

The phone rang, and I swiveled my chair around to get it. It was Lon Cohen of the *Gazette*. He wanted to know how much I would take for an exclusive on who roped Wade Eisler and why, and I told him I did and when I typed my confession I would make an extra carbon for him but at the moment I was busy.

As I reached to cradle the receiver Wolfe's voice sounded

behind me, not loud but clear enough though it was coming through the waterfall that covered the hole. "Archie, don't move. Don't turn around. She has taken a gun from her bag and is pointing it at you. Miss Jay. Your purpose is clear. With Mr. Goodwin dead there will be no one to disclose what you told Mr. Barrow at breakfast yesterday but Mr. Barrow himself, and you will deny it. You will of course be doomed since you can't hope to escape the due penalty for killing Mr. Goodwin, but you accept it in order to save Mr. Barrow from the doom you think you have contrived for him. A desperate expedient but a passable one; but it's no good now because I have heard you. You can't kill me too; you don't know where I am. Drop the gun. I will add that Mr. Goodwin has worked with me many years; I know him well; and I accept his conclusion that Mr. Barrow did not kill Wade Eisler. He is not easily gulled. Drop the gun."

I had stayed put, but it wasn't easy. Of course tingles were chasing up and down my spine, but worse than that I felt so damned silly, sitting there with my back to her while Wolfe made his speech. When he stopped it was too much. I swiveled. Her hand with the gun was resting on her knee, and she was staring at it, apparently wondering how it got there. I got up and took it, an old snub-nosed Graber, and flipped the cylinder. Fully loaded.

As I jiggled the cartridges out Wolfe entered from the hall. As he approached he spoke. "Archie. Does Mr. Barrow cherish this woman?"

"Sure he does. This could even key him up to mentioning it."

"Heaven help him." He glared down at her. "Madam, you are the most dangerous of living creatures. However, here you are, and I may need you." He turned his head and roared, "Fritz!" Fritz must have been in the hall; he appeared immediately. "This is Miss Laura Jay," Wolfe told him. "Show her to the south room, and when lunch is ready take her a tray."

"I'm going," Laura said. "I'm going to—I'm going."

"No. You'd be up to some mischief within the hour. I am going to expose a murderer, and I have accepted Mr. Goodwin's conclusion that it will not be Mr. Barrow, and you will probably be needed. This is Mr. Fritz Brenner. Go with him."

"But I must—"

"Confound it, will you go? Mr. Cramer would like to know why you came to see Mr. Goodwin. Do you want me to ring him and tell him?"

She went. I got her jacket from the couch and handed it

to Fritz, and he convoyed her out and to the elevator. Wolfe commanded me, "Get Mr. Dunning," and went to his desk and sat. I put the Graber and the cartridges in a drawer, looked in the book for the number of the Paragon Hotel, got at the phone, and dialed. The girl said Dunning's room didn't answer, and I asked her to have him paged. When he couldn't be found I left a message, and tried Madison Square Garden, and finally got him.

Wolfe took his phone. I stayed on mine. "Mr. Dunning? This is Nero Wolfe. We met yesterday at the home of Miss Lily Rowan. Miss Rowan has hired me to investigate what she calls an abuse of her hospitality—the death by violence of one of her guests—and I would like to see you. If you will please come to my office, say at a quarter past two?"

"I can't," Dunning said. "Impossible. Anyway, I've told the police everything I know. I suppose Miss Rowan has a right to hire you if she wants to, but I don't see why . . . anyhow, I can't. It's a nightmare, this is, a nightmare, but we're going to have a performance tonight if I live that long."

"Murder hatches nightmares. Did you tell the police about Miss Karlin's visit to Mr. Eisler's apartment Sunday night?"

Silence. Five seconds.

"Did you?"

"I don't know what you're talking about."

"That won't do, Mr. Dunning. I can ask the police that question if I must, but I would rather not. I would prefer to discuss it with you, and with Miss Karlin and Mr. Fox. If you will please be here with them at a quarter past two? A yes or no will be sufficient. It might be unwise to discuss it on the phone."

Another silence. Six seconds.

"I'll be there."

"With Miss Karlin and Mr. Fox?"

"Yes."

"Good. I'll expect you." He hung up and looked at me. "Archie. Will that woman try climbing out a window?"

"No. She's hooked."

"Very well." He looked up at the wall clock. "Lunch in forty minutes. Report."

IV

When the company arrived I wasn't there to let them in. They came five minutes early, at ten after two, and I was upstairs with Laura Jay. The south room is two flights up, on the same floor as my room, in the rear, above Wolfe's room. I left the lunch table before Wolfe finished his coffee, and mounted the two flights, partly to make sure she was still there, partly to see if she had eaten anything from the tray Fritz had taken up, and partly to tell her that Nan and Mel and Roger Dunning were expected and if Wolfe wanted her to join the party later I would either come and get her or send Fritz for her. All three purposes were served. She was there, standing at a window, the sun setting fire to her honey-colored hair. There was only one Creole fritter left on the plate and no salad in the bowl. I had expected her to insist on going down with me instead of waiting for a sum-mons, but she didn't. Just for curiosity I asked her if she had intended to pull the trigger as soon as I hung up or wait until I turned around, and she said I ought to know she wouldn't shoot a man in the back.

When I descended to the office they were there—Roger Dunning in the red leather chair, and Nan Karlin and Mel Fox in two of the yellow ones facing Wolfe's desk. When I entered and circled around them I got no glances; they were too intent on Wolfe, who was speaking.

". . . and the source of my information is not important. If you persist in your denial you will merely be postponing your embarrassment. The police have learned, not from me, that Eisler took a woman to his apartment Sunday night, and they are going over it for fingerprints. Almost certainly they will find some of yours, Miss Karlin, and Mr. Goodwin has told me that all of you permitted them to take samples last evening. You're in a pickle. If you refuse to discuss it with me I advise you to tell the police about it at once, be-fore they confront you with it."

Nan turned her head to look at Mel, and I had her full-face. Even without her pink silk shirt and Levis and boots, in a blouse and skirt and pumps, she would have been spotted by any New Yorker as an alien. The skin of a girl's face doesn't get that deep tone from week ends at the beach or even a two weeks' go-now-pay-later trip to Bermuda.

Mel Fox, meeting her look, said, "What the hell."

Nan went back to Wolfe. "Laura told you," she said. "Laura Jay. She's the only one that knew about it except Roger Dunning and he didn't."

"He *says* he didn't," Mel said. His eyes went to Dunning. "You wouldn't be letting out anybody's cinch, would you, Roger?"

"Of course not," Dunning said. It came out a little squeaky, and he cleared his throat. His narrow, bony face was just a sliver. I have noticed over and over that under strain a fat face gets fatter and a long face gets longer. He asked Wolfe, "Did I tell you?"

"No." To Nan: "You say that Miss Jay and Mr. Dunning are the only ones who knew about it. When did you tell them?"

"Sunday night when I got back to the hotel. Laura's room is next to mine and I went in and told her. I thought I ought to tell Roger and so did she, and when I went to my room I phoned him and he came and I told him."

"Why him? Are you on terms of intimacy with him?"

"With *him?* Good lord. Him?"

"The question arises. It is conceivable that he was so provoked by the outrage that he decided to kill Eisler, moved perhaps by an unavowed passion. Is it not?"

"Look at him," Nan said.

We did so. With no desire to slander him, it must be admitted that he didn't look like a man apt to burn with passion, avowed or unavowed.

"I never killed a man yet," he said. "Why Nan told me, she thought she ought to and she was absolutely right. It was partly my fault she had gone with Eisler to his apartment, I had asked the girls to let him have a little rope as long as he didn't get too frisky, I knew they could take care of themselves, and Nan wanted to tell me that if he ever came near her again she would give him worse than a scratch, and I couldn't blame her."

"Why did you ask them to give him rope?"

"Well." Dunning licked his lips. "In a way I was hog-tied. If Eisler hadn't put up the money we wouldn't have made it to New York this year, or anyhow it wouldn't have been easy. I didn't know much about him when I first signed up with him except that he had the money. Anyhow he was all right except with the girls, and I didn't know he was that kind. I knew if he didn't pull up there might be trouble, but I figured it wouldn't do any good to tell him so. What could I do? I couldn't fence him out. When Nan told me about Sunday night I thought that might stop him, it might show him that a girl that can handle a bronc can handle his kind."

"Did you tell him that?"

"No, I didn't. I hoped I wouldn't have to. But I decided I would keep my eyes open. Up there yesterday when I noticed he wasn't on the terrace I looked around for him some, inside and outside. When I couldn't find him and I saw all the girls were there I thought he had up and gone, and that suited me fine."

"What time was that? When you looked around and couldn't find him."

Dunning shook his head. "I can't make it close. The police

wanted me to and I did the best I could, but all I can say, it wasn't long after Miss Rowan went in for some more coffee —maybe three minutes, maybe more than that. Then when I went back in after looking outside Cal Barrow said his rope was gone and he was looking for it, and I wondered if Eisler had took it but I couldn't guess why."

"How many people did you tell about Miss Karlin's experience at Eisler's apartment?"

"How many?" Dunning frowned. "No people at all. What good would that do?"

"You told no one?"

"No."

"And you haven't told the police?"

"No." He licked his lips. "I figured it would just sick them on Nan, and I couldn't see any sense in that. What you asked her about her and me, there's nothing to that, she's just one of the girls, but I know her pretty well and she wouldn't kill a man just because he had pawed at her. I'd like to ask you a question. You say Miss Rowan has hired you to investigate?"

"Yes."

"You weren't there when it happened, and neither was Goodwin. Is that right?"

"Yes."

"But Miss Rowan was, and she hires you. She's paying you. So you're not going to investigate *her*, naturally. I got the idea there yesterday that she didn't like Eisler any too well. I don't suppose you're interested in that? I suppose you think it has to be one of us, the boys and girls and me?"

Wolfe grunted. He turned his head. "Archie. I haven't asked you. Did Miss Rowan kill Mr. Eisler?"

"No, sir."

"Then that's settled. Mr. Dunning, obviously it was one of you. By the way, Miss Karlin, I haven't asked you: did you kill Mr. Eisler?"

"No."

"Mr. Fox. Did you?"

"No."

"When did you first learn of Miss Karlin's visit to Eisler's apartment Sunday night?"

"Today. Two hours ago. Roger told me after you phoned him. If I'd knew about it Sunday night or yesterday morning Eisler wouldn't of got killed there yesterday because he wouldn't of been there. He would of been in bed or maybe in the hospital."

"Then it's a pity you didn't know."

"Yeah. Roger told me because you told him to bring me

along, he didn't know why and I don't either, but I can make a guess. You're a friend of Harvey Greve's."

"Mr. Goodwin is."

"Yeah. So Harvey tells him things. He tells him about Nan and me, that we're fixing to get hitched, which we are, and you—"

"Not Harvey," Nan said. "Laura. Laura told him. Because they've arrested Cal."

"All right, maybe Laura." Mel stayed at Wolfe. "So that looks like a good setup. Eisler went after my girl and I killed him. So you tell Roger to bring me along. I understand you're about as slick as they come, you can bend a loop around a corner, but let's see you try. Here's Roger says he didn't tell anybody about Nan going there. Here's Nan says she didn't tell anybody but Laura and Roger. So I didn't know about it unless Eisler told me himself, and that don't seem practical, and he's dead. So here I am and it's your move."

"You did know about it!"

It was Laura Jay's voice and it came from the waterfall that covered the hole, which was only a couple of arms' lengths from Roger Dunning, and he jerked around. I bounced up and started for the hall, but had got only halfway when here came Laura.

She went straight to Mel and stopped, facing him, and spoke. "You knew about it because I told you." She turned to Wolfe: "Yesterday. I told him yesterday morning. I thought he—"

She was interrupted. Nan flew at her and smacked her on the side of the head.

V

Somehow when two women tie into each other it's harder to separate them than it is two men. It's not just that you don't want to hurt a woman if you can help it; they're actually more wriggly and you're more apt to get scratched or bit; and when it's two active cowgirls it's a real problem. However, I had help. Roger and Mel were closer than I was, and Roger had Laura's shoulders, and Mel had Nan around the waist, when I reached them. They yanked them apart, and I merely stepped in between. Laura wriggled free from Roger, but I was there. Mel had Nan wrapped up.

"Pfui," Wolfe said. "Miss Jay, your talent for turmoil is extraordinary. Archie, put her—"

"She's a liar," Nan said. She was panting a little, and her eyes were blazing. "I knew it was her. I knew she—"

"Hold it, Nan," Mel commanded her. His eyes were narrowed at Wolfe. "So you had it rigged good, huh? So you had her all primed, huh?"

"I did not." Wolfe was emphatic. "This is becoming farcical. You were right, up to a point, Miss Karlin. Miss Jay, concerned on account of Mr. Barrow, came to see Mr. Goodwin, to tell him of your experience at Eisler's apartment. She stated that you made her promise not to tell Mr. Fox, and that she had kept the promise. Thinking it well to have her at hand, I had her shown to a room upstairs and told her to stay there. Her abrupt entry surprised me as much as you. Miss Jay, did you tell Mr. Goodwin that you had not told Mr. Fox?"

"Yes." Laura's chin was up.

"But you now say you had?"

"Yes."

"Precisely where and when?"

"Yesterday morning at the hotel. In the lobby after breakfast."

"You had breakfast with Mr. Barrow. Was he present?"

"No. He went to buy some cigarettes, and I saw Mel there and went and told him."

"Look here, Laura," Mel said. "Look at me."

Her head came around, slowly, and she met his eyes, straight.

"You know darned well that ain't so," he said. "This slicker talked you into it. He told you that was the way to get Cal out of trouble. Didn't he?"

"No."

"You mean you can stand there and look me in the eye and lie like that?"

"I don't know, Mel, I never tried."

"Listen, Laura," Roger Dunning said, to her back. "If it's on account of Cal, I don't think you have to. I've got a lawyer on it and he'll soon have him out on bail, thirty thousand dollars. He may be out already. They can't charge him with murder unless they can show some reason why he wanted to kill Eisler, and there wasn't any."

"It's not just her," Mel said. He had backed Nan up and moved in front of her. He turned to me. "You're slick too, huh?"

"Not very," I said. "I manage somehow."

"I bet you do. I bet you're pretty good at answering questions. What if I asked you where you was yesterday while someone was killing Eisler?"

"That's easy. I was driving a car. Driving Mr. Wolfe home and then back to Sixty-third Street."

"Was anybody else along?"

"Nope. Just us two."

"Did you see anybody on the way that knows you?"

"No."

"Did anybody here see you except Wolfe?"

"No, I didn't come in. I wanted to get back in time for the roping—I mean the contest, not roping Eisler. You're asking pretty good questions, but you'll hit the same snag with me as with Cal Barrow. You'll have to show some reason why I wanted to kill Eisler."

"Yeah. Or why Wolfe would want you to, the man you work for. Or why that Miss Rowan would, the woman that's hired him." He turned to Wolfe. "You better look out with this Laura Jay. She ain't cut out for a liar." He turned to Laura. "I'll be having a talk with you, Laura. Private." He turned to Roger Dunning. "This lawyer you got to get bail for Cal, is he any good?"

Roger's long narrow face was even longer. "I think he's all right. He seems to know his way around."

"I want to see him. Come on, Nan. You come along. We're not going to get——"

The doorbell rang. Mel had Nan under control, so I went. A glance through the glass of the front door showed me a hundred and ninety pounds of sergeant out on the stoop—Sergeant Purley Stebbins of Homicide. I proceeded, put the chain bolt on, opened the door to the two-inch crack the chain permitted, and said politely, "No clues today. Out of stock."

"Open up, Goodwin." Like a sergeant. "I want Nan Karlin."

"I don't blame you. She's very attractive——"

"Can it. Open up. I've got a warrant for her and I know she's here."

There was no use making an issue of it, since there had probably been an eye on the house ever since Cramer left. As for the warrant, of course the prints she had left at Eisler's apartment had caught up with her. But Wolfe doesn't approve of cops' taking anyone in his house, no matter who. "What if you brought the wrong warrant?" I asked.

He got it from a pocket and stuck it through the crack, and I took it and looked it over. "Okay," I said, "but watch her, she might bite." Removing the chain, swinging the door open, and handing him the warrant as he crossed the sill, I followed him to the office. He didn't make a ceremony of it. He marched across to Nan, displayed the paper, and spoke. "Warrant to take you as a material witness in the murder of Wade Eisler. You're under arrest. Come along."

My concern was Laura. As like as not, she would blurt

out that he should take Mel too because she had told him about it, so I lost no time getting to her, but she didn't utter a peep. She stood stiff, her teeth clamped on her lip. Wolfe let out a growl, but no words. Nan gripped Mel's arm. Mel took the warrant, read it through, and told Stebbins, "This don't say what for."

"Information received."

"Where you going to take her?"

"Ask the District Attorney's office."

"I'm getting a lawyer for her."

"Sure. Everybody ought to have a lawyer."

"I'm going along."

"Not with us. Come on, Miss Karlin."

Wolfe spoke. "Miss Karlin. You will of course be guided by your own judgment and discretion. I make no suggestion. I merely inform you that you are under no compulsion to speak until you have consulted an attorney."

Stebbins and Mel Fox both spoke at once. Stebbins said, "She didn't ask you anything." Mel said, "You goddam snake." Stebbins touched Nan's elbow and she moved. I stayed with Laura as they headed out, Nan and Stebbins in front and Mel and Roger following; seeing them go might touch her off. She still had her teeth on her lip. When I heard the front door close I went and took a look and came back.

I expected to find Wolfe scowling at her, but he wasn't. He was leaning back with his eyes closed and his lips moving. He was pushing out his lips, puckered, and then drawing them in—out and in, out and in. He only does that, and always does it, when he has found a crack somewhere, or thinks he has, and is trying to see through. I am not supposed to interrupt the process, so I crossed to my desk, but didn't sit, because Laura was still on her feet, and a gentleman should not seat himself when a lady or a wildcat is standing.

Wolfe opened his eyes. "Archie."

"Yes, sir."

"It would help to know whether Miss Jay had told Mr. Fox or not. Is there any conceivable way of finding out?"

I raised a brow. If that was the crack he had been trying to see through he was certainly hard up for cracks. "Not bare-handed," I said. "It would take a scientist. I know where you can get one with a lie detector. Or you might try a hypnotist."

"Pfui. Miss Jay, which is it now, now that Miss Karlin is in custody? Had you told Mr. Fox?"

"Yes."

"Yesterday morning in the hotel lobby?"

"Yes."

"I suppose you understand what that will let you in for —or rather, I suppose you don't. You will be—"

The phone rang. I got it. "Nero Wolfe's office, Archie Goodwin speaking."

"This is Cal, Archie. Do you know where Laura is?"

"I might have an idea. Where are you?"

"I'm at the hotel. I'm out on bail. They say she went out this morning and she hasn't been back, and she's not at the Garden. I thought maybe she might have been to see you."

"Hold the wire a minute. I'll go to another phone."

I got my memo pad, wrote on it, *Cal Barrow out on bail looking for Laura, get him here & you can check her*, tore off the sheet, and handed it to Wolfe. He read it and looked up at the clock. His afternoon date with the orchids was at four.

"No," he said. "You can. Get her out of here. Of course you must see him first."

I resumed at the phone. "I think I know where to find her. It's a little complicated, and the best way—"

"Where is she?"

"I'll bring her. What's your room number?"

"Five-twenty-two. Where is she?"

"I'll have her there in half an hour, maybe less. Stay in your room."

I hung up and faced Laura. "That was Cal. He's out on bail and he wants to see you. I'll take—"

"Cal! Where is he?"

"I'll take you to him, but I'm going to see him first. I don't ask you to promise because you'd promise anything, but if you try any tricks I'll show you a new way to handle a calf. Where's your jacket?"

"It's upstairs."

"Go get it. If I went for it you might not be here when I came back."

VI

The Paragon Hotel, around the corner from Eighth Avenue on 54th Street, not exactly a dump but by no means a Waldorf, is convenient for performers at the Garden—of course not including the stars. When Larua and I entered there were twenty or more cow-persons in the lobby, both male and female, some in costume and some not. We went to the elevator, and to my surprise she stuck to the program as agreed upon in the taxi, getting out at the fourth floor to

go to her room. I stayed in, left at the fifth, found Room
522 and knocked on the door, and it opened before I was
through knocking.

"Oh," Cal said. "Where is she?"

He was still in the same outfit he had worn yesterday
—bright blue shirt, blue jeans, and fancy boots. His face
wasn't any fresher than his clothes.

"She's in her room," I said. "She wanted to fix her hair.
Before she joins us I want to ask you something. Do I see a
chair in there?"

"Why sure. Come on in and sit." He gave me room and I
entered. There were two chairs, about all there was space for,
what with the bed and chest of drawers and a little table.
I took one. Cal stood and yawned, wide.

"Excuse me," he said. "I'm a little short on sleep."

"So am I. Some things have been happening, but Laura can
tell you about them. Miss Rowan has hired Nero Wolfe to
investigate, and he knows about what you told me yesterday.
Laura can tell you how he found out. I haven't told the
cops or anyone else."

He nodded. "I figured you hadn't or they would have
asked me. I guess you've got your tongue in straight. I'm
mighty glad. I guess I picked the right man to tell."

"Frankly, you could have done worse. Now you can tell
me something else. Yesterday morning you met Laura downstairs and had breakfast with her. Remember?"

"Sure I remember."

"Mel Fox says that when you and Laura went into the
lobby after breakfast you left her and went to the cigar
counter to buy cigarettes, and he went and had a little talk
with you. Remember that?"

"I don't seem to." He frowned. "I didn't buy no cigarettes. I got a carton here in my room. Mel must of
got mixed up."

"I'd like to be sure about this, Cal. Go back to it, it was
only yesterday. You and Laura had breakfast in the coffee
shop?"

"Yes."

"Then you went into the lobby together. If you didn't
leave her to buy cigarettes, maybe it was to buy a paper. The
newsstand is—"

"Wait a minute. We didn't go into the lobby. We left the
coffee shop by the street door. We went down to the Garden
to look at some things."

"Then it might have been when you came back. You went
into the lobby then."

"We didn't come back. When we left the Garden we went

up to that Miss Rowan's. I guess you might tell me why this is so particular. What does Mel say we talked about?"

"You'll know pretty soon. I had to be sure—"

There was a knock at the door, and he lost no time getting to it. It was Laura. She was running true to form. We had agreed on fifteen minutes, and it had been only ten. The reunion was mighty dramatic. Cal said, "Well, hello." Laura said, "Hello, Cal." He stood aside so she wouldn't have to brush against him as she entered. I arose and said, "You fudged a little but I expected you to." Cal shut the door and came and said, "Gosh, you look like you got throwed by a camel."

I took command. "Look," I told them, "when I leave you'll have all the time there is, but now I've got some talking to do and you can listen. Sit down."

"You've already talked," Laura said. "What did you tell him?"

"Nothing yet but I'm going to. If you don't want to listen I know who will—Inspector Cramer if I phone him and say I'm ready to unload. Sit down!"

Laura sat in the other chair. Cal sat on the edge of the bed. "I guess you got the drop on us, Archie," he said. "I hope you don't feel as mean as you sound."

"I don't feel mean at all." I sat. "I'm going to tell you a love story. I take valuable time to tell it because if I don't God only knows what Laura will be up to next. Yesterday she told you a colossal lie. Today she told me she killed Wade Eisler. Then she—shut up, both of you! Then she pointed a loaded gun at my back and would have plugged me if she hadn't been interrupted. Then she told another lie, trying to frame Mel Fox for the murder. That's—"

"No!" Laura cried. "That was the truth!"

"Nuts. You and Cal didn't go to the lobby after breakfast. You went to the Garden and from there to Miss Rowan's. You didn't tell Mel Fox what you said you did. You were framing him, or trying to."

"You're talking pretty fast," Cal said. "Maybe you'd better slow down and back it up a little. If you can. What was the lie she told me yesterday?"

"That she had gone to Eisler's apartment Sunday night. She hadn't. She has never been there. It was Nan Karlin that Eisler took there Sunday night, and Nan told Laura about it when she got back to the hotel. Laura told you *she* had been there for two reasons: she didn't want to admit she had been careless about a horse and got her ear bruised, and the real reason, she hoped it would make you realize it was time to break out the bridle. All for love. You are her dream man.

She wants to hook you. She wants you to take her for better or for worse, and she has done her damnedest to make it worse."

"I didn't say that!" Laura cried.

"Not in those words. Was that why you told him that lie or wasn't it? Try telling the truth once."

"All right, it was!"

Cal stood up. "You might go and leave us alone awhile. You can come back."

"This is a respectable hotel. A gentleman isn't supposed to be in his room alone with a lady. I'll go pretty soon, after I fill in a little. Sit down. She came today and told me she killed Eisler because she thought you had—she still thinks so—and it was her fault and she wanted to take the rap. When I showed her that wouldn't work she took a gun from her bag—she had thoughtfully brought it along—when my back was turned, and got set to let me have it, the idea being that I was the only one who knew you had a motive. She can tell you why that didn't work either. Then—"

"She wouldn't of shot you," Cal said.

"The hell she wouldn't. Then Mel and Nan and Roger came, and she got another idea. She announced that she had told Mel about Nan going to Eisler's place Sunday night, the idea being to give Mel a motive for killing Eisler. She said she told him yesterday morning when you and she went to the lobby after breakfast and you went to buy cigarettes. I have now stepped on that one." I turned to Laura. "You'd better see Mel and tell him. Tell him you had a fit."

I returned to Cal. "Of course that's fairly thick, trying to dump a murder on a guy, but after all, she would have dumped it on herself if she could. She tried that first, so I admit I should make allowances. I'm telling you all this for three reasons: first, so you'll know what she's capable of and you'll head her off. No one else can. If she keeps on having ideas there'll be hell to pay and you'll probably do the paying. Second, I want you both to realize that whoever killed Eisler is going to get tagged, and the sooner the better. It's one of six people: Nan Karlin, Anna Casado, Harvey Greve, Mel Fox, and Roger Dunning and his wife. If you know of any reason, anything at all, why one of them might have wanted Eisler dead, I expect you to tell me and tell me now."

"You say Laura still thinks I killed him," Cal said.

"She may be losing her grip on that. After the way her other ideas have panned out she must be shaky on that one." I looked at her. "Make it hypothetical, Laura. If Cal didn't, who did?"

"I don't know."

"What about Harvey Greve? He's a friend of mine, but I'll overlook that if he's it. Could he have had a motive?"

"I don't know."

"What about Roger Dunning? Did Eisler make passes at his wife?"

"If he did I never saw him. Neither did anybody else. She's not—well, you saw her—why would he? With all the girls to paw at. She must be nearly fifty."

Ellen Dunning probably wasn't a day over forty, but I admit she was a little faded. I turned to Cal. "Your turn. If you didn't kill him who did?"

He shook his head. "You got me. Does it have to be one of them six?"

"Yes."

"Then I pass. I just couldn't guess."

"It will take more than a guess. My third reason for taking up your time, not to mention mine: I wanted to have another look at you and listen to you some more. You're the only one with a known motive, and I'm the one that knows it. Nero Wolfe has bought my conclusion that you're out, and I haven't told the cops, and if I'm wrong I'm sunk. Besides, Laura would have the laugh on me, and I'd hate that. Did you kill him?"

"I'll tell you, Archie." He was actually grinning at me, and there was nothing but me between him and a murder trial. "I wouldn't want her to have the laugh on me, either. And she won't."

"Okay." I got up. "For God's sake keep an eye on her. Do you know Harvey's room number?"

"Sure. He's down the hall. Five-thirty-one."

I went.

Knocking on the door of Room 531, first normal and then loud, got no result. I intended to see Harvey. He might be down in the lobby, and if he wasn't I would try the Garden. There was no hurry about getting back to the office, since it was only four-thirty and Wolfe wouldn't be down from the plant rooms until six. Taking the elevator down, I found that there were more people in the lobby than when I came. Moving around, I didn't see Harvey, but I saw a man I knew, standing over in a corner chinning with a couple of cowboys. It was Fred Durkin. Fred, a free-lance, was second-best of the three operatives whom Wolfe considers good enough to trust with errands when we need help on a job. I looked at my watch: 4:34. Nearly an hour and a half since I had left with Laura, time enough for Wolfe to get Fred on the phone, brief him, and put him to work. Had he? Of course it could be that Fred was there on a job for one of the agencies that used him, but that would have been quite a coincidence and I don't like coincidences.

That question would have to wait for an answer. Knowing that Harvey Greve liked a drink when one was handy, I crossed the lobby and entered the bar. The crowd there was smaller but noisier. No Harvey, but there were booths along the wall, and I strolled back for a look, and found him. He was in a booth, deep in conversation with a man. Neither of them saw me, and I went on by, circled and backtracked, returned to the lobby, and on out to the street.

The man with Harvey was Saul Panzer. Saul is not only the first-best of the three men Wolfe uses for errands, he is the best operative south of the North Pole. That settled it. Fred could have been a coincidence, but not both of them. Wolfe had got busy on the phone the minute I was out of the house, or darned soon after. What had stung him? No answer. At Ninth Avenue I flagged a taxi. When I gave the hackie the number on West 35th Street, he said, "What a honor. Archie Goodwin in person. Your name in the paper again but no pitcher this time. Stranglin' a guy with a lasso right on Park Avenue, can you beat that? Whodunit?"

I'm all for fame, but I was too busy guessing to smirk.

The hackie had another honor coming. When the cab rolled to a stop in front of the old brownstone and I climbed out, a man appeared from behind a parked car and spoke to him. It was Sergeant Purley Stebbins. He said to the hackie, "Hold it, driver. Police." He said to me, "You're under arrest. I've got a warrant." He took a paper from a pocket and offered it.

He was enjoying it. He would have enjoyed even more to see me squirm, so I didn't. I didn't bother to look at the paper. "Information received?" I asked politely. "Or just on general principles?"

"The inspector will tell you. We'll use this cab. Get in."

I obeyed. He climbed in beside me and told the driver, "Two-thirty West Twentieth," and we rolled.

I chose to snub him. He was of course expecting me to try some appropriate cracks, so of course I didn't. I didn't open my trap from the time I climbed in the cab until he ushered me into the office of Inspector Cramer, which is on the third floor of the dingy old building that houses the precinct. I didn't open it even then. I waited until I was in a chair at the end of Cramer's desk, and he said, "I've been going over your statement, Goodwin, and I want to know more about your movements yesterday afternoon. The District Attorney does too, but I'll have a go at it first. You left with Wolfe, to drive him home, at twelve minutes after three. Right?"

I spoke. "It's all in my statement, and I answered a thousand questions, some of them a dozen times. That's enough. I am now clamming, unless and until you tell me why I am suddenly grabbed. If you think you dug up something, what?"

"That will develop as we go along. You left with Wolfe at three-twelve?"

I leaned back and yawned.

He regarded me. He looked up at Stebbins, who was standing. Stebbins said, "You know him. He hasn't said a word since I took him."

Cramer looked at me. "A woman phoned headquarters this afternoon and said she saw you there yesterday at half past three on the terrace in the rear of the penthouse. She was sure about the time. She didn't give her name. I don't have to tell you that if Wolfe came home in a taxi we'll find the driver. You left with him at three-twelve?"

"Thanks for the warning. What time did the woman phone?"

"Three-thirty-nine."

I looked at it. Laura and I had got to the hotel about twenty-five to four. The first thing on my program when I got loose would be to wring her neck and toss her in the river. "Okay," I said, "naturally you're curious. You say the DA is too, so it will be a long discussion. I'll talk after I make a phone call. May I use your phone?"

"In my hearing."

"Certainly, it's your phone."

He moved it across and I got it and dialed. Fritz answered and I asked him to buzz the plant rooms. After a wait Wolfe's voice came, cranky, as it always is when he is interrupted up there.

"Yes?"

"Me. I'm with Cramer in his office. When I got home Stebbins was waiting for me out front with a warrant. A woman, name unknown, phoned the police that she saw me at half past three yesterday afternoon on Miss Rowan's terrace. If you think you'll need me tomorrow you'd better get Parker. Of the two contradictory statements you sent me to check, the first one is true. Tell Fritz to save some of the veal knuckle for me. He can warm it over tomorrow."

"At half past three yesterday afternoon you were with me in the car."

"I know it, but they don't. Cramer would give a month's pay to prove I wasn't."

I hung up and sat back. "Where were we? Oh yes. I left with Mr. Wolfe at three-twelve. Next question?"

VII

At 10:39 Wednesday morning, standing at the curb on Leonard Street waiting for an empty taxi, I said to Nathaniel Parker, the lawyer, "It's a dirty insult. Did you say five *hundred?*"

He nodded. "It is rather a slap, isn't it? As your attorney, I could hardly suggest a higher figure. And of course the cost will be much—here comes one." He stepped off the curb and raised an arm to stop an approaching cab.

The insult, having my bail set at a measly five C's, one-sixtieth of Cal Barrow's, was merely an insult. The injuries were what I would some day, preferably that one, get even for. I had spent fourteen hours in a detention room with too much heat and not enough air; I had asked for corned-beef sandwiches and got ham and rubbery cheese; I had been asked the same question over and over by four different county and city employees, none of whom had a sense of humor; I had been served lukewarm coffee in a paper thing that leaked; I had not been allowed to use the phone; I had been told three times to take a nap on a bumpy couch and had been roused for more questions just as I was fading out; and I had been asked to sign a statement that had four mistakes in content, three misspelled words, and five typographical errors. And at the end of it all, which must have cost the taxpayers at least a thousand bucks, counting overhead, they were exactly where they had been when they started.

After climbing out of the taxi in front of the old brownstone and thanking Parker for the lift, I mounted the stoop, let myself in, and headed for the office to tell Wolfe that I would be available as soon as I had showered, shaved, brushed my teeth, cleaned my nails, brushed my hair, dressed, and had breakfast. It was five minutes past eleven, so he would be down from the plant rooms.

But he wasn't. The overgrown chair behind his desk was empty. Four of the yellow chairs were grouped in front of his desk, facing it, and Fritz was emerging from the front room carrying two more of them. On the couch at the far side at right angles to my desk two people sat holding hands —Cal Barrow and Laura Jay. As I entered Cal jerked his hand away and stood up.

"We came a little early," he said. "We thought you might tell us what's up."

"Roping contest," I said. "I run down the block and you snare me from the stoop. Orchids for prizes." I turned to Fritz. "There's a mermaid in the sink." I wheeled and went to the kitchen, and in a moment he came.

"Where is he?" I demanded.

"In his room with Saul and Fred. Your tie's crooked, Archie, and your—"

"I fell off a horse. Having a party?"

"Yes. Mr. Wolfe—"

"What time?"

"I was told they would come at half past eleven. The lady and gentleman on the couch—"

"Came early to hold hands. Excuse my manners, I spent the night with louts and it rubbed off on me. I've got to rinse it off. Could you possibly bring up toast and coffee in eight minutes?"

"Easy. Seven. Your orange juice is in the refrigerator." He went to the range.

I got the glass of juice from the refrigerator, got a spoon and stirred it, took a healthy sip, and headed for the hall and the stairs. One flight up the door of Wolfe's room was at the left, but I kept going and mounted another flight to my room, which was to the right, at the front of the house.

Ordinarily, what with my personal morning fog, it takes me around forty minutes to get rigged for the day, but that time I made it in thirty, with time out for the juice, toast and jam, and coffee. When Fritz came with the tray I asked him to tell Wolfe I was there, and he said he had done so on his way up, and Wolfe was pleased. I don't mean Wolfe said he was pleased; Fritz said he was. Fritz thinks he is a diplomat. At 11:42, cleaner and neater but not gayer, I went down to the office.

They were all there, all of Lily's Monday luncheon guests but Wade Eisler. Lily was in the red leather chair. Cal and Laura were still on the couch, but not holding hands. The other six were on the yellow chairs, Mel Fox, Nan Karlin, and Harvey Greve in front, and Roger Dunning, his wife, and Anna Casado in the rear. Saul Panzer and Fred Durkin were off at the side, over by the big globe.

Wolfe, at his desk, was speaking as I entered. He stopped to dart a glance at me. I halted and inquired politely, "Am I intruding?"

Lily said, "You look pretty spruce for a man who spent the night in jail."

Wolfe said, "I have told them why you were delayed. Now

that you're here I'll proceed." As I circled around the company to get to my desk he went on, to them, "I repeat, I have been employed by Miss Rowan and am acting in her interest, but I am solely responsible for what I am about to say. If I defame I alone am liable; she is not. You are here at my invitation, but you came, of course, not to please me but to hear me. I won't keep you longer than I must."

"We have to be at the Garden by a quarter after one," Roger Dunning said. "The show starts at two."

"Yes, sir, I know." Wolfe's eyes went right and then left. "I think it likely that one of you won't be there. I am not prepared to say to one of you, 'You killed Wade Eisler and I can prove it,' but I can offer a suggestion. All of you had the opportunity and the means; you were there, the steel rod was there, the rope was there. None of you was eliminated with a certainty by a check of your movements. I made no such check, but the police did, and at that sort of thing they are inimitable. So it was a question of motive, as it often is."

He pinched his nose with a thumb and forefinger, and I suppressed a grin. He is convinced that when a woman is present, let alone four of them, the air is tainted with perfume. Sometimes it is, naturally, but not then and there. I have a good nose and I hadn't smelled any on the cowgirls, and you have to get a good deal closer to Lily than Wolfe was to catch hers. But he pinched his nose.

He resumed. "From the viewpoint of the police two facts pointed to Mr. Barrow: it was his rope, and he found the body. Rather, it seemed to me, they pointed away from him, but let that pass. He had a motive, but no one knew it but Miss Jay and Mr. Goodwin. If the police had known it he would have been charged with murder. I learned of it only yesterday, and I ignored it because Mr. Goodwin told me to. He was convinced that Mr. Barrow was innocent, and he is not easy to convince. Mr. Barrow, you and I are in his debt —you because he saved you from a mortal hazard, and I because he saved me from wasting time and trouble on you."

"Yes, sir," Cal said. "That's not all I owe him." He looked at Laura, and for a second I thought he was going to take her hand in public, but he reined in.

"I also learned yesterday," Wolfe went on, "that Miss Karlin had had a motive, and, according to Miss Jay, that Mr. Fox had had one. But later Miss Jay recanted. Miss Jay, did you tell Mr. Fox of Miss Karlin's experience at Eisler's apartment?"

"No. I must have been—"

"The 'no' is enough. But you did phone the police yester-

day that you saw Mr. Goodwin on Miss Rowan's terrace at
half past three Monday afternoon?"

"What?" Laura stared. "I never phoned the police anything!"

"You must have. It is of no consequence now, but—"

"I phoned the police," Ellen Dunning said. "I phoned them
and told them that because it was true, and I thought they
ought to know."

"But you didn't identify yourself."

"No, I didn't. I was afraid to. I didn't know what they
might do because I hadn't told about it before. But I thought
they ought to know."

I wouldn't have dreamed that the day would ever come
when I would owe Laura an apology.

"I doubt," Wolfe said, "if you have earned their gratitude.
Certainly not mine or Mr. Goodwin's. To go back to Mr. Fox
—by the way, Miss Karlin, you were released on bail this
morning?"

"Yes," Nan said.

"You were questioned at length?"

"I certainly was."

"Did they worm it out of you that you had told Mr. Fox
of your visit to Eisler's apartment?"

"Of course not! I *hadn't* told him! He didn't know about it
until yesterday!"

Wolfe's eyes moved. "Do you confirm that, Mr. Fox?"

"I sure do." Mel was on the edge of his chair, leaning forward, his elbows on his knees, his head tilted up. "If this is
the suggestion you said you'd offer you can stick it somewhere."

"It isn't. I'm merely clearing away the brush. Even if you
and Miss Karlin are lying, if she did tell you, it can't be
proven. Therefore it is impossible to establish a motive for
you. No, that is not my suggestion. I only—"

"Wait a minute," Roger Dunning blurted. "I've held off
up to now, but I might have known I couldn't forever. I
told Mel about it—about Nan going to Eisler's place and
what he did."

"When?"

"I told him Sunday night. I thought he ought to know because I knew he—"

"You're a dirty liar. Get on your feet." Mel was on his.
Dunning's chair was right behind his, and Mel had turned
to face him.

"I'm sorry, Mel," Dunning said. "I'm damn sorry, but you
can't expect—"

"On your feet!"

"That won't help any, Mel. That won't—"

Mel smacked him on the jaw with his open hand, his right, and his left was on the way to countersmack him as his head swayed, but Saul Panzer and Fred Durkin were there. I was up, but they were closer. They got his arms and backed him up and turned him, and Wolfe spoke.

"If you please, Mr. Fox. I'll deal with him. I know he's lying."

Mel squinted. "How the hell do *you* know he's lying?"

"I know a cornered rat when I see one. Move your chair and sit down. Saul, see if Mr. Dunning has a weapon. We don't need any melodrama."

Dunning was on his feet, focused on Wolfe. "You said Miss Rowan's not responsible," he said, louder than necessary. "You said you are." He turned to Lily. "You hired him. I advise you to fire him quick."

Lily looked at me. I shook my head. Fred moved behind Dunning and took his arms, and Saul went over him. Mel Fox moved his chair away and sat. Cal said something to Laura, and Anna Casado spoke to Harvey Greve. Saul turned and told Wolfe, "No gun." Dunning said to his wife, "Come on, Ellen, we're going." She reached and grabbed his sleeve.

Wolfe spoke. "You are not going, Mr. Dunning. When you do go you will be under escort. I repeat, I can't say to you, 'You killed Wade Eisler and I can prove it,' but I do say that the probability of your guilt is so great that I stake my reputation on it. I must confess that this is impetuous, but your motive couldn't be established without warning you; and I wished to gratify a caprice of my client, Miss Rowan, who invited me to her table for a memorable meal. She wants to deliver you to the District Attorney. Mr. Panzer and Mr. Durkin will go along to give him some information they have gathered. You are going willy-nilly. Do you want to challenge me here and now?"

Dunning turned his head to see where his chair was, and sat. He pulled his shoulders up and lifted his chin. "What information?" he asked.

"I'll tell you its nature," Wolfe said. "I doubt if the District Attorney would want me to give you the particulars. But first, what fixed my attention on you? You did—something that you said when you were here yesterday morning. I didn't worm it out of you, you volunteered it, that on Monday at Miss Rowan's place you noticed that Mr. Eisler wasn't on the terrace and you looked around for him, inside and outside. I asked you when, and you said—I quote you verbatim: 'It wasn't long after Miss Rowan went in for some more coffee—maybe three minutes, maybe more than that.'

That was entirely too pat, Mr. Dunning. You were accounting for your absence in case it had been remarked by anyone, and more important, you were accounting for your appearance in the rear of the penthouse in case you had been observed. And you did it gratuitously; I hadn't asked for it."

"I said it because it was true." Dunning licked his lips.

"No doubt. But it suggested the question, what if, instead of looking for him, you were killing him? What if, having got the rope from the closet and concealed it under your jacket, you got Eisler to go with you to that shack on some pretext, or to meet you there? That attracted me. Of the persons there you were the only one whose absence during that period could be established; you yourself avowed it. But then the question, what impelled you? Had you had a cogent motive? To avenge his misconduct with Miss Karlin or with another woman or women?"

Wolfe shook his head. "That seemed unlikely, though not impossible. More probably it had been some other factor of your relations with him. But when I put Mr. Panzer and Mr. Durkin on your trail I told them to explore all avenues, and they did so. They found no hint that you had a personal interest in any of the young women Mr. Eisler had pestered, but they gathered facts that were highly suggestive. By the way, a detail: on the phone last evening I asked Miss Rowan if you knew of that shack in the rear of the penthouse, and she said that you not only knew of it, you had been in it. You went there on Sunday to make sure that the terrace would be cleared of obstructions so the ropes could be manipulated, and she took you to the shack to see the grouse that were hanging there. Is that correct, Miss Rowan?"

Lily said yes. She didn't look happy. Since it was beginning to look as if she was going to get her money's worth, she should have been pleased, but she didn't look it.

"That's a lie," Dunning said. "I didn't know about that shack. I never saw it."

Wolfe nodded. "You're desperate. You knew I wouldn't arrange this gathering unless I had discovered something of consequence, so you start wriggling; you try to implicate Mr. Fox, your word against his, and you deny you knew of the shack, your word against Miss Rowan's. Indeed, you started wriggling yesterday, when you had your wife phone the police in an effort to implicate Mr. Goodwin. Probably you have learned that something has been taken from your hotel room. Have you inspected the contents of your suitcase since ten o'clock last evening? The old brown one in the closet that you keep locked?"

"No." Dunning swallowed. "Why should I?'"

"I think you have. I have reason to believe that an envelope now in my safe came from that suitcase. I have examined its contents, and while they don't prove that you killed Wade Eisler they are highly suggestive of a possible motive. I said I'll tell you the nature of the information I have but not the particulars. However, you may have one detail." His head turned. "Mr. Greve. You told Mr. Panzer that in the past two years you have purchased some three hundred horses, two hundred steers and bulls, and a hundred and fifty calves, in behalf of Mr. Dunning. Is that correct?"

Harvey didn't look happy either. "That's about right," he said. "That's just rough figures."

"From how many different people did you buy them?"

"Maybe a hundred, maybe more. I scouted around."

"How did you pay for them?"

"Some I gave them a check, but mostly cash. They like cash."

"Your own checks?"

"Yes. Roger made deposits in my account, eight or ten thousand dollars at a time, and I paid out of that."

"Did Mr. Dunning tell you not to divulge the amounts you paid for the animals?"

Harvey screwed up his mouth. "I don't like this."

"Neither do I. I am earning a fee. You are exposing a man who made you a party to a swindle and who is almost certainly a murderer. Did he tell you not to divulge the amounts?"

"Yes, he did."

"Has anyone asked you to?"

"Yes. Wade Eisler. About ten days ago. I told him Roger had all the records and he'd have to ask him."

"Did you tell Mr. Dunning that Mr. Eisler had asked you?"

"Yes."

"That's a lie," Dunning said.

Wolfe nodded. "Again one person's word against yours. But I have the envelope, and I have the names of three other men who have made purchases for you under similar arrangements, and Mr. Durkin and Mr. Panzer have spoken with them. Two of them were asked for figures recently by Wade Eisler, as was Mr. Greve. I don't know how much you cheated Eisler out of, but from the contents of the envelope I surmise that it was many thousands." His head turned. "Saul and Fred, you will escort Mr. Dunning to the District Attorney's office and deliver the envelope and the information you have collected. Archie, get the envelope from the safe."

I moved. As I passed behind Dunning's chair he started up, but Saul's hand on one shoulder and Fred's on the other stopped him. As I opened the safe door Wolfe said, "Give it to Saul. Miss Rowan, do you want Mr. Goodwin to phone the District Attorney to expect you?"

I had never seen Lily so completely got. "Good lord," she said, "I didn't realize. You couldn't drag me. I wish I hadn't . . . No, I don't . . . but I didn't realize how—how *hard* it is."

"You're not going?"

"Of course not!"

"You, Mr. Greve? You might as well. If you don't you'll be sent for later."

"Then I'll go later." Harvey was on his feet. "We've got a show on." He looked at Cal and Mel. "What about it? Think you can handle a calf if I hold his tail?"

"But we can't," Nan Karlin said. "Just go and—we *can't!*"

"The hell we can't," Cal Barrow said. "Come on, Laura."

VIII

One snowy morning in January I got a letter from Cal Barrow.

Dear Archie:
    You used them two dots like that when you wrote me on the typewriter so if you can I can. I read in the paper today about Roger Dunning getting convicted and Laura said I ought to write you and I said she ought to and she said did I want her writing letters to the man she should have married instead of me: and so it went. Remember when I said about that blowout I didn't want to stink it up, well it sure got stunk up. We are making out pretty well here in Texas but it is cold enough to freeze the tits on a steer if he had any. Laura says to give you her love but don't believe it. Best regards.

Yours truly:
Cal